SAN FRANCISCO

Thrillers

SAN FRANCISCO

Thrillers

True Crimes and Dark Mysteries
from the City by the Bay

EDITED BY JOHN MILLER AND TIM SMITH

INTRODUCTION BY MARTIN CRUZ SMITH

PHOTOGRAPHS BY FRANCIS BRUGUIÉRE

CHRONICLE BOOKS

SAN FRANCISCO

Compilation ©1995 by John Miller.
Introduction ©1995 by Martin Cruz Smith
Photographs ©1919 by Francis Bruguiére.
All rights reserved. No part of this book may be reproduced in any
form without written permission from the publisher.
Printed in the United States of America.
Page 252 constitutes a continuation of the copyright page.

Library of Congress Cataloging-in-Publication Data
San Francisco thrillers : true crimes and dark mysteries from
the City by the Bay / Edited by John Miller & Tim Smith.
      p.   cm.
    ISBN 0-8118-1043-7
      1. Detective and mystery stories, American.
    2. Crime—California—San Francisco—Fiction.
  3. San Francisco, (Calif.)—Fiction. 4. American fiction—
        20th century. 5. Horror tales, American.
    I. Miller, John, 1959-   . II. Smith, Tim, 1962-
            PS648.D4S26   1995
813'.087208327946l—dc20   95-12957
                                      CIP

Book and cover design: Big Fish Books
Composition: Jennifer Petersen, Big Fish Books
Cover photograph: Francis Bruguiére

Distributed in Canada by Raincoast Books,
8680 Cambie Street
Vancouver BC V6P 6M9

10 9 8 7 6 5 4 3 2 1

Chronicle Books
275 Fifth Street
San Francisco, CA 94103

Special thanks to

Kirsten Miller

Shelley Berniker

Len Gilbert

Bill Pronzini

and Bruce Taylor of the S.F. Mystery Bookstore

Contents

Introduction

Martin Cruz Smith

SAN FRANCISCO, THAT most elusive and feminine of American cities, inspires murder. From across the bay, the city lies white and pristine on its hills, shimmers in a Mediterranean light, fades and vanishes in summer fog. Why does it make a writer want to pick up a gun?

What strange spell is this? Spanish explorers sailed by the bay without seeing it for fifty years, until the cutthroat Sir Francis Drake saw the harbor open up for him. At that pre-landfill time, the hills were even more spectacular, covered by redwood and oak that marched in ranks down to the water. Now the city has a seductive languor that ends in the bracelet of the Golden Gate Bridge, the grandest piece of Art Deco ever created. Add a mist that, at whim, hides any part of town at any hour, changes the light as if spinning the hands of a clock, and transforms a North Beach cafe into a cabin at 35,000 feet and you have imagination hanging in the air.

Consider the elements.

Light. In "The Second Coming," Joe Gores describes a day as "one of those chilly California brights with blue sky

Martin Cruz Smith is the author of a string of best-selling thrillers, including *Gorky Park*, *Red Square*, and *Polar Star*. He lives in Northern California.

and cold sunshine." If Poussin wrote murder stories, he'd have written that.

Fog. Jim Thompson in *Ironside* calls it the "nearly opaque nightfog," a phrase so perfect that it leaves the eye looking for a streetlamp that's never mentioned.

Wind. "The California winter was on," in Ambrose Bierce's "Beyond the Wall," and "three or four trees, writhing and moaning in the torment of the tempest, appeared to be trying to escape their dismal environment and take the chance of finding a better one at sea."

There's no reality when streets, sea, and mist mix so easily. Where Alcatraz, once the ugliest prison in America, is the pearl of the bay. Typically, when prisoners broke out of Alcatraz it was often not known whether they survived the swim and escaped or were swept out to sea; they just disappeared.

There is no normality when the streets themselves rise and fall in dizzying succession. Where the moral level of the citizens was established not by Puritans but by adventurers—Americans, French, Chinese, Chileans—lured by gold. A San Franciscan enjoys the fact that the city is by fact and psyche a peninsula appended to the rest of the continent, that on three side streets lead to water and, often enough, fog. In "The Demon in the Belfry" Hildegarde Teilhet identifies a victim as being "from across the bay." Could be from another world.

The most popular vista point for this spectacular setting is the Golden Gate Bridge, which also happens to be the most popular site for suicides on earth. An estimated thousand people have jumped off the bridge. Think of the view. Green pines of the Presidio on one side of the span, Marin's golden headland on the other. Sunshine filling sails all the way to Oakland. Heaven! The bridge itself droning to the rhythm of the traffic. A scramble over the rail and quick scan of the target below, though with that much water, how can you miss? Then, as soon as you let go, a sure sense of how black and cold the waves will be.

I don't know a writer here who hasn't thought about it. Imagined it, I should say. Marcia Muller's *Deceptions* contains a one-line description you will never forget of boats searching for a jumper.

We're overwhelmed by San Francisco. Who is the main character of Alfred Hitchcock's *Vertigo* if not the shimmering, heavenly city that Jimmy Stewart dreamily stalks in search of Kim Novak? What other city announces itself with the deep, evocative call of a foghorn? Occasionally suffers, like any high-bred beauty, from tremors? Has been known to go up in flames?

The reason San Francisco has played such a role in leading mystery writing away from the florid style of the nineteenth century is that writers, in the face of such seductiveness of place, reacted against it and treated the city like a slut, abandoning adjectives like so many unnecessary bouquets. They developed their own style, adapting first the flat, professional attitude of Hammett's Continental Op and then the noir, amoral voice of Jim Thompson.

But no one's fooled. She wipes the dirt off her face and her white dress, smiles and seduces us again and again and again.

It's a Lousy World

Bill Pronzini

COLLY BABCOCK WAS shot to death on the night of September 9, in an alley between Twenty-ninth and Valley streets in the Glen Park District of San Francisco. Two police officers, cruising, spotted him coming out the rear door of Budget Liquors there, carrying a metal box. Colly ran when he saw them. The officers gave chase, calling out for him to halt, but he just kept running; one of the cops fired a warning shot, and when Colly didn't heed it the officer pulled up and fired again. He was aiming low, trying for the legs, but in the half-light of the alley it was a blind shot. The bullet hit Colly in the small of the back and killed him instantly.

I read about it the following morning over coffee and undercooked eggs in a cafeteria on Taylor Street, a block and a half from my office. The store was on an inside page, concise and dispassionate; they teach that kind of objective writing in

Award-winning author BILL PRONZINI is one of San Francisco's most popular and successful mystery novelists. First published in 1968, his story "It's a Lousy World" marks the first appearance of the Nameless Detective, a character who has appeared in twenty-two of Pronzini's forty novels.

the journalism classes. Just the cold facts. A man dies, but he's nothing more than a statistic, a name in black type, a faceless nonentity to be considered and then forgotten along with your breakfast coffee.

Unless you knew him.

Unless he was your friend.

Very carefully I folded the newspaper and put it into my coat pocket. Then I stood from the table, went out to the street. The wind was up, blowing in off the Bay; rubble swirled and eddied in the Tenderloin gutters. The air smelled of salt and dark rain and human pollution.

I walked into the face of the wind, toward my office.

"How's the job, Colly?"

"Oh, fine, just fine."

"No problems?"

"No, none at all."

"Stick with it, Colly."

"Sure. I'm a new man."

"Straight all the way?"

"Straight all the way."

Inside the lobby of my building, I found an out-of-order sign taped to the closed elevator doors. Yeah, that figured. I went around to the stairs, up to the second floor and along the hallway to my office.

The door was unlocked, standing open a few inches. I tensed when I saw it like that, and reached out with the tips of my fingers and pushed it all the way open. But there was no trouble. The woman sitting in the chair in front of my desk had never been trouble for anyone.

Colly Babcock's widow.

I moved inside, shut the door and crossed toward her. "Hello, Lucille."

Her hands were clasped tightly in the lap of a plain black dress. She said, "The man down the hall, the CPA—he let me in. He said you wouldn't mind."

"I don't mind."

"You heard, I guess? About Colly?"

"Yes," I said. "What can I say, Lucille?"

"You were his friend. You helped him."

"Maybe I didn't help him enough."

"He didn't do it," Lucille said. "He didn't steal that money. He didn't do all those robberies like they're saying."

"Lucille . . ."

"Colly and I were married thirty-one years," she said. "Don't you think I would have known?"

I did not say anything.

"I always knew," she said.

I sat down, looking at her. She was a big woman, hand-some—a strong woman. There was strength in the line of her mouth, and in her eyes, round and gray, tinged with red now from the crying. She had stuck by Colly through two prison terms and twenty-odd years of running, and hiding, and looking over her shoulder. Yes, I thought, she would always have known.

But I said, "The papers said Colly was coming out the back door of the liquor store carrying a metal box. The police found a hundred and six dollars in the box, and the door jimmied open."

"I know what the papers said, and I know what the police are saying. But they're wrong. *Wrong.*"

"He was there, Lucille."

"I know that," she said. "Colly liked to walk in the evenings. A long walk and then a drink when he came home; it helped him to relax. That was how he came to be there."

I shifted position on my chair, not speaking.

Lucille said, "Colly was always nervous when he was doing burglaries. That was one of the ways I could tell. He'd get irritable, and he couldn't sleep."

"He wasn't like that lately?"

"You saw him a few weeks ago," she said. "Did he look that way to you?"

"No," I said, "he didn't."

"We were happy," Lucille said. "No more running. And no more waiting. We were truly happy."

My mouth felt dry. "What about his job?"

"They gave Colly a raise last week. A fifteen-dollar raise. We went to dinner to celebrate, down on the Wharf."

"You were getting along all right on what he made?" I said. "Nothing came up?"

"Nothing. We even had a little bank account started." She bit her lower lip. "We were going to Hawaii next year, or the year after. Colly always wanted to go to Hawaii."

I looked at my hands. They seemed big and awkward resting on the desk top; I took them away and put them in my lap. "These Glen Park robberies started a month and a half ago," I said. "The police estimate the total amount taken at close to five thousand dollars. You could get to Hawaii pretty well on that kind of money."

"Colly didn't do those robberies," she said.

What could I say? God knew, and Lucille knew, that Colly had never been a saint; but this time she was convinced he'd been innocent. Nothing, it seemed, was going to change that in her eyes.

I got a cigarette from my pocket and made a thing of lighting it. The smoke added more dryness to my mouth. Without looking at her, I said, "What do you want me to do, Lucille?"

"I want you to prove Colly didn't do what they're saying he did."

"I'd like nothing better, you know that. But how can I do it? The evidence—"

"Damn the evidence!" Her wide mouth trembled with the sudden emotion. "Colly was innocent, I tell you! I won't have him buried with this last mark against his name. I won't have it."

"Lucille, listen to me . . ."

"I won't listen," she said. "Colly was your friend. You

stood up for him with the parole board. You helped him find his job. You talked to him, gave him guidance. He was a different man, a new man, and you helped make him that way. Will you sit here and tell me you believe he threw it all away for five thousand dollars?"

I didn't say anything; I still could not meet her eyes. I stared down at the burning cigarette in my fingers, watching the smoke rise, curling, a gray spiral in the cold air of the office.

"Or don't you care whether he was innocent or not?" she said.

"I care, Lucille."

"Then help me. Find out the truth."

"All right," I said. Her anger and grief, and her absolute certainty that Colly had been innocent, had finally got through to me; I could not have turned her down now if there had been ten times the evidence there was. "All right, Lucille, I'll see what I can do."

IT WAS DRIZZLING when I got to the Hall of Justice. Some of the chill had gone out of the air, but the wind was stronger now. The clouds overhead looked black and swollen, ready to burst.

I parked my car on Bryant Street, went past the sycamores on the narrow front lawn, up the concrete steps and inside. The plainclothes detective division, General Works, was on the fourth floor; I took the elevator. Eberhardt had been promoted to lieutenant not too long ago and had his own private office now, but I caught myself glancing over toward his old desk. Force of habit; it had been a while since I'd visited him at the Hall.

He was in and willing to see me. When I entered his office he was shuffling through some reports and scowling. He was my age, pushing fifty, and he seemed to have been fashioned of an odd contrast of sharp angles and smooth, blunt planes: square forehead, sharp nose and chin, thick and blocky upper body, long legs and angular hands. Today he was wearing a brown suit that hadn't been pressed in a month; his tie was crooked; there was a collar button missing from his shirt. And he had a fat, purplish bruise over his left eye.

"All right," he said, "make it quick."

"What happened to your eye?"

"I bumped into a doorknob."

"Sure you did."

"Yeah," he said. "You come here to pass the time of day, or was there something?"

"I'd like a favor, Eb."

"Sure. And I'd like three weeks' vacation."

"I want to look at an Officer's Felony Report."

"Are you nuts? Get the hell out of here."

The words didn't mean anything. He was always gruff and grumbly while he was working; and we'd been friends for more years than either of us cared to remember, ever since we went through the Police Academy together after World War II and then joined the force here in the city.

I said, "There was a shooting last night. Two squad-car cops killed a man running away from the scene of a burglary in Glen Park."

"So?"

"The victim was a friend of mine."

He gave me a look. "Since when do you have burglars for friends?"

"His name was Colly Babcock," I said. "He did two stretches in San Quentin, both for burglary; I helped send him up the first time. I also helped get him out on parole the second time and into a decent job."

"Uh-huh. I remember the name. I also heard about the shooting last night. Too bad this pal of yourse turned bad again, but then a lot of them do—as if you didn't know."

I was silent.

"I get it," Eberhardt said. "You don't think so. That's why you're here."

"Colly's wife doesn't think so. I guess maybe I don't either."

"I can't let you look at any reports. And even if I could, it's not my department. Robbery'll be handling it. Internal Affairs, too."

"You could pull some strings."

"I could," he said, "but I won't. I'm up to my ass in work. I just don't have the time."

I got to my feet. "Well, thanks anyway, Eb." I went to the door, put my hand on the knob, but before I turned it he made a noise behind me. I turned.

"If things go all right," he said, scowling at me, "I'll be off duty in a couple of hours. If I happen to get down by Robbery on the way out, maybe I'll stop in. Maybe."

"I'd appreciate it if you would."

"Give me a call later on. At home."

"Thanks, Eb."

"Yeah," he said. "So what are you standing there for? Get the hell out of here and let me work."

I FOUND TOMMY Belknap in a bar called Luigi's, out in the Mission District.

He was drinking whiskey at the long bar, leaning his head on his arms and staring at the wall. Two men in work clothes were drinking beer and eating sandwiches from lunch pails at the other end, and in the middle an old lady in a black shawl sipped red wine from a glass held with arthritic fingers. I sat on a stool next to Tommy and said hello.

He turned his head slowly, his eyes moving upward. His face was an anemic white, and his bald head shone with beaded perspiration. He had trouble focusing his eyes; he swiped at them with the back of one veined hand. He was pretty drunk. And I was pretty sure I knew why.

"Hey," he said when he recognized me, "have a drink, will you?"

"Not just now."

He got his glass to his lips with shaky fingers, managed to drink without spilling any of the whiskey. "Colly's dead," he said.

"Yeah. I know."

"They killed him last night," Tommy said. "They shot him in the back."

"Take it easy, Tommy."

"He was my friend."

"He was my friend, too."

"Colly was a nice guy. Lousy goddamn cops had no right to shoot him like that."

"He was robbing a liquor store," I said.

"Hell he was!" Tommy said. He swiveled on the stool and pushed a finger at my chest. "Colly was straight, you hear that? Just like me. Ever since we both got out of Q."

"You sure about that, Tommy?"

"Damn right I am."

"Then who did those burglaries in Glen Park?"

"How should I know?"

"Come on, you get around. You know people, you hear things. There must be something on the earie."

"Nothing," he said. "Don't know."

"Kids?" I said. "Street punks?"

"Don't *know*."

"But it wasn't Colly? You'd know if it was Colly?"

"Colly was straight," Tommy said. "And now he's dead."

He put his head down on his arms again. The bartender came over; he was a fat man with a reddish handlebar mustache. "You can't sleep here, Tommy," he said. "You ain't even supposed to *be* in here while you're on parole."

"Colly's dead," Tommy said, and there were tears in his eyes.

"Let him alone," I said to the bartender.

"I can't have him sleeping in here."

I took out my wallet and put a five-dollar bill on the

bar. "Give him another drink," I said, "and then let him sleep it off in the back room. The rest of the money is for you."

The bartender looked at me, looked at the fin, looked at Tommy. "All right," he said. "What the hell."

I went out into the rain.

D. E. O'MIRA and Company, Wholesale Plumbing Supplies, was a big two-storied building that took up three-quarters of a block on Berry Street, out near China Basin. I parked in front and went inside. In the center of a good-sized office was a switchboard walled in glass, with a card taped to the front that said Information. A dark-haired girl wearing a set of headphones was sitting inside, and when I asked her if Mr. Templeton was in she said he was at a meeting uptown and wouldn't be back all day. Mr. Templeton was the office manager, the man I had spoken to about giving Colly Babcock a job when he was paroled from San Quentin.

Colly had worked in the warehouse, and his immediate supervisor was a man I had never met named Harlin. I went through a set of swing doors opposite the main entrance, down a narrow, dark passage screened on both sides. On my left when I emerged into the warehouse was a long service counter; behind it were display shelves, and behind them long rows of bins that stretched the length and width of the building. Straight ahead, through an open doorway, I could see the loading dock and a yard cluttered with soil pipe and other supplies. On my right was a windowed office with two desks, neither occupied; an old man in a pair of baggy brown slacks, a brown vest and a battered slouch hat stood before a side counter under the windows.

The old man didn't look up when I came into the office. A foul-smelling cigar danced in his thin mouth as he shuffled papers. I cleared my throat and said, "Excuse me."

He looked at me then, grudgingly. "What is it?"

"Are you Mr. Harlin?"

"That's right."

I told him who I was and what I did. I was about to ask him about Colly when a couple of guys came into the office and one of them plunked himself down at the nearest desk. I said to Harlin, "Could we talk someplace private?"

"Why? What're you here about?"

"Colly Babcock," I said.

He made a grunting sound, scribbled on one of his papers with a pencil stub and then led me out onto the dock. We walked along there, past a warehouseman loading crated cast-iron sinks from a pallet into a pickup truck, and up to the wide, double-doored entrance to an adjoining warehouse.

The old man stopped and turned to me. "We can talk here."

"Fine. You were Colly's supervisor, is that right?"

"I was."

"Tell me how you felt about him."

"You won't hear anything bad, if that's what you're looking for."

"That's not what I'm looking for."

He considered that for a moment, then shrugged and said, "Colly was a good worker. Did what you told him, no fuss. Quiet sort, kept to himself mostly."

"You knew about his prison record?"

"I knew. All of us here did. Nothing was ever said to Colly about it, though. I saw to that."

"Did he seem happy with the job?"

"Happy enough," Harlin said. "Never complained if that's what you mean."

"No friction with any of the other men?"

"No. He got along fine with everybody."

A horn sounded from inside the adjoining warehouse and a yellow forklift carrying a pallet of lavatories came out. We stepped out of the way as the thing clanked and belched past.

I asked Harlin, "When you heard about what happened to Colly last night—what was your reaction?"

"Didn't believe it," he answered. "Still don't. None of us do."

I nodded. "Did Colly have any particular friend here? Somebody he ate lunch with regularly—like that?"

"Kept to himself for the most part, like I said. But he stopped with Sam Biehler for a beer a time or two after work; Sam mentioned it."

"I'd like to talk to Biehler, if it's all right."

"Is with me," the old man said. He paused, chewing on his cigar. "Listen, there any chance Colly didn't do what the papers say he did?"

"There might be. That's what I'm trying to find out."

"Anything I can do," he said, "you let me know."

"I'll do that."

We went back inside and I spoke to Sam Biehler, a tall, slender guy with a mane of silver hair that gave him, despite his work clothes, a rather distinguished appearance.

"I don't mind telling you," he said, "I don't believe a damned word of it. I'd have had to be there to see it with my own eyes before I'd believe it, and maybe not even then."

"I understand you and Colly stopped for a beer occa-sionally?"

"Once a week maybe, after work. Not in a bar; Colly couldn't go to a bar because of his parole. At my place. Then afterward I'd give him a ride home."

"What did you talk about?"

"The job, mostly," Biehler said. "What the company could do to improve things out here in the warehouse. I guess you know the way fellows talk."

"Uh-huh. Anything else?"

"About Colly's past, that what you're getting at?"

"Yes."

"Just once," Biehler said. "Colly told me a few things. But I never pressed him on it. I don't like to pry."

"What was it he told you?"

"That he was never going back to prison. That he was through with the kind of life he'd led before." Biehler's eyes sparkled, as if challenging me. "And you know something? I been on this earth for fifty-nine years and I've known a lot of men in that time. You get so you can tell."

"Tell what, Mr. Biehler?"

"Colly wasn't lying," he said.

I SPENT AN hour at the main branch of the library in Civic Center, reading through back issues of the *Chronicle* and the *Examiner*. The Glen Park robberies had begun a month and a half ago, and I had paid only passing attention to them at the time.

When I had acquainted myself with the details I went back to my office and checked in with my answering service. No calls. Then I called Lucille Babcock.

"The police were here earlier," she said. "They had a search warrant."

"Did they find anything?"

"There was nothing to find."

"What did they say?"

"They asked a lot of questions. They wanted to know about bank accounts and safe-deposit boxes."

"Did you cooperate with them?"

"Of course."

"Good," I said. I told her what I had been doing all day, what the people I'd talked with had said.

"You see?" she said. "Nobody who knew Colly can believe he was guilty."

"Nobody but the police."

"Damn the police," she said.

I sat holding the phone. There were things I wanted to say, but they all seemed trite and meaningless. Pretty soon I told her I would be in touch, leaving it at that, and put the receiver back in its cradle.

It was almost five o'clock. I locked up the office, drove home to my flat in Pacific Heights, drank a beer and ate a pastrami sandwich, and then lit a cigarette and dialed Eberhardt's home number. It was his gruff voice that answered.

"Did you stop by Robbery before you left the Hall?" I asked.

"Yeah. I don't know why."

"We're friends, that's why."

"That doesn't stop you from being a pain in the ass sometimes."

"Can I come over, Eb?"

"You can if you get here before eight o'clock," he said. "I'm going to bed then, and Dana has orders to bar all the doors and windows and take the telephone off the hook. I plan to get a good night's sleep for a change."

"I'll be there in twenty minutes," I said.

EBERHARDT LIVED IN Noe Valley, up at the back end near Twin Peaks. The house was big and painted white, a two-storied frame job with a trimmed lawn and lots of flowers in front. If you knew Eberhardt, the house was sort of symbolic; it typified everything the honest, hardworking cop was dedicated to protecting. I had a hunch he knew it, too; and if he did, he got a certain amount of satisfaction from the knowledge. That was the way he was.

I parked in his sloping driveway and went up and rang the bell. His wife Dana, a slender and very attractive brunette with a lot of patience, let me in, asked how I was and showed me into the kitchen, closing the door behind her as she left.

Eberhardt was sitting at the table having a pipe and a cup of coffee. The bruise over his eye had been smeared with some kind of pinkish ointment; it made him look a little silly, but I knew better than to tell him so.

"Have a seat," he said, and I had one. "You want some coffee?"

"Thanks."

He got me a cup, then indicated a manila envelope lying on the table. Without saying anything, sucking at his pipe, he made an elaborate effort to ignore me as I picked up the envelope and opened it.

Inside was the report made by the two patrolmen, Avinisi and Carstairs, who had shot and killed Colly Babcock in the act of robbing the Budget Liquor Store. I read it over carefully—and my eye caught on one part, a couple of sentences, under "Effects." When I was through I put the report back in the envelope and returned it to the table.

Eberhardt looked at me then. "Well?"

"One item," I said, "that wasn't in the papers."

"What's that?"

"They found a pint of Kesslers in a paper bag in Colly's coat pocket."

He shrugged. "It was a liquor store, wasn't it? Maybe he slipped it into his pocket on the way out?"

"And put it into a paper bag first?"

"People do funny things," he said.

"Yeah," I said. I drank some of the coffee and then got on my feet. "I'll let you get to bed, Eb. Thanks again."

He grunted. "You owe me a favor. Just remember that."

"I won't forget."

"You and the elephants," he said.

IT WAS STILL raining the next morning—another dismal day. I drove over to Chenery Street and wedged my car into a downhill parking slot a half-block from the three-room apartment Lucille and Colly Babcock had called home for the past year. I hurried through the rain, feeling the chill of it on my face, and mounted sagging wooden steps to the door.

Lucille answered immediately. She wore the same black dress she'd had on yesterday, and the same controlled mask of grief; it would be a long time before that grief faded and she was able to get on with her life. Maybe never, unless somebody proved her right about Colly's innocence.

I sat in the old, stuffed leather chair by the window: Colly's chair. Lucille said, "Can I get you something?"

I shook my head. "What about you? Have you eaten anything today? Or yesterday?"

"No," she answered.

"You have to eat, Lucille."

"Maybe later. Don't worry, I'm not suicidal. I won't starve myself to death."

I managed a small smile. "All right," I said.

"Why are you here?" she asked. "Do you have any news?"

"No, not yet." I had an idea, but it was only that, and too early. I did not want to instill any false hopes. "I just wanted to ask you a few more questions."

"Oh. What questions?"

"You mentioned yesterday that Colly liked to take walks in the evening. Was he in the habit of walking to any particular place, or in any particular direction?"

"No," Lucille said. "He just liked to walk. He was gone for a couple of hours sometimes."

"He never told you where he'd been?"

"Just here and there in the neighborhood."

Here and there in the neighborhood, I thought. The alley where Colly had been shot was eleven blocks from this apartment. He could have walked in a straight line, or he could have gone roundabout in any direction.

I asked, "Colly liked to have a nightcap when he came back from these walks, didn't he?"

"He did, yes."

"He kept liquor here, then?"

"One bottle of bourbon. That's all."

I rotated my hat in my hands. "I wonder if I could have a small drink, Lucille. I know it's early, but . . ."

She nodded and got up and went to a squat cabinet

near the kitchen door. She bent, slid the panel open in front, looked inside. Then she straightened. "I'm sorry," she said. "We . . . I seem to be out."

I stood. "It's okay. I should be going anyway."

"Where will you go now?"

"To see some people." I paused. "Would you happen to have a photograph of Colly? A snapshot, something like that?"

"I think so. Why do you want it?"

"I might need to show it around," I said. "Here in the neighborhood."

She seemed satisfied with that. "I'll see if I can find one for you."

I waited while she went into the bedroom. A couple of minutes later she returned with a black-and-white snap of Colly, head and shoulders, that had been taken in a park somewhere. He was smiling, one eyebrow raised in mock raffishness.

I put the snap into my pocket and thanked Lucille and told her I would be in touch again pretty soon. Then I went to the door and let myself out.

The skies seemed to have parted like the Red Sea. Drops of rain as big as hail pellets lashed the sidewalk. Thunder rumbled in the distance, edging closer. I pulled the collar of my overcoat tight around my neck and made a run for my car.

IT WAS AFTER four o'clock when I came inside a place called Tay's Liquors on Whitney Street and stood dripping water on the floor. There was a heater on a shelf just inside the door, and I allowed myself the luxury of its warmth for a few seconds. Then I crossed to the counter.

A young guy wearing a white shirt and a Hitler mustache got up from a stool near the cash register and walked over to me. He smiled, letting me see crooked teeth that weren't very clean. "Wet enough for you?" he said.

No, I thought, I want it to get a lot wetter so I can drown. Dumb question, dumb answer. But all I said was,

"Maybe you can help me."

"Sure," he said. "Name your poison."

He was brimming with originality. I took the snapshot of Colly Babcock from my pocket, extended it across the counter and asked, "Did you see this man two nights ago, sometime around eleven o'clock?" It was the same thing I had done and the same question I had asked at least twenty times already. I had been driving and walking the streets of Glen Park for four hours now, and I had been to four liquor stores, five corner groceries, two large chain markets, a delicatessen and half a dozen bars that sold off-sale liquor. So far I had come up with nothing except possibly a head cold.

The young guy gave me a slanted look. "Cop?" he asked, but his voice was still cheerful.

I showed him the photostat of my investigator's license. He shrugged, then studied the photograph. "Yeah," he said finally, "I did see this fellow a couple of nights ago. Nice old duck. We talked a little about the Forty-niners."

I stopped feeling cold and I stopped feeling frustrated. I said, "About what time did he come in?"

"Let's see. Eleven-thirty or so, I think,"

Fifteen minutes before Colly had been shot in an alley three and a half blocks away. "Do you remember what he bought?"

"Bourbon—a pint. Medium price."

"Kesslers."

"Yeah, I think it was."

"Okay, good. What's your name?"

"My name? Hey, wait a minute, I don't want to get involved in anything . . . "

"Don't worry, it's not what you're thinking."

It took a little more convincing, but he gave me his name finally and I wrote it down in my notebook. And I thanked him and hurried out of there.

I had something more than an idea now.

EBERHARDT SAID, "I ought to knock you flat on your ass."

He had just come out of his bedroom, eyes foggy with sleep, hair standing straight up, wearing a wine-colored bathrobe. Dana stood beside him looking fretful.

"I'm sorry I woke you up, Eb," I said. "But I didn't think you'd be in bed this early. It's only six o'clock."

He said something I didn't hear, but that Dana heard. She cracked him on the arm to show her disapproval, then turned and left us alone.

Eberhardt went over and sat on the couch and glared at me. "I've had about six hours' sleep in the past forty-eight," he said. "I got called out last night after you left, I didn't get home until three A.M., I was up at seven, I worked all goddamn day and knocked off early so I could get some *sleep*, and what happens? I'm in bed ten minutes and you show up."

"Eb, it's important."

"What is?"

"Colly Babcock."

"Ah, Christ, you don't give up, do you?"

"Sometimes I do, but not this time. Not now." I told him what I had learned from the guy at Tay's Liquors.

"So Babcock bought a bottle there," Eberhardt said. "So what?"

"If he was planning to burglarize a liquor store, do you think he'd have bothered to *buy* a bottle fifteen minutes before?"

"Hell, the job might have been spur-of-the-moment."

"Colly didn't work that way. When he was pulling them, they were all carefully planned well in advance. Always."

"He was getting old," Eberhardt said. "People change."

"You didn't know Colly. Besides, there are a few other things."

"Such as?"

"The burglaries themselves. They were all done the same way—back door jimmied, marks on the jamb and lock made with a hand bar or something." I paused. "They didn't find any tool like that on Colly. Or inside the store either."

"Maybe he got rid of it."

"When did he have time? They caught him coming out the door."

Eberhardt scowled. I had his interest now. "Go ahead," he said.

"The pattern of the burglaries, like I was saying, is doors jimmied, drawers rifled, papers and things strewn about. No fingerprints, but it smacks of amateurism. Or somebody trying to make it look like amateurism."

"And Babcock was a professional."

"He could have done the book," I said. "He used lock picks and glass cutters to get into a place, never anything like a hand bar. He didn't ransack; he always knew exactly what he was after. He never deviated from that, Eb. Not once."

Eberhardt got to his feet and paced around for a time. Then he stopped in front of me and said, "So what do you think, then?"

"You figure it."

"Yeah," he said slowly, "I can figure it, all right. But I don't like it. I don't like it at all."

"And Colly?" I said. "You think he liked it?"

Eberhardt turned abruptly, went to the telephone. He spoke to someone at the Hall of Justice, then someone else. When he hung up, he was already shrugging out of his bathrobe.

He gave me a grim look. "I hope you're wrong, you know that."

"I hope I'm not," I said.

I WAS SITTING in my flat, reading one of the pulps from my collection of several thousand issues, when the telephone rang just before eleven o'clock. It was Eberhardt, and the first thing he said was, "You weren't wrong."

I didn't say anything, waiting.

"Avinisi and Carstairs," he said bitterly. "Each of them on the force a little more than two years. The old story: bills, long hours, not enough pay—and greed. They cooked up the idea one night while they were cruising Glen Park, and it worked just fine until two nights ago. Who'd figure the cops for it?"

"You have any trouble with them?"

"No. I wish they'd given me some so I could have slapped them with a resisting-arrest charge, too."

"How did it happen with Colly?"

"It was the other way around," he said. "Babcock was cutting through the alley when he saw them coming out the rear door. He turned to run and they panicked and Avinisi shot him in the back. When they went to check, Carstairs found a note from Babcock's parole officer in one of his pockets, identifying him as an ex-con. That's when they decided to frame him."

"Look, Eb, I—"

"Forget it," he said. "I know what you're going to say."

"You can't help it if a couple of cops turn out that way . . ."

"I said forget it, all right?" And the line went dead.

I listened to the empty buzzing for a couple of seconds. It's a lousy world, I thought. But sometimes, at least, there is justice.

Then I called Lucille Babcock and told her why her husband had died.

THEY HAD A nice funeral for Colly.

The services were held in a small nondenominational church on Monterey Boulevard. There were a lot of flowers, carnations mostly; Lucille said they had been Colly's favorites. Quite a few people came. Tommy Belknap was there, and Sam Biehler and old man Harlin and the rest of them from D. E. O'Mira. Eberhardt, too, which might have seemed surprising unless you knew him. I also saw faces I didn't recognize; the whole thing had gotten a big play in the media.

Afterward, there was the funeral procession to the cemetery in Colma, where we listened to the minister's final words and watched them put Colly into the ground. When it was done I offered to drive Lucille home, but she said no, there were some arrangements she wanted to make with the care-taker for upkeep of the plot; one of her neighbors would stay with her and see to it she got home all right. Then she held my hand and kissed me on the cheek and told me again how grate-ful she was.

I went to where my car was parked. Eberhardt was waiting; he had ridden down with me.

"I don't like funerals," he said.

"No," I said.

We got into the car. "So what are you planning to do when we get back to the city?" Eberhardt asked.

"I hadn't thought about it."

"Come over to my place. Dana's gone off to visit her sister, and I've got a refrigerator full of beer."

"All right."

"Maybe we'll get drunk," he said.

I nodded. "Maybe we will at that."

Fly Paper

Dashiell Hammett

IT WAS A wandering daughter job.

The Hambletons had been for several generations a wealthy and decently prominent New York family. There was nothing in the Hambleton history to account for Sue, the youngest member of the clan. She grew out of childhood with a kink that made her dislike the polished side of life, like the rough. By the time she was twenty-one, in 1926, she definitely preferred Tenth Avenue to Fifth, drifters to bankers, and Hymie the Riveter to the Honorable Cecil Windown, who had asked her to marry him.

The Hambletons tried to make Sue behave, but it was too late for that. She was legally of age. When she finally told them to go to hell and walked out on them there wasn't much they could do about it. Her father, Major Waldo Hambleton, had given up all the hopes he ever had of salvaging her, but he didn't want her to run into any grief that could be avoided. So he came into the Continental Detective Agency's New York office and asked to have an eye kept on her.

Hymie the Riveter was a Philadelphia racketeer who had moved north to the big city, carrying a Thompson subma-

SAMUEL DASHIELL HAMMETT, the founder of American hard-boiled detective fiction, left an indelible mark on the San Francisco mystery scene. Hammett's rare story "Fly Paper" was first published in his short story collection *The Big Knockover* in 1928.

chine gun wrapped in blue-checkered oil cloth, after a dis-
agreement with his partners. New York wasn't so good a field
as Philadelphia for machine gun work. The Thompson lay idle
for a year or so while Hymie made expenses with an automatic,
preying on small-time crap games in Harlem.

Three or four months after Sue went to live with
Hymie he made what looked like a promising connection with
the first of the crew that came into New York from Chicago to
organize the city on the western scale. But the boys from Chi
didn't want Hymie; they wanted the Thompson. When he
showed it to them, as the big item in his application for
employment, they shot holes in the top of Hymie's head and
went away with the gun.

Sue Hambleton buried Hymie, had a couple of lonely
weeks in which she hocked a ring to eat, and then got a job as
hostess in a speakeasy run by a Greek named Vassos.

One of Vassos' customers was Babe McCloor, two
hundred and fifty pounds of hard Scotch-Irish-Indian bone and
muscle, a black-haired, blue-eyed, swarthy giant who was resting up after doing a fifteen-year hitch in Leavenworth for ruining most of the smaller post offices between New Orleans and
Omaha. Babe was keeping himself in drinking money while he
rested by playing with pedestrians in dark streets.

Babe like Sue. Vassos like Sue. Sue like Babe. Vassos
didn't like that. Jealousy spoiled the Greek's judgment. He kept
the speakeasy door locked one night when Babe wanted to come
in. Babe came in, bringing pieces of the door with him. Vassos
got his gun out, but couldn't shake Sue off his arm. He stopped
trying when Babe hit him with the part of the door that had the
brass knob on it. Babe and Sue went away from Vassos' together.

Up to that time the New York office had managed to
keep in touch with Sue. She hadn't been kept under constant
surveillance. Her father hadn't wanted that. It was simply a
matter of sending a man around every week or so to see that she
was still alive, to pick up whatever information he could from

her friends and neighbors, without, of course, letting her know she was being tabbed. All that had been easy enough, but when she and Babe went away after wrecking the gin mill, they dropped completely out of sight.

After turning the city upside-down, the New York office sent a journal on the job to the other Continental branches throughout the country, giving the information above and enclosing photographs and descriptions of Sue and her new playmate. That was late in 1927.

We had enough copies of the photographs to go around, and for the next month or so whoever had a little idle time on his hands spent it looking through San Francisco and Oakland for the missing pair. We didn't find them. Operatives in other cities, doing the same thing, had the same luck.

Then, nearly a year later, a telegraph came to us from the New York office. Decoded, it read:

> MAJOR HAMBLETON TODAY RECEIVED
> TELEGRAM FROM DAUGHTER IN SAN
> FRANCISCO QUOTE PLEASE WIRE ME THOU-
> SAND DOLLARS CARE APARTMENT TWO
> HUNDRED SIX NUMBER SIX HUNDRED ONE
> EDDIS STREET STOP I WILL COME HOME IF
> YOU WILL LET ME STOP PLEASE TELL ME IF I
> CAN COME BUT PLEASE PLEASE WIRE
> MONEY ANYWAY UNQUOTE HAMBLETON
> AUTHORIZES PAYMENT OF MONEY TO HER
> IMMEDIATELY STOP DETAIL COMPETENT
> OPERATIVE TO CALL ON HER WITH MONEY
> AND ARRANGE FOR HER RETURN HOME
> STOP IF POSSIBLE HAVE MAN AND WOMAN
> OPERATIVE ACCOMPANY HER HERE STOP
> HAMBLETON WIRING HER STOP REPORT
> IMMEDIATELY BY WIRE.

The Old Man gave me the telegram and a check, say‑
ing, "You know the situation. You'll know how to handle it."

I pretended I agreed with him, went down to the
bank, swapped the check for a bundle of bills of several
sizes, caught a streetcar, and went up to 601 Eddis Street,
a fairly large apartment building on the corner of Larkin.

The name on Apartment 206's vestibule mailbox was
J. M. Wales.

I PUSHED 206'S button. When the locked door buzzed off
I went into the building, past the elevator to the stairs, and up
a flight. 206 was just around the corner from the stairs.

The apartment door was opened by a tall, slim man of
thirty‑something in neat dark clothes. He had narrow dark eyes
set in a long pale face. There was some gray in the dark hair
brushed flat to his scalp.

"Miss Hambleton," I said.

"Uh—what about her?" His voice was smooth, but not
too smooth to be agreeable.

"I'd like to see her."

His upper eyelids came down a little and the brows
over them came a little closer together. He asked, "Is it—?" and
stopped, watching me steadily.

I didn't say anything. Presently he finished his ques‑
tion, "Something to do with a telegram?"

"Yeah."

His long face brightened immediately. He asked,
"You're from her father?"

"Yeah."

He stepped back and swung the door wide open, say‑
ing, "Come in. Major Hambleton's wire came to her only a few
minutes ago. He said someone would call."

We went through a small passageway into a sunny
living room that was cheaply furnished, but neat and clean
enough.

"Sit down," the man said, pointing at a brown rocking chair.

I sat down. He sat on the burlap-covered sofa facing me. I looked around the room. I didn't see anything to show that a woman was living there.

He rubbed the long bridge of his nose with a longer forefinger and asked slowly, "You brought the money?"

I said I'd feel more like talking with her there.

He looked at the finger with which he had been rubbing his nose, and then up at me, saying softly, "But I'm her friend."

I said, "Yeah?" to that.

"Yes," he repeated. He frowned slightly, drawing back the corners of his thin-lipped mouth. "I've only asked whether you've brought the money."

I didn't say anything.

"The point is," he said quite reasonably, "that if you brought the money she doesn't expect you to hand it over to anybody except her. If you didn't bring it she doesn't want to see you. I don't think her mind can be changed about that. That's why I asked if you had brought it."

"I brought it."

He looked doubtfully at me. I showed him the money I had got from the bank. He jumped up briskly from the sofa.

"I'll have her here in a minute or two," he said over his shoulder as his long legs moved him toward the door. At the door he stopped to ask, "Do you know her? Or shall I have her bring means of identifying herself?"

"That would be best," I told him.

He went out, leaving the corridor door open.

IN FIVE MINUTES he was back with a slender blonde girl of twenty-three in pale green silk. The looseness of her small mouth and the puffiness around her blue eyes weren't yet pronounced enough to spoil her prettiness.

I stood up.

"This is Miss Hambleton," he said.

She gave me a swift glance and then lowered her eyes again, nervously playing with the strap of a handbag she held.

"You can identify yourself?" I asked.

"Sure," the man said. "Show them to him, Sue."

She opened the bag, brought out some papers and things, and held them up for me to take.

"Sit down, sit down," the man said as I took them.

They sat on the sofa. I sat in the rocking chair again and examined the things she had given me. There were two letters addressed to Sue Hambleton here, her father's telegram welcoming her home, a couple of receipted department store bills, an automobile driver's license, and a savings account pass book that showed a balance of less than ten dollars.

By the time I had finished my examination the girl's embarrassment was gone. She looked levelly at me, as did the man beside her. I felt in my pocket, found my copy of the photograph New York had sent us at the beginning of the hunt, and looked from it to her.

"Your mouth could have shrunk, maybe," I said, "but how could your nose have got that much longer?"

"If you don't like my nose," she said, "how'd you like to go to hell?" Her face had turned red.

"That's not the point. It's a swell nose, but it's not Sue's." I held the photograph out to her. "See for yourself."

She glared at the photograph and then at the man.

"What a smart guy you are," she told him.

He was watching me with dark eyes that had a brittle shine to them between narrow-drawn eyelids. He kept on watching me while he spoke to her out the side of his mouth, crisply. "Pipe down."

She piped down. He sat and watched me. I sat and watched him. A clock ticked seconds away behind me. His eyes began shifting their focus from one of my eyes to the other. The girl sighed.

He said in a low voice, "Well?"

I said, "You're in a hole."

"What can you make out of it?" he asked casually.

"Conspiracy to defraud."

The girl jumped up and hit one of his shoulders angrily with the back of a hand, crying, "What a smart guy you are, to get me in a jam like this. It was going to be duck soup—yeh! Eggs in the coffee—yeh! Now look at you. You haven't even got guts enough to tell this guy to go chase himself." She spun around to face me, pushing her red face down at me—I was still sitting in the rocker—snarling, "Well, what are you wait- ing for? Waiting to be kissed goodbye? We don't owe you any- thing, do we? We didn't get any of your lousy money, did we? Outside, then. Take the air. Dangle."

"Stop it, sister," I growled. "You'll bust something."

The man said, "For God's sake stop that bawling, Peggy, and give somebody else a chance." He addressed me, "Well, what do you want?"

"How'd you get into this?" I asked.

He spoke quickly, eagerly, "A fellow named Kenny gave me that stuff and told me about this Sue Hambleton, and her old man having plenty. I thought I'd give it a whirl. I fig- ured the old man would either wire the dough right off the reel or wouldn't send it at all. I didn't figure on this send-a- man stuff. Then when his wire came, saying he was sending a man to see her, I ought to have dropped it.

"But hell! Here was a man coming with a grand in cash. That was too good to let go of without a try. It looked like there still might be a chance of copping, so I got Peggy to do Sue for me. If the man was coming today, it was a cinch he belonged out here on the Coast, and it was an even bet he wouldn't know Sue, would only have a description of her. From what Kenny had told me about her, I knew Peggy would come pretty close to fitting her description. I still don't see how you got that photograph. I only wired the old

man yesterday, so we'd have them with the other identification stuff to get the money from the telegraph company on."

"Kenny gave you the old man's address?"

"Sure he did."

"Did he give you Sue's?"

"No."

"How'd Kenny get hold of the stuff?"

"He didn't say."

"Where's Kenny now?"

"I don't know. He was on his way east, with something else on the fire, and couldn't fool with this. That's why
he passed it on to me."

"Big-hearted Kenny," I said. "You know Sue Hambleton?"

"No," emphatically. "I'd never even heard of her till
Kenny told me."

"I don't like this Kenny," I said, "though without him
your story's got some good points. Could you tell it leaving
him out?"

He shook his head slowly from side to side, saying, "It
wouldn't be the way it happened."

"That's too bad. Conspiracies to defraud don't mean as
much to me as finding Sue. I might have made a deal with you."

He shook his head again, but his eyes were thoughtful,
and his lower lip moved up to overlap the upper a little.

The girl had stepped back so she could see both of us as
we talked, turning her face, which showed she didn't like us,
from one to the other as we spoke our pieces. Now she fastened
her gaze on the man, and her eyes were growing angry again.

I got up on my feet, telling him, "Suit yourself. But if
you want to play it that way I'll have to take you both in."

He smiled with indrawn lips and stood up.

The girl thrust herself in between us, facing him.

"This is a swell time to be dummying up," she spit at
him. "Pop off, you lightweight, or I will. You're crazy if you
think I'm going to take the fall with you."

"Shut up," he said in his throat.

"Shut me up," she cried.

He tried to, with both hands. I reached over her shoulders and caught one of his wrists, knocked the other hand up.

She slid out from between us and ran around behind me, screaming, "Joe does know her. He got the things from her. She's at the St. Martin on O'Farrell Street—her and Babe McCloor."

While I listened to this I had to pull my head aside to let Joe's right hook miss me, had got his left arm twisted behind him, had turned my hip to catch his knee, and had got the palm of my left hand under his chin. I was ready to give his chin the Japanese tilt when he stopped wrestling and grunted, "Let me tell it."

"Hop to it," I consented, taking my hands away from him and stepping back.

He rubbed the wrist I had wrenched, scowling past me at the girl. He called her four unlovely names, the mildest of which was "a dumb twist," and told her, "He was bluffing about throwing us in the can. You don't think old man Hambleton's hunting for newspaper space, do you?" That wasn't a bad guess.

He sat on the sofa again, still rubbing his wrist. The girl stayed on the other side of the room, laughing at him through her teeth.

I said, "All right, roll it out, one of you."

"You've got it all," he muttered. "I glaumed that stuff last week when I was visiting Babe, knowing the story and hating to see a promising layout like that go to waste."

"What's Babe doing now?" I asked.

"I don't know."

"Is he still puffing them?"

"I don't know."

"Like hell you don't."

"I don't," he insisted. "If you know Babe you know you can't get anything out of him about what he's doing."

"How long have he and Sue been here?"

"About six months that I know of."

"Who's he mobbed up with?"

"I don't know. Any time Babe works with a mob he picks them up on the road and leaves them on the road."

"How's he fixed?"

"I don't know. There's always enough grub and liquor in the joint."

Half an hour of this convinced me that I wasn't going to get much information about my people here.

I went to the phone in the passageway and called the Agency. The boy on the switchboard told me MacMan was in the operative's room. I asked to have him sent up to me, and went back to the living room. Joe and Peggy took their heads apart when I came in.

MacMan arrived in less than ten minutes. I let him in and told him, "This fellow says his name's Joe Wales, and the girl's supposed to be Peggy Carroll who lives in 421. We've got them cold for conspiracy to defraud, but I've made a deal with them. I'm going out to look at it now. Stay here with them, in this room. Nobody goes in or out, and nobody but you gets to the phone. There's a fire escape in front of the window. The window's locked now. I'd keep it that way. If the deal turns out O.K. we'll let them go, but if they cut up on you while I'm gone there's no reason why you can't knock them around as much as you want."

MacMan nodded his hard round head and pulled a chair out between them and the door. I picked up my hat.

Joe Wales called, "Hey, you're not going to uncover me to Babe, are you? That's got to be part of the deal."

"Not unless I have to."

"I'd just as leave stand the rap," he said. "I'd be safer in jail."

"I'll give you the best break I can," I promised, "but you'll have to take what's dealt you."

WALKING OVER TO the St. Martin—only half a dozen blocks from Wales's place—I decided to go up against McCloor and the girl as a Continental op who suspected Babe of being in on a branch bank stick-up in Alameda the previous week. He hadn't been in on it—if the bank people had described half-correctly the men who had robbed them—so it wasn't likely my supposed suspicions would frighten him much. Clearing himself, he might give me some information I could use. The chief thing I wanted, of course, was a look at the girl, so I could report to her father that I had seen her. There was no reason for supposing that she and Babe knew her father was trying to keep an eye on her. Babe had a record. It was natural enough for sleuths to drop in now and then and try to hang something on him.

The St. Martin was a small three-story apartment house of red brick between two taller hotels. The vestibule register showed R. K. McCloor, 313, as Wales and Peggy had told me.

I pushed the bell button. Nothing happened. Nothing happened any of the four times I pushed it. I pushed the button labeled *Manager*.

The door clicked open. I went indoors. A beefy woman in a pink-striped cotton dress that needed pressing stood in an apartment doorway just inside the street door.

"Some people named McCloor live here?" I asked.

"Three-thirteen," she said.

"Been living here long?"

She pursed her fat mouth, looked intently at me, hesitated, but finally said, "Since last June."

"What do you know about them?"

She balked at that, raising her chin and her eyebrows.

I gave her my card. That was safe enough; it fit in with the pretext I intended using upstairs.

Her face, when she raised it from reading the card, was oily with curiosity.

"Come in here," she said in a husky whisper, backing through the doorway.

I followed her into her apartment. We sat on a chester-
field and she whispered, "What is it?"

"Maybe nothing." I kept my voice low, playing up to her
theatricals. "He's done time for safe burglary. I'm trying to get a
line on him now, on the off chance that he might have been tied
up in a recent job. I don't know that he was. He may be going
straight for all I know." I took his photograph—front and profile,
taken at Leavenworth—out of my pocket. "This him?"

She seized it eagerly, nodded, said, "Yes, that's him, all
right," turned it over to read the description on the back, and
repeated, "Yes, that's him, all right."

"His wife is here with him?" I asked.

She nodded vigorously.

"I don't know her," I said. "What sort of girl is she?"

She described a girl who could have been Sue
Hambleton. I couldn't show Sue's picture; that would have
uncovered me if she and Babe heard about it.

I asked the woman what she knew about the McCloors.
What she knew wasn't a great deal: paid their rent on time, kept
irregular hours, had occasional drinking parties, quarreled a lot.

"Think they're in now?" I asked. "I got no answer on the
bell."

"I don't know," she whispered. "I haven't seen either of
them since night before last, when they had a fight."

"Much of a fight?"

"Not much worse than usual."

"Could you find out if they're in?" I asked.

She looked at me out of the ends of her eyes.

"I'm not going to make any trouble for you," I assured
her. "But if they've blown I'd like to know it, and I reckon you
would too."

"All right, I'll find out." She got up, patting a pocket in
which keys jingled. "You wait here."

"I'll go as far as the third floor with you," I said, "and
wait out of sight there."

"All right," she said reluctantly.

On the third floor, I remained by the elevator. She disappeared around a corner of the dim corridor, and presently a muffled electric bell rang. It rang three times. I heard her keys jingle and one of them grate in a lock. The lock clicked. I heard the doorknob rattle as she turned it.

Then a long moment of silence was ended by a scream that filled the corridor from wall to wall.

I jumped for the corner, swung around it, saw an open door ahead, went through it, and slammed the door shut behind me.

The scream stopped.

I was in a small dark vestibule with three doors beside the one I had come through. One door was shut. One opened into a bathroom. I went to the other.

The fat manager stood just inside it, her round back to me. I pushed past her and saw what she was looking at.

Sue Hambleton, in pale yellow pajamas trimmed with black lace, was lying across the bed. She lay on her back. Her arms were stretched out over her head. One leg was bent under her, one stretched out so that its bare foot rested on the floor. That bare foot was whiter than a live foot could be. Her face was white as her foot, except for a mottled swollen area from the right eyebrow to the right cheekbone and dark bruises on her throat.

"Phone the police," I told the woman, and began poking into corners, closets and drawers.

It was late afternoon when I returned to the Agency. I asked the file clerk to see if we had anything on Joe Wales and Peggy Carroll, and then went into the Old Man's office.

He put down some reports he had been reading, gave me a nodded invitation to sit down, and asked, "You've seen her?"

"Yeah. She's dead."

The Old Man said, "Indeed," as if I had said it was raining, and smiled with polite attentiveness while I told him about it—from the time I had rung Wales's bell until I had joined the fat manager in the dead girl's apartment.

"She had been knocked around some, was bruised on the face and neck," I wound up. "But that didn't kill her."

"You think she was murdered?" he asked, still smiling gently.

"I don't know. Doc Jordan says he thinks it could have been arsenic. He's hunting for it in her now. We found a funny thing in the joint. Some thick sheets of dark gray paper were stuck in a book—*The Count of Monte Cristo*—wrapped in a month-old newspaper and wedged into a dark corner between the stove and the kitchen wall."

"Ah, arsenical fly paper," the Old Man murmured. "The Maybrick-Seddons trick. Mashed in water, four to six grains of arsenic can be soaked out of a sheet—enough to kill two people."

I nodded, saying, "I worked on one in Louisville in 1916. The mulatto janitor saw McCloor leaving at half-past nine yesterday morning. She was probably dead before that. Nobody's seen him since. Earlier in the morning the people in the next apartment had heard them talking, her groaning. But they had too many fights for the neighbors to pay much attention to that. The landlady told me they had a fight the night before that. The police are hunting for him."

"Did you tell the police who she was?"

"No. What do we do on that angle? We can't tell them about Wales without telling them all."

"I dare say the whole thing will have to come out," he said thoughtfully. "I'll wire New York."

I went out of his office. The file clerk gave me a couple of newspaper clippings. The first told me that fifteen months ago Joseph Wales, alias Holy Joe, had been arrested on the complaint of a farmer named Toomey that he had been taken for twenty-five hundred dollars on a phony "business opportunity" by Wales and three other men. The second clipping said the case had been dropped when Toomey failed to appear against Wales in court—bought off in the customary manner by the return of part or all of his money. That was all our files held on Wales, and they had nothing on Peggy Carroll.

MACMAN OPENED THE door for me when I returned to Wales's apartment.

"Anything doing?" I asked him.

"Nothing—except they've been belly-aching a lot."

Wales came forward, asking eagerly, "Satisfied now?"

The girl stood by the window, looking at me with anxious eyes.

I didn't say anything.

"Did you find her?" Wales asked, frowning. "She was where I told you?"

"Yeah," I said.

"Well, then." Part of his frown went away. "That lets Peggy and me out, doesn't—" He broke off, ran his tongue over his lower lip, put a hand to his chin, asked sharply, "You didn't give them the tip-off on me, did you?"

I shook my head, no.

He took his hand from his chin and asked irritably, "What's the matter with you, then? What are you looking like that for?"

Behind him the girl spoke bitterly. "I knew damned well it would be like this," she said. "I knew damned well we weren't going to get out of it. Oh, what a smart guy you are!"

"Take Peggy into the kitchen, and shut both doors," I told MacMan. "Holy Joe and I are going to have a real heart-to-heart talk."

The girl went out willingly, but when MacMan was closing the door she put her head in again to tell Wales, "I hope he busts you in the nose if you try to hold out on him."

MacMan shut the door.

"Your playmate seems to think you know something," I said.

Wales scowled at the door and grumbled, "She's more

help to me than a broken leg." He turned his face to me, trying to make it look frank and friendly. "What do you want? I came clean with you before. What's the matter now?"

"What do you guess?"

He pulled his lips in between his teeth. "What do you want to make me guess for?" he demanded. "I'm willing to play ball with you. But what can I do if you won't tell me what you want? I can't see inside your head."

"You'd get a kick out of it if you could."

He shook his head wearily and walked back to the sofa, sitting down bent forward, his hands together between his knees. "All right," he sighed. "Take your time about asking me. I'll wait for you."

I went over and stood in front of him. I took his chin between my left thumb and fingers, raising his head and bending my own down until our noses were almost touching. I said, "Where you stumbled, Joe, was in sending the telegram right after the murder."

"He's dead?" It popped out before his eyes had even had time to grow round and wide.

The question threw me off balance. I had to wrestle with my forehead to keep it from wrinkling, and I put too much calmness in my voice when I asked, "Is who dead?"

"Who? How do I know? Who do you mean?"

"Who did you think I meant?" I insisted.

"How do I know? Oh, all right! Old Man Hambleton, Sue's father."

"That's right," I said, and took my hand away from his chin.

"And he was murdered, you say?" He hadn't moved his face an inch from the position into which I had lifted it. "How?"

"Arsenic fly paper."

"Arsenic fly paper." He looked thoughtful. "That's a funny one."

"Yeah, very funny. Where'd you go about buying some if you wanted it?"

"Buying it? I don't know. I haven't seen any since I was a kid. Nobody uses fly paper here in San Francisco anyway. There aren't enough flies."

"Somebody used some here," I said, "on Sue."

"Sue?" He jumped so that the sofa squeaked under him.

"Yeah. Murdered yesterday morning—arsenical fly paper."

"Both of them?" he asked incredulously.

"Both of who?"

"Her and her father."

"Yeah."

He put his chin far down on his chest and rubbed the back of one hand with the palm of the other. "Then I am in a hole," he said slowly.

"That's what," I cheerfully agreed. "Want to try talking yourself out of it?"

"Let me think."

I let him think, listening to the tick of the clock while he thought. Thinking brought drops of sweat out on his gray-white face. Presently he sat up straight, wiping his face with a fancily colored handkerchief. "I'll talk," he said. "I've got to talk now. Sue was getting ready to ditch Babe. She and I were going away. She—Here, I'll show you."

He put his hand in his pocket and held out a folded sheet of thick note paper to me. I took it and read:

Dear Joe:—

I can't stand this much longer—we've simply got to go soon. Babe beat me again tonight. Please, if you really love me, let's make it soon.

Sue

The handwriting was a nervous woman's, tall, angular, and piled up.

HAMMETT

"That's why I made the play for Hambleton's grand," he said. "I've been shatting on my uppers for a couple of months, and when that letter came yesterday I just had to raise dough somehow to get her away. She wouldn't have stood for tapping her father, though, so I tried to swing it without her knowing."

"When did you see her last?"

"Day before yesterday, the day she mailed that letter. Only I saw her in the afternoon—she was here—and she wrote it that night."

"Babe suspect what you were up to?"

"We didn't think he did. I don't know. He was jealous as hell all the time, whether he had any reason to be or not."

"How much reason did he have?"

Wales looked me straight in the eye and said, "Sue was a good kid."

I said, "Well, she's been murdered."

He didn't say anything.

Day was darkening into evening. I went to the door and pressed the light button. I didn't lose sight of Holy Joe Wales while I was doing it.

As I took my finger away from the button, something clicked at the window. The click was loud and sharp.

I looked at the window.

A man crouched there on the fire escape, looking in through the glass and lace curtain. He was a thick-featured dark man whose size identified him as Babe McCloor. The muzzle of a big black automatic was touching the glass in front of him. He had tapped the glass with it to catch our attention.

He had our attention.

There wasn't anything for me to do just then. I stood there and looked at him. I couldn't tell whether he was looking at me or at Wales. I could see him clearly enough, but the lace curtain spoiled my view of details like that. I imagined he wasn't neglecting either of us, and I didn't imagine the lace curtain hid much from him. He was closer to the curtain then we, and I had turned on the room's lights.

Wales, sitting dead-still on the sofa, was looking at McCloor. Wales's face wore a peculiar, stiffly sullen expression. His eyes were sullen. He wasn't breathing.

McCloor flicked the nose of his pistol against the pane, and a triangular piece of glass fell out, tinkling apart on the floor. It didn't, I was afraid, make enough noise to alarm MacMan in the kitchen. There were two closed doors between here and there.

Wales looked at the broken pane and closed his eyes. He closed them slowly, little by little, exactly as if he were falling asleep. He kept his stiffly sullen blank face turned straight to the window.

McCloor shot him three times.

The bullets knocked Wales down on the sofa, back against the wall. Wales's eyes popped open, bulging. His lips crawled back over his teeth, leaving them naked to the gums. His tongue came out. Then his head fell down and he didn't move anymore.

When McCloor jumped away from the window I jumped to it. While I was pushing the curtain aside, unlocking the window and raising it, I heard his feet land on the cement paving below.

MacMan flung the door open and came in, the girl at his heels.

"Take care of this," I ordered as I scrambled over the sill. "McCloor shot him."

WALES'S APARTMENT WAS on the second floor. The fire escape ended there with a counter-weighted iron ladder that a man's weight would swing down into a cement-paved court.

I went down as Babe McCloor had gone, swinging down on the ladder till within dropping distance of the court, and then letting go.

There was only one street exit to the court. I took it.

A startled-looking, smallish man was standing in the middle of the sidewalk close to the court, gaping at me as I dashed out.

I caught his arm, shook it. "A big guy running." Maybe I yelled. "Where?"

He tried to say something, couldn't, and waved his arm at billboards standing across the front of a vacant lot on the other side of the street.

I forgot to say, "Thank you," in my hurry to get over there.

I got behind the billboards by crawling under them instead of going to either end, where there were openings. The lot was large enough and weedy enough to give cover to any-body who wanted to lie down and bushwack a pursuer—even anybody as large as Babe McCloor.

While I considered that, I heard a dog barking at one corner of the lot. He could have been barking at a man who had run by. I ran to that corner of the lot. The dog was in a board-fenced backyard, at the corner of a narrow alley that ran from the lot to a street.

I chinned myself on the board fence, saw a wire-haired terrier alone in the yard, and ran down the alley while he was charging at my part of the fence.

I put my gun back into my pocket before I left the alley for the street.

A small touring car was parked at the curb in front of a cigar store some fifteen feet from the alley. A policeman was talking to a slim dark-faced man in the cigar store doorway.

"The big fellow that come out of the alley a minute ago," I said. "Which way did he go?"

The policeman looked dumb. The slim man nodded his head down the street, said, "Down that way," and went on with his conversation.

I said, "Thanks," and went on down to the corner. There was a taxi phone there and two idle taxis. A block and a half below, a street car was going away. "Did the big fellow who came down here a minute ago take a taxi or the streetcar?" I asked the two taxi chauffeurs who were leaning against one of the taxis.

The rattier-looking one said, "He didn't take a taxi."

I said, "I'll take one. Catch that streetcar for me."

The streetcar was three blocks away before we got going. The street wasn't clear enough for me to see who got on and off it. We caught it when it stopped at Market Street.

"Follow along," I told the driver as I jumped out.

On the rear platform of the streetcar I looked through the glass. There were only eight or ten people aboard.

"There was a great big fellow got on at Hyde Street," I said to the conductor. "Where'd he get off?"

The conductor looked at the silver dollar I was turning over in my fingers and remembered that the big man got off at Taylor Street. That won the silver dollar.

I dropped off as the streetcar turned into Market Street. The taxi, close behind, slowed down, and its door swung open. "Sixth and Mission," I said as I hopped in.

McCloor could have gone in any direction from Taylor Street. I had to guess. The best guess seemed to be that he would make for the other side of Market Street.

It was fairly dark by now. We had to go down to Fifth Street to get off Market, then over to Mission, and back up to Sixth. We got to Sixth Street without seeing McCloor. I couldn't see him on Sixth Street—either way from the crossing.

"On up to Ninth," I ordered, and while we rode told the driver what kind of man I was looking for.

We arrived at Ninth Street. No McCloor. I cursed and pushed my brains around.

The big man was a yegg. San Francisco was on fire for him. The yegg instinct would be to use a rattler to get away from trouble. The freight yards were in this end of town. Maybe he would be shifty enough to lie low instead of trying to powder. In that case, he probably hadn't crossed Market Street at all. If he stuck, there would still be a chance of picking him up tomorrow. If he was high-tailing, it was catch him now or not at all.

"Down to Harrison," I told the driver.

We went down to Harrison Street, and down Harrison to Third, up Bryant to Eighth, down Brannan to Third again, and over to Townsend—and we didn't see Babe McCloor.

"That's tough, that is," the driver sympathized as we stopped across the street from the Southern Pacific passenger station.

"I'm going over and look around in the station," I said. "Keep your eyes open while I'm gone."

When I told the copper in the station my trouble he introduced me to a couple of plain-clothes men who had been planted there to watch for McCloor. That had been done after Sue Hambleton's body was found. The shooting of Holy Joe Wales was news to them.

I went outside again and found my taxi in front of the door, its horn working overtime, but too asthmatically to be heard indoors. The ratty driver was excited.

"A guy like you said come up out of King Street just now and swung on a Number 16 car as it pulled away," he said.

"Going which way?"

"Thataway," pointing southeast.

"Catch him," I said, jumping in.

The streetcar was out of sight around a bend in Third Street two blocks below. When we rounded the bend, the streetcar was slowing up, four blocks ahead. It hadn't slowed up very much when a man leaned far out and stepped off. He was a tall man, but didn't look tall on account of his shoulder spread. He didn't check his momentum, but used it to carry him across the sidewalk and out of sight.

We stopped where the man left the car.

I gave the driver too much money and told him, "Go back to Townsend Street and tell the copper in the station that I've chased Babe McCloor into the S. P. yards."

I THOUGHT I was moving silently down between two strings of box cars, but I had gone less than twenty feet when a light flashed in my face and a sharp voice ordered, "Stand still, you."

I stood still. Men came from between cars. One of them spoke my name, adding, "What are you doing here? Lost?" It was Harry Pebble, a police detective.

I stopped holding my breath and said, "Hello, Harry. Looking for Babe?"

"Yes. We've been going over the rattlers."

"He's here. I just tailed him in from the street."

Pebble swore and snapped the light off.

"Watch, Harry," I advised. "Don't play with him. He's packing plenty of gun and he's cut down one boy tonight."

"I'll play with him," Pebble promised, and told one of the men with him to go over and warn those on the other side of the yard that McCloor was in, and then to ring for reinforcements.

"We'll just sit on the edge and hold him in till they come," he said.

That seemed a sensible way to play it. We spread out and waited. Once Pebble and I turned back a lanky bum who tried to slip into the yard between us, and one of the men below us picked up a shivering kid who was trying to slip out. Otherwise nothing happened until Lieutenant Duff arrived with a couple of carloads of coppers.

Most of our force went into a cordon around the yard. The rest of us went through the yard in small groups, working it over car by car. We picked up a few hoboes that Pebble and his men had missed earlier, but we didn't find McCloor.

We didn't find any trace of him until somebody stumbled over a railroad bum huddled in the shadow of a gondola. It took a couple of minutes to bring him to, and he couldn't talk then. His jaw was broken. But when we asked if McCloor had slugged him, he nodded, and when we asked in which direction McCloor had been headed, he moved a feeble hand to the east.

We went over and searched the Santa Fe yards.

We didn't find McCloor.

I RODE UP to the Hall of Justice with Duff. MacMan was in the captain of detectives' office with three or four police sleuths.

"Wales die?" I asked.

"Yep."

"Say anything before he went?"

"He was gone before you were through the window."

"You held on to the girl?"

"She's here."

"She say anything?"

"We were waiting for you before we tapped her," detective sergeant O'Gar said, "not knowing the angle on her."

"Let's have her in. I haven't had any dinner yet. How about the autopsy on Sue Hambleton?"

"Chronic arsenic poisoning."

"Chronic? That means it was fed to her little by little, and not in a lump?"

"Uh-huh. From what he found in her kidneys, intestines, liver, stomach and blood, Jordan figures there was less than a grain of it in her. That wouldn't be enough to knock her off. But he says he found arsenic in the tips of her hair, and she'd have to be given some at least a month ago for it to have worked out that far."

"Any chance that it wasn't arsenic that killed her?"

"Not unless Jordan's a bum doctor."

A policewoman came in with Peggy Carroll.

The blonde girl was tired. Her eyelids, mouth corners and body drooped, and when I pushed a chair out toward her she sagged down in it.

O'Gar ducked his grizzled bullet head at me.

"Now, Peggy," I said, "tell us where you fit into this mess."

"I don't fit into it." She didn't look up. Her voice was tired. "Joe dragged me into it. He told you."

"You his girl?"

"If you want to call it that," she admitted.

"You jealous?"

"What," she asked, looking up at me, her face puzzled, "has that got to do with it?"

"Sue Hambleton was getting ready to go away with him when she was murdered."

The girl sat up straight in the chair and said deliberately, "I swear to God I didn't know she was murdered."

"But you did know she was dead," I said positively.

"I didn't," she replied just as positively.

I nudged O'Gar with my elbow. He pushed his undershot jaw at her and barked, "What are you trying to give us? You knew she was dead. How could you kill her without knowing it?"

While she looked at him I waved the others in. They crowded close around her and took up the chorus of the sergeant's song. She was barked, roared, and snarled at plenty in the next few minutes.

The instant she stopped trying to talk back to them I cut in again. "Wait," I said, very earnestly. "Maybe she didn't kill her."

"The hell she didn't," O'Gar stormed, holding the center of the stage so the others could move away from the girl without their retreat seeming too artificial. "Do you mean to tell me this baby—"

"I didn't say she didn't," I remonstrated. "I said maybe she didn't."

"Then who did?"

I passed the question to the girl. "Who did?"

"Babe," she said immediately.

O'Gar snorted to make her think he didn't believe her.

I asked, as if I were honestly perplexed, "How do you know that if you didn't know she was dead?"

"It stands to reason he did," she said. "Anybody can see that. He found out she was going away with Joe, so he killed her and then came to Joe's and killed him. That's just exactly what Babe would do when he found it out."

"Yeah? How long have *you* known they were going away together?"

"Since they decided to. Joe told me a month or two ago."

"And you didn't mind?"

"You've got this all wrong," she said. "Of course I did-n't mind. I was being cut in on it. You know her father had the bees. That's what Joe was after. She didn't mean anything to him but an in to the old man's pockets. And I was to get my dib. And you needn't think I was crazy enough about Joe or anybody else to step off in the air for them. Babe got next and fixed the pair of them. That's a cinch."

"Yeah? How do you figure Babe would kill her?"

"That guy? You don't think he'd—"

"I mean how would he go about killing her?"

"Oh!" She shrugged. "With his hands, likely as not."

"Once he'd made up his mind to do it, he'd do it quick and violent?" I suggested.

"That would be Babe," she agreed.

"But you can't see him slow-poisoning her—spreading it out over a month?"

Worry came into the girl's blue eyes. She put her lower lip between her teeth, then said slowly, "No, I can't see him doing it that way. Not Babe."

"Who can you see doing it that way?"

She opened her eyes wide, asking, "You mean Joe?"

I didn't say anything.

"Joe might have," she said persuasively. "God only knows what he'd want to do it for, why he'd want to get rid of the kind of meal ticket she was going to be. But you couldn't always guess what he was getting at. He pulled plenty of dumb ones. He was too slick without being smart. If he was going to kill her, though, that would be about the way he'd go about it."

"Were he and Babe friendly?"

"No."

"Did he go to Babe's much?"

"Not at all that I know about. He was too leery of Babe to take a chance on being caught there. That's why I moved upstairs, so Sue could come over to our place to see him."

"Then how could Joe have hidden the fly paper he poisoned her with in her apartment?"

"Fly paper!" Her bewilderment seemed honest enough.

"Show it to her," I told O'Gar.

He got a sheet from the desk and held it close to the girl's face.

She stared at it for a moment and then jumped up and grabbed my arm with both hands.

"I didn't know what it was," she said excitedly. "Joe had some a couple of months ago. He was looking at it when I came in. I asked him what it was for, and he smiled that wisenheimer smile of his and said, 'You make angels out of it,' and wrapped it up again and put it in his pocket. I didn't pay much attention to him; he was always fooling with some kind of tricks that were supposed to make him wealthy, but never did."

"Ever see it again?"

"No."

"Did you know Sue very well?"

"I didn't know her at all. I never even saw her. I used to keep out of the way so I wouldn't gum Joe's play with her."

"But you know Babe?"

"Yes, I've been on a couple of parties where he was. That's all I know him."

"Who killed Sue?"

"Joe," she said. "Didn't he have that paper you say she was killed with?"

"Why did he kill her?"

"I don't know. He pulled some awful dumb tricks sometimes."

"You didn't kill her?"

"No, no, no!"

I jerked the corner of my mouth at O'Gar.

"You're a liar," he bawled, shaking the fly paper in her face. "You killed her." The rest of the team closed in, throwing accusations at her. They kept it up until she was groggy and the policewoman was beginning to look worried.

Then I said angrily, "All right. Throw her in a cell and let her think it over." To her, "You know what you told Joe this afternoon: this is no time to dummy up. Do a lot of thinking tonight."

"Honest to God I didn't kill her," she said.

I turned my back to her. The policewoman took her away.

"Ho-hum," O'Gar yawned. "We gave her a pretty good ride at that, for a short one."

"Not bad," I agreed. "If anybody else looked likely, I'd say she didn't kill Sue. But if she's telling the truth, then Holy Joe did it. And why should he poison the goose that was going to lay nice yellow eggs for him? And how and why did he cache the poison in their apartment? Babe had the motive, but damned if he looks like a slow-poisoner to me. You can't tell, though; he and Holy Joe could even have been working together on it."

"Could," Duff said. "But it takes a lot of imagination to get that one down. Anyway you twist it, Peggy's our best bet so far. Go up against her again, hard, in the morning?"

"Yeah," I said. "And we've got to find Babe."

The others had had dinner. MacMan and I went out

and got ours. When we returned to the detective bureau an hour later it was practically deserted of the regular operatives.

"All gone to Pier 42 on a tip that McCloor's there," Steve Ward told us.

"How long ago?"

"Ten minutes."

MacMan and I got a taxi and set out for Pier 42. We didn't get to Pier 42.

On First Street, half a block from the Embarcadero, the taxi suddenly shrieked and slid to a halt.

"What—?" I began, and saw a man standing in front of the machine. He was a big man with a big gun. "Babe," I grunted, and put my hand on MacMan's arm to keep him from getting his gun out.

"Take me to—" McCloor was saying to the frightened driver when he saw us. He came around to my side and pulled the door open, holding the gun on us.

He had no hat. His hair was wet, plastered to his head. Little streams of water trickled down from it. His clothes were dripping wet.

He looked surprised at us and ordered, "Get out."

As we got out he growled at the driver, "What the hell you got your flag up for if you had fares?"

The driver wasn't there. He had hopped out the other side and was scooting down the street. McCloor cursed him and poked his gun at me, growling, "Go on, beat it."

Apparently he hadn't recognized me. The light here wasn't good, and I had a hat on now. He had seen me for only a few seconds in Wales's room.

I stepped aside. MacMan moved to the other side.

McCloor took a backward step to keep us from getting him between us and started an angry word.

MacMan threw himself on McCloor's gun arm.

I socked McCloor's jaw with my fist. I might just as well have hit somebody else for all it seemed to bother him.

He swept me out of his way and pasted MacMan in the mouth. MacMan fell back till the taxi stopped him, spit out a tooth, and came back for more.

I was trying to climb up McCloor's left side.

MacMan came in on his right, failed to dodge a chop of the gun, caught it square on the top of the noodle, and went down hard. He stayed down.

I kicked McCloor's ankle, but couldn't get his foot from under him. I rammed my right fist into the small of his back and got a left-handful of his wet hair, swinging on it. He shook his head, dragging me off my feet.

He punched me in the side and I could feel my ribs and guts flattening together like leaves in a book.

I swung my fist against the back of his neck. That bothered him. He made a rumbling noise down in his chest, crunched my shoulder in his left hand, and chopped at me with the gun in his right.

I kicked him somewhere and punched his neck again.

Down the street, at the Embarcadero, a police whistle was blowing. Men were running up First Street toward us.

McCloor snorted like a locomotive and threw me away from him. I didn't want to go. I tried to hang on. He threw me away from him and ran up the street.

I scrambled up and ran after him, dragging my gun out.

At the first corner he stopped to squirt metal at me—three shots. I squirted one at him. None of the four connected.

He disappeared around the corner. I swung wide around it, to make him miss if he were flattened to the wall waiting for me. He wasn't. He was a hundred feet ahead, going into a space between two warehouses. I went in after him, and out after him at the other end, making better time with my hundred and ninety pounds than he was making with his two-fifty.

He crossed a street, turning up, away from the water-front. There was a light on the corner. When I came into its glare he wheeled and leveled his gun at me. I didn't hear it click, but I knew it had when he threw it at me. The gun went past with a couple of feet to spare and raised hell against a door behind me.

McCloor turned and ran up the street. I ran up the street after him.

I put a bullet past him to let the others know where we were. At the next corner, he started to turn to the left, changed his mind, and went straight on.

I sprinted, cutting the distance between us to forty or fifty feet, and yelped, "Stop or I'll drop you."

He jumped sidewise into a narrow alley.

I passed it on the jump, saw he wasn't waiting for me, and went in. Enough light came in from the street to let us see each other and our surroundings. The alley was blind—walled on each side and at the other end by tall concrete buildings with steel-shuttered windows and doors.

McCloor faced me, less than twenty feet away. His jaw stuck out. His arms curved down free of his sides. His shoulders were bunched.

"Put them up," I ordered, holding my gun level.

"Get out of my way, little man," he grumbled, taking a stiff-legged step toward me. "I'll eat you up."

"Keep coming," I said, "and I'll put you down."

"Try it." He took another step, crouching a little. "I can still get to you *with* slugs in me."

"Not where I'll put them." I was wordy, trying to talk him into waiting till the others came up. I didn't want to have to kill him. We could have done that from the taxi. "I'm no Annie Oakley, but if I can't pop your kneecaps with two shots at this distance, you're welcome to me. And if you think smashed kneecaps are a lot of fun, give it a whirl."

"Hell with that," he said and charged.

I shot his right knee.

He lurched toward me.

I shot his left knee.

He tumbled down.

"You would have it," I complained.

He twisted around, and with his arms pushed himself into a sitting position facing me.

"I didn't think you had sense enough to do it," he said through his teeth.

I TALKED TO McCloor in the hospital. He lay on his back in bed with a couple of pillows slanting his head up. The skin was pale and tight around his mouth and eyes, but there was nothing else to show he was in pain.

"You sure devastated me, bo," he said when I came in.

"Sorry," I said, "but—"

"I ain't beefing. I asked for it."

"Why'd you kill Holy Joe?" I asked, offhand, as I pulled a chair up beside the bed.

"Uh-uh—you're tooting the wrong ringer."

I laughed and told him I was the man in the room with Joe when it happened.

McCloor grinned and said, "I thought I'd seen you somewheres before. So that's where it was. I didn't pay no attention to your mug, just so your hands didn't move."

"Why'd you kill him?"

He pursed his lips, screwed up his eyes at me, thought something over and said, "He killed a broad I knew."

"He killed Sue Hambleton?" I asked.

He studied my face a while before he replied, "Yep."

"How do you figure that out?"

"Hell," he said, "I don't have to. Sue told me. Give me a butt."

I gave him a cigarette, held a lighter under it, and objected. "That doesn't exactly fit in with other things I know. Just what happened and what did she say? You might start back with the night you gave her the goog."

He looked thoughtful, letting smoke sneak slowly out of his nose, then said, "I hadn't ought to hit her in the eye, that's a fact. But, see, she had been out all afternoon and wouldn't tell me where she'd been, and we had a row about it. What's this—Thursday morning? That was Monday, then. After the row I went out and spent the night in a dump over on Army Street. I got home about seven the next morning. Sue was sick as hell, but she wouldn't let me get a croaker for her. That was kind of funny, because she was scared stiff."

McCloor scratched his head meditatively and suddenly drew in a great lungful of smoke, practically eating up the rest of the cigarette. He let the smoke leak out of mouth and nose together, looking dully through the cloud at me. Then he said brusquely, "Well, she went under. But before she went she told me she'd been poisoned by Holy Joe."

"She say he'd given it to her?"

McCloor shook his head.

"I'd been asking her what was the matter, and not getting anything out of her. Then she starts whining that she's poisoned. 'I'm poisoned, Babe,' she whines. 'Arsenic. That damned Holy Joe,' she says. Then she won't say anything else, and it's not a hell of a while after that that she kicks off."

"Yeah? Then what'd you do?"

"I went gunning for Holy Joe. I knew him but didn't know where he jungled up, and didn't find out till yesterday. You was there when I came. You know about that. I had picked up a boiler and parked it over on Turk Street, for the getaway. When I got back to it, there was a copper standing close to it. I figured he might have spotted it as a hot one and was waiting to see who came for it, so I let it alone, and caught a streetcar instead, and cut for the yards. Down there I ran into a whole flock of hammer and saws and had to go overboard in China Basin, swimming up to a pier, being ranked again by a watchman there, swimming off to another, and finally getting through the line only to run into another bad break. I wouldn't of flagged that taxi if the *For Hire* flag hadn't been up."

"You knew Sue was planning to take a run-out on you with Joe?"

"I don't know it yet," he said. "I knew damned well she was cheating on me, but I didn't know who with."

"What would you have done if you had known that?" I asked.

"Me?" He grinned wolfishly. "Just what I did."

"Killed the pair of them," I said.

He rubbed his lower lip with a thumb and asked calmly, "You think I killed Sue?"

"You did."

"Serves me right," he said. "I must be getting simple in my old age. What the hell am I doing barbering with a lousy dick? That never got nobody nothing but grief. Well, you might just as well take it on the heel and toe now, my lad. I'm through spitting."

And he was. I couldn't get another word out of him.

THE OLD MAN sat listening to me, tapping his desk lightly with the point of a long yellow pencil, staring past me with mild blue rimless-spectacled eyes. When I had brought my story up to date, he asked pleasantly, "How is MacMan?"

"He lost two teeth, but his skull wasn't cracked. He'll be out in a couple of days."

The Old Man nodded and asked, "What remains to be done?"

"Nothing. We can put Peggy Carroll on the mat again, but it's not likely we'll squeeze much more out of her. Outside of that, the returns are pretty well all in."

"And what do you make of it?"

I squirmed in my chair and said, "Suicide."

The Old Man smiled at me, politely but skeptically.

"I don't like it either," I grumbled. "And I'm not ready to write in a report yet. But that's the only total that what we've got will add up to. The fly paper was hidden behind the kitchen stove. Nobody would be crazy enough to try to hide something from a woman in her own kitchen like that. But the woman might hide it there.

"According to Peggy, Holy Joe had the fly paper. If Sue hid it, she got it from him. For what? They were planning to go away together, and were only waiting till Joe, who was on the nut, raised enough dough. Maybe they were afraid of Babe, and had the poison there to slip him if he tumbled to their plan before they went. Maybe they meant to slip it to him before they went away.

"When I started talking to Holy Joe about murder, he thought Babe was the one who had been bumped off. He was surprised, maybe, but as if he was surprised that it had happened so soon. He was more surprised when he heard that Sue had died too, but even then he wasn't so surprised as when he saw McCloor alive at the window.

"She died cursing Holy Joe, and she knew she was poisoned, and she wouldn't let McCloor get a doctor. Can't that mean she had turned against Joe, and had taken the poison herself instead of feeding it to Babe? The poison was hidden from Babe. But even if he found it, I can't figure him as a poisoner. He's too rough. Unless he caught her trying to poison him and made her swallow the stuff. But that doesn't account for the month-old arsenic in her hair."

"Does your suicide hypothesis take care of that?" the Old Man asked.

"It could," I said. "Don't be kicking holes in my theory. It's got enough as it stands. But, if she committed suicide this time, there's no reason why she couldn't have tried it once before—say after a quarrel with Joe a month ago—and failed to bring it off. That would have put the arsenic in her. There's no real proof that she took any between a month ago and day before yesterday."

"No real proof," the Old Man protested mildly, "except the autopsy's finding—chronic poisoning."

I was never one to let experts' guesses stand in my way. I said, "They base that on the small amount of arsenic they found in her remains—less than a fatal dose. And the amount they find in your stomach after you're dead depends on how much you vomit before you die."

The Old Man smiled benevolently at me and asked, "But you're not, you say, ready to write this theory into a report? Meanwhile, what do you propose doing?"

"If there's nothing else on tap, I'm going home, fumigate my brains with Fatimas, and try to get this thing straightened out in my head. I think I'll get a copy of *The Count of Monte Cristo* and run through it. I haven't read it since I was a kid. It looks like the book was wrapped up with fly paper to make a bundle large enough to wedge tightly between the wall and the stove, so it wouldn't fall down. But there might be something in the book. I'll see anyway."

"I did that last night," the Old Man murmured.

I asked, "And?"

He took a book from his desk drawer, opened it where a slip of paper marked a place, and held it out to me, one pink finger marking a paragraph.

"Suppose you were to take a milligramme of this poison the first day, two milligrammes the second day, and so on. Well, at the end of ten days you would have taken a centigramme; at the end of twenty days increasing another milligramme, you would have taken three hundred centigrammes; that is to say; a dose you would support without inconvenience, and which would be very dangerous for any other person who had not taken the same precautions as yourself. Well, then, at the end of the month, when drinking water from the same carafe, you would kill the person who had drunk this water, without your perceiving otherwise than from slight inconvenience that there was any poisonous substance mingled with the water."

"That does it," I said. "That does it. They were afraid to go away without killing Babe, too certain he'd come after them. She tried to make herself immune from arsenic poisoning by getting her body accustomed to it, taking steadily increasing doses, so when she slipped the big shot in Babe's food she could eat it with him without danger. She'd be taken sick, but wouldn't die, and the police couldn't hang his death on her because she too had eaten the poisoned food.

"That clicks. After the row Monday night, when she wrote Joe the note urging him to make the getaway soon, she tried to hurry up her immunity, and increased her preparatory doses too quickly, took too large a shot. That's why she cursed Joe at the end; it was his plan."

"Possibly she overdosed herself in an attempt to speed it along," the Old Man agreed, "but not necessarily. There are people who can cultivate an ability to take large doses of arsenic without trouble, but it seems to be sort of a natural gift with them, a matter of some constitutional peculiarity. Ordinarily, anyone who tried it would do what Sue Hambleton did— slowly poison themselves until the cumulative effect was strong enough to cause death."

Babe McCloor was hanged, for killing Holy Joe Wales, six months later.

The Demon in the Belfry

Hildegarde Teilhet

EVEN NOW, AFTER all these years, she still comes back to us. We can see her as through one of those old-fashioned looking glasses, the details blurred a little, the outlines stamped with a kind of melancholy transparency. On that Wednesday, April 3, 1895, the morning was windy and sweeping the fog from the San Francisco hills when Blanche Lamont left the house of her uncle Charley and aunt Tryphena to get herself so unnecessarily killed.

Her photograph reveals her as she must have looked half a century ago. But it cannot convey to us anything of the secret excitement she must have felt from the knowledge Theo Durrant was waiting for her at Mission Street, some blocks distant, far enough away from the house at 209 Twenty-first Street to allay any suspicions of her aunt's.

Blanche was a tall, supple, twenty-one-year-old lass from Montana, of exceedingly white skin, round eyes, long

San Francisco newspaper reporter **HILDEGARDE TEILHET** presents a true account of the brutal 1895 murders of two young Bay Area women. Teilhet's 1936 report of the media spectacle which ensued demonstrates that much has remained the same in the past 100 years.

lashes, smooth oval face, and soft dark brown hair; with something of a complacent look staring out at us from the faded photograph. A year before, in Dillon, Montana, Blanche had not been well; it was thought she might even be tubercular. In the hope of regaining her health, she came west with her sister to live with her aunt and uncle, Tryphena and Charles G. Noble.

Of course, the restricted and dull life two socially inclined girls might have had in a little Montana town, as compared to the possibilities of a city such as San Francisco—with cable cars running up and down the hills, ships in the harbor, the schools, the parties, the churches, and the opportunities to meet interesting people—might well have helped two young ladies to find themselves afflicted with a vague illness in order to seek a change of scenery. San Francisco seems to have been effective as a medicine. Within a year of her arrival, Blanche was actively engaged in a fairly strenuous school and social curriculum; and, despite this, she had added six pounds to the one hundred and fourteen she brought with her from Montana.

When Blanche departed for school a little before eight on that Wednesday morning in April, she had attired herself in a very attractive outfit. She wore a flowing black skirt, short enough to reveal pretty ankles, and a fashionable basque jacket. Over the brown hair was a large floppy hat, with feathers stuck in it and ribbons. It was not the hat, even for those days, a girl might be expected to wear to school on a windy day, unless she had a very special reason for wishing to look her best.

In brief, she was worth looking at as she left the house. In the Nineties girls may have been warned more frequently than now that good looks could be a hazard to them. In Blanche's case, as it turned out, her appearance was more of a hazard to her murderer. For her fair face and figure in passing along the streets that day was such as to evoke the memory of her passing, days later, by a great horde of witnesses, who came forward of their own volition from all parts of the city, to say what they had seen and by their joint action to reveal the murderer.

She met Theo Durrant at Twenty-first and Mission at fifteen minutes after eight. She had approximately eight and a half hours more in which to breathe, to laugh, to know it was good to be in San Francisco, to listen to all Theo urged her to do—but certainly not to be frightened enough to run from him while she still had the chance.

No, Blanche listened to him. On the electric car, his hand was around her shoulder and he was talking very sweetly with her. Car conductor Henry Shellmont later recalled on the stand, "He was fooling with her gloves which she had removed. He was fooling with them in this manner over hands; and he seemed to be talking very sweetly to her." A fellow medical student of Theo's was on that same car, too, and some time afterwards, to his surprise, found himself on the stand swearing he had seen them both. If Theo had been contemplating murder in advance, a man of his intelligence would have done his best to prevent such a horde of witnesses marking him and his victim step by step to the very minute when he and Blanche disappeared into the church and encountered the demon.

William Henry Theodore Durrant was a medical student and the assistant superintendent of Sunday School at the Emanuel Baptist Church. He was, by all accounts, devout. He was amiable and well liked. His mother testified he invariably kissed her upon going out and returning. He was an usher at church. He had a talented sister, Eullah, who had journeyed to Berlin two months previously in order to study music. His father was a foreman in a shoe factory, the Durrant family having lived in San Francisco the past sixteen years, coming from Canada where Theo had been born twenty-four years earlier in Toronto.

Theo had attended private school instead of public; he had graduated from Cogswell's Polytechnic School at nineteen. In 1895 he was in his senior year at the Cooper Medical College. He had been a member of the Emanuel

Baptist Church since 1891. Theo had the church keys and was accustomed to dropping in at the Emanuel Baptist Church during week days, to make repairs, to fix doors, to put up a stage for entertainment, often with his nineteen-year-old friend, George King, the church organist.

When the time came for Theo's character to be examined publicly, witnesses to his purity and innocence were not wanting. One of his fellow medical students stated unequivocally that at least up until two years previously, by Theo's own confession, evidently in one of the innumerable bull-sessions of those days, he had no intimate knowledge of women. In truth, he had been a pure young man. As with many a pure young man, after a certain age, evidently he went in for wider instruction.

Witnesses to this later phase were available also. In September of that same year, the *Examiner's* reporter discovered that a Miss Annie Welming had escaped from an attack by Durrant. Durrant had conducted her into the church, evidently on a week day, and left her in the library, to return in a moment mother-naked, his intentions plainly not those expected of an assistant Sunday School superintendent; and Miss Welming had departed with much haste. She related this to a friend, a Miss Clayton, who passed the word around in such a way that the reporter got hold of it and then when the scandalous account was printed, she immediately and indignantly repudiated it, as might be expected from a proper young lady of those days. The intended recipient of Theo Durrant's clumsy attempt at love making, Miss Welming, then vanished and was unable to be located for questioning.

Even as good a girl as Blanche Lamont was reputed to be could not have been quite so dense as to have missed the growing rumors of the gay times some of the young people were having during week days and early evenings in the church rooms, when the rooms were supposed to be empty. A certain Alexander Zenger, who had known Theo for years, and whose wife was a member of the Emanuel Baptist Church, claimed definitely he had "heard stories . . . of strange actions on the part of some of the young people of the church."

So, there were rumors. In addition, it is highly probable that Blanche Lamont knew and had discussed Theo with a fellow church member, a certain Miss Minnie Williams, an unhappily obsessed young woman from across the Bay who was quite cognizant of the young man's latent possibilities.

Furthermore, there is a strong suspicion if not positive conviction that before this April morning, Blanche, herself, had experienced direct proof that Theo did not always act as an assistant Sunday School superintendent should. Neither her aunt nor her sister were very specific, at a later date, about what happened between Blanche and Theo during a twilight walk in December through Golden Gate Park. He brought her back safely. He apologized to the aunt for keeping her so late—and, after that, there was a sudden interval of a number of weeks before she seems to have allowed him to see her again. It may have been nothing of consequence, a desire on Theo's part to put his arm around her, to toy with her gloves. Whatever it was, she had to make up her mind about it before seeing him again. . . .

But to return to that Wednesday morning: Blanche and Theo rode as far as Polk Street, near the Boys' High School. There they got off. According to Theo's statement she went on foot to the high school and he continued on to his college; and, he claimed on his oath, after that moment he never saw her alive again.

By her schoolmates' evidence, Blanche went to the high school and in the afternoon appeared at cooking classes in the Normal School. Here she dutifully remained until about five minutes before three. None of her companions noticed anything unusual in her behavior. She simply sat there quietly during the lectures, a tall, dreamy-eyed girl, no doubt thinking about Theo pleasantly and happily.

At 2:55 P.M., when the cooking lectures ended, three other students, Minnie Edwards, Alice Pleasant, and

May Lanigan, saw her go out and meet Theo. She went straight to him.

Now, Theo was so impatient to be with Blanche that he came back early. He remained in front of the Normal School from two o'clock on. Old Mrs. Mary Vogel, who was afraid of burglars, and who lived diagonally across from the school at 919 Powell, was looking out her window. She saw him standing there. Because he remained so long she became convinced he was a burglar sizing up her place to rob later on at night. With that in her mind, it is no wonder she was later able to identify him without hesitation.

He stayed there until the girls started coming out of school. Suddenly he ran, "like a boy," said old Mrs. Vogel, to the cable car at Clay and Powell where he got his breath and put on his hat. Miss Lanigan, one of the three schoolmates, remembered that Theo tipped his hat and then got on the cable car *before* Blanche did; and that Blanche followed him and sat down beside him—not the action of a young lady being coerced. Theo was dressed very smartly, too, that day, in a blue coat and vest of cheviot, and matching pants of another material, and a knobby hat. As the cable car went on down the hill the observant Miss Lanigan had a clear view of him next to Blanche, again engaged in conversation. "His long hair attracted my attention at that time. He did not have much of a mustache, just a short growth. I noticed the way he had his hair cut. It struck me as unusual to see a gentleman with such long hair."

The time is growing short for Blanche.

Mrs. Elizabeth D. Crosset, well in her prime, who had known Theo for about four years, happened to be passing by in a street car going in the opposite direction. She saw him accurately enough to describe how he was dressed—accurately enough to describe his attractive companion, Blanche. As Mrs. Crosset got off her car she noticed they had descended at Twenty-second and Valencia and she watched them, and later she remembered the wind blew fiercely, the young lady clutching her hat; and, "her clothes blew considerably around her limbs—her form—her dress," explained Mrs. Crosset, rather primly. Those added six pounds on Blanche gave her a figure to catch every eye, and cause old ladies to wonder whom that Durrant boy was going with now.

They continued directly toward the Emanuel Baptist Church, without stopping, conversing amiably with each other, two young people knowing exactly where they were going. On their way they crossed Twenty-second Street, passing Attorney Martin Quinlan, who was watching workmen lay new paving.

Mrs. Caroline Leak, sixty-six years old, lived at 124 Bartlett, opposite the Emanuel Baptist Church. She attended the church and had known Theo for the past several years. She happened to be waiting for her daughter. The time was between four and four-thirty, and now Blanche had scarcely ten or fifteen minutes more to live. From the windows of the rooms Mrs. Leak occupied, as she waited for her daughter, she saw Theo and the tall girl with the floppy hat, carrying her school books, pass in front of the church and go in the side gate at Twenty-third Street. Blanche entered the gate first. Theo followed her, closing the gate, a minor point perhaps— but still, Blanche did follow after Theo in the street car and did go first into the empty church. Mrs. Leak was the last in the extraordinary chain of witnesses to see Blanche.

Very little of what happened to Blanche, and what happened to Theo, in the dim lower hall of the church or, more probably, in the library, depends upon conjecture. The subsequent examination of Blanche's body by Dr. J. S. Barrett tells us precisely what Theo did and did not do to her; and, by implication, something of her reply to Theo's proposal when at last she was compelled to a specific answer.

Did she try to run, as the other girl had run from Theo in the library? Did she threaten to expose Theo? What was the spark that set him off this time? We do not know. In a passion of frustration, the demon was released. Blanche had no more time left now, as Theo's hands came around her throat and choked her to death.

Reading the police reconstruction of what followed, it is clear that Durrant dragged her by the hair to the alcove in the library, through the door to the staircase upwards, into the Sunday School room; and on upwards, to the gallery floor, higher still, through door and belfry staircase into the belfry tower. Here he dropped the body on the top landing of the southeastern corner of the tower and, evidently still caught by his frenzy, fell upon her, not to ravish the dead, according to Dr. Barrett, but to strip off her clothes.

The fetish symbolism of the act is perfect, as revelatory of Theo's state of mind as any confession he never made. He stuffed clothes and hat into the corners and between the beams. He returned to the body. He placed two small wooden blocks under her head to hold it in position; and, afterwards, he did much the most significant thing of all. He knelt within the awful silence of the belfry and crossed her hands over her.

At five o'clock he went downstairs and encountered his young friend, George King, church organist, just arrived—who testified Theo appeared composed and self-possessed, although extremely pale and fatigued. To explain his appearance Theo told George the paleness was caused by breathing escaping gas from a gas-jet he had been fixing upstairs and he lay down while George hastened out to fetch for his friend, of all remedies for the special nature of Theo's weakness, a bromo-seltzer.

Once more before Dr. Barrett took her body and separated its illusion into the elements of flesh and bone, is there a final far-away vision of this girl. Ten days later, detective officer E. L. Gibson entered the cool dimness of the belfry and saw her there and even then she must have been very beautiful to have stirred a comment like a fragment of poetry from this hardened detective, for he said afterwards, "The body was white, like a piece of marble. . . ."

MINNIE FLORA WILLIAMS, the unhappy young woman from across the Bay, of whom previous mention has been made, was of a different cut altogether from Blanche, although Minnie went to her death by the same hands, if not for the same sad reason.

There she is in her photograph, her hair a black curly mop; she has lively eyes, pert clear features, the childish sweetness of the shortened upper lip young women not infrequently retain five to fifteen years after adolescence—and, beyond that, indefinable but still caught and held by the old photograph, that slightly sharp, slightly gay air which the young blades of the Nineties were apt easily to characterize as "minx-like."

Minnie, however, was something more than a minx. In the social hierarchy of the Emanuel Baptist Church, which she also attended, she was in the secondary ranks. Born in Canada, as was Theo, she didn't meet him until long after, when she was twenty-one. All her acquaintances have emphasized her gay and cheerful nature. The Reverend Mr. Cressy said cautiously that she was "very quiet and retiring." Her intimate friends emphasize more than that. Dora Fales, interviewed in the November sixth *San Francisco Call*, remembered that Minnie was "an exceedingly discreet girl." Although Minnie weighed only ninety pounds, she was strong enough to lift this same Dora whom the *Call* intimated was on the fat side. Jennie Turnbull, a confidante, said she was "smart in concocting plans."

Minnie had many devious and unusual plans, which she so smartly concocted. The newspapers discovered that six years earlier this vivacious, lively minx of a girl, then aged fourteen, decided her father was being unfaithful to her mother. A decision of this sort, remember, was very precocious in those days for a girl of fourteen. Only the most enterprising of fourteen-year-olds, of feminine lineage at least, ever knew about such things.

This industrious little fourteen-year-old thereupon proceeded to shadow her father. She actually learned the identity of her father's mistress. She induced a little sister to become a playmate of the other woman's daughter and through that strategy, to spy and report upon the household. When the case was complete, Minnie not only denounced her father to her mother but calmly took her mother to a church rendezvous Mr. Williams was having with the other woman. After reading these volumes of old transcripts I am almost become of the opinion that in the Nineties San Francisco churches at times had their functions confused with those of dwellings along the Barbary Coast. However—

Minnie's minx-like maneuvers wrecked her family, emotionally and financially. The woman discovered in the church with Mr. Williams had previously gained control of most of his property. She refused to return it. Mr. Williams was unable to support his estranged family, even if he wished to. Eventually the sympathetic congregation of the unfortunate Emanuel Baptist Church, led by undoubtedly one of the most obtuse pastors in all creation, financed the journey of Mrs. Williams and her three youngest children back to her parents' home in Canada. Minnie, cute, gay, clever little Minnie, from fourteen years on remained on her own in San Francisco.

Minnie continued to attend the Emanuel Baptist Church. Church circles cared for her. She became a maid. As she grew older she took a job in a casket factory across the Bay in Alameda under Clark H. Morgan, a man of some years. Later, she entered his household in the not clearly defined position of half companion to Mrs. Morgan and half housemaid.

As with Theo, Minnie seems to have developed two sides to her life. With her women employers she was quiet. She was well-behaved. She spoke of little but church functions. The women who employed her are unable to recall she mentioned any men in particular except a dentist, Dr. Vogel, whose home was a meeting place for the Christian Endeavor; and the medical student, Theodore Durrant.

On the other hand, by the understandably reticent tes-timonies of casket-maker Morgan, most bearded, most respectable of men in appearance, there is ample indication that Minnie's precocious qualities had not ceased broadening from the age of discretion. She discussed men and life with Morgan, evidently in detail, on the pretext of wanting advice.

In 1895, she was having dates with Theo when Theo wasn't accompanying that haughty Miss Lamont or various other young ladies having the good fortune to live in San Francisco, with families to support them. She even con-fessed to the casket-maker Morgan how Theo had taken her to Fruitvale and in a lonely spot had wanted intimate rela-tions with her. She refused. He took her home from that lonely spot. After all these years, and trying to be perfectly objective about it, it is impossible not to feel pity for Theo's recurrent frustrations, all alike: Taking attractive young ladies to private places, there being refused by them; and then, except for the last two times in his life, taking them home again, evidently resigning himself so gracefully to the refusals that usually he was allowed to call afterwards. Under ordinary circumstances he had not become a serious threat to the young ladies' honors, as most of them con-sciously or instinctively realized, since they permitted him to see them again.

Minnie Williams was well acquainted with Blanche Lamont, although at the trial both Blanche's sister and aunt Tryphena denied it. They were lying. Blanche and Minnie attended the same church and both went to the Christian Endeavor meetings. According to the record, at one time Blanche's sister had suggested that her aunt hire little Minnie. Auntie refused; she said Minnie "looked too frail."

Moreover, the San Francisco Chronicle crime reporter of that era dug up through various church members, too chary to permit their names to be quoted, the astounding fact that at one time or another Minnie had repeated to her friends the relationship between Theo and Blanche was "of a nature to startle" anyone.

Minnie, here, was probably exaggerating, being jealous of Blanche. But Minnie did know her; did know Theo was seeing her; and from what we know of Theo, it does not seem unlikely that he might have boasted to Minnie, who liked to have men talk to her of such matters, of successes he had had only in his imagination.

Before that day of April 3rd Minnie had been seeing Theo; she knew Theo was dancing after Blanche, she had told casket-maker Morgan of her adventures with various men; she had confided to a young servant girl, Jennie Turnbull, her adventures with Theo and another mysterious man, older, who possessed elegant rooms in a San Francisco hotel. She had even admitted to Jennie someone had deceived her.

But, stated Jennie later, "From what she told me I could not fully understand just how she had been deceived. . . ." Evidently in 1895, before the era of standardization, deception had not yet become a single, run-of-the-mill article.

THE DAY OF April third is over. Blanche lies undiscovered in the dim belfry tower.

Where is Theo? What passes behind the snub-nosed, sulky, intelligent face of the photograph? The thing has been done. The demon is out. Blanche is dead. All that is known of his erratic course after April third comes from glimpses, indistinct, unconnected, until at last a clear sequence is established for the day of April twelfth, nine long days for the body to lie unmolested in the belfry tower. It has never been fully established why Theo sought out Minnie Williams during those nine days. In 1895 it would have been said that Minnie appealed to Theo's lower self.

Blanche Lamont was killed before five o'clock, Wednesday, April third. Within the next twenty hours, somehow, someway, Theo was driven to confide or intimate to Minnie at least a part of what had happened. The next day, April fourth, Thursday, Minnie appeared at the bakery shop of her good friend Frank Young, in Alameda. In court the baker testified she looked downcast and worried. She blurted out, "I know too much about the disappearance of Blanche. . . ."

And the servant girl, Jennie Turnbull, testified, "Since the disappearance of Blanche Lamont, Miss Williams said her chum [was Blanche actually Minnie's 'chum'?] had met with foul play. She positively declined to reveal the nature of her information. . . ."

According to Morgan, the casket maker, sometime before the following Friday, Durrant called to see Minnie in Alameda. Theo asked her to meet him in San Francisco, as he had "something special to say to her." And he made no effort to keep Morgan from overhearing him.

Minnie replied that Theo might state what he had to say "then and there"—or, providing him with an alternative right before her employer, Theo could meet her at the Christian Endeavor meeting at Dr. Vogel's, the following Friday night. The following Friday was April twelfth.

On that day, Minnie left Morgan's home to go to Mrs. A. D. Voy's, in San Francisco, as companion and housemaid. She sent off her trunk in the morning. At three-thirty in the afternoon she went to a hairdresser in Alameda to make herself pretty for the Christian Endeavor meeting that evening at Dr. Vogel's. When she left, she said she meant to catch the four o'clock ferryboat across the Bay to San Francisco.

Once more there is the resurgence of an extraordinary chain of witnesses.

At three in the afternoon, over in San Francisco, three fellow medical students saw Theo waiting at the Ferry Depot. He explained to them he was going across to Mt. Diablo for Signal Corps militia exercises and requested one of them to answer for him next day at roll call in school.

At four o'clock Frank Sademan, janitor of the Emanuel Baptist Church, was in the neighborhood of the Ferry Building, saw Theo in a long coat—in April it can be cold around the ferry terminus—and stopped to talk with him. Theo explained being there by some nonsense about a clue he was seeking in regard to Blanche's disappearance.

At five o'clock, Adolph Hobe, Oakland commuter, saw Theo conversing at the Ferry Building with a very small, slight young woman, dressed in a cape. Obviously, this was Minnie.

Between six and seven that evening Minnie went to Mrs. Voy's house. Theo was not with her. She told Mrs. Voy she was going to the Christian Endeavor meeting at Dr. Vogel's house. She never got there.

At eight o'clock Ann McKay, a hard working Scotch girl, a laundress, on her way home passed the Emanuel Church and saw a man in a long coat, whom she later identified as Theo, and a small girl in a cape. The man was pleading; the girl was protesting. . . . At ten minutes past eight J. P. Hodgkins, freight-claim adjuster, coming home from a cigar store, saw Theo and Minnie. Theo was wildly excited and Hodgkins later testified he was acting so much "in a manner unbecoming of a gentleman" that Hodgkins turned back to come gallantly to the rescue. Theo suddenly broke off; Minnie took his arm (note here: *she* took his arm—still not frightened) and when Hodgkins continued on his way the two young people were about three hundred feet from the church.

No murderer ever had such wretched luck in attracting witnesses as Theo had. I think now I may have emphasized Blanche's charms too greatly as the reason why so many people recalled seeing her and Theo. Perhaps Theo himself was fated to have hordes, swarms of people at his heels each time he did murder.

A little after eight Theo was seen by a boy, C. Y. Hilly, entering the back door of the church. I don't know why so many witnesses didn't stumble into each other. It is obvious once again that Theo's thoughts were so far from murder a whole brass band could have paraded down the street and Minnie and he would have stayed there and looked at it before going into the church. In addition to young Hilly, Alexander Zengler also appeared, his purpose to find out for himself about the rumored gay times in the church rooms. He knew both Theo and Minnie. From his vantage point he saw them pass under the light at the rear entrance to the church. Zengler "wanted to know how long young people stayed in the church" and to find how long, he actually waited there until Theo reappeared some time later. Thereupon, satisfied, Mr. Zengler went his own way, believing for some reason other people were also in the church and that Minnie had stayed with them.

That ends the witnesses.

What happened in the church? We must again refer to Dr. Barrett, who also took Minnie's body apart. From his probings we have these facts: 1. Theo and Minnie did exactly what Mr. Zengler apparently was afraid young people were coming week days and nights to the church to do; 2. Afterwards Theo ripped pieces from her dress and stuffed them into her mouth. He took one of several table knives which apparently were lying about handily in the library room, and slashed her wrists, forehead, and body. Dr. Barrett said, "The girl died from asphyxiation and hemorrhage." He is of the opinion that Theo outraged the body afterwards. Minnie's blood spurted all over the walls. When photographed later this became one of the elements of the standard phenomenon of mass-horror, the newspapers terming the murders "The Crime of the Century."

After all this, Theo's frenzy left him. At nine-thirty that evening he appeared at the Christian Endeavor meeting, perspiration still on his face, his hands grimy. Dr. Vogel remembers he asked permission to wash his hands. Then he joined the young people, pleasant and amiable as usual, and went home with them, none of them recalling anything about his attitude that was unusual.

EXCEPT FOR THE mystery as to why Minnie was willing to accompany Theo to the deserted church, when all along she must have suspected him of having either knowledge or a hand in Blanche's disappearance, and one last singular item, there is little more to be said. On Saturday, the next day, April thirteenth, a group of women church members came to decorate the church for Easter services and found it already gruesomely decorated by the mutilated body of Minnie Williams stuffed behind an open closet door.

When the police were called in they made a search of the church and found the body of Blanche Lamont. The newspapers did the rest. Indeed, the police admitted the press was primarily responsible for locating the murderer. The witnesses read about Blanche and Minnie, all the hordes of witnesses, remembered what they had seen, and flocked in to give testimony. Theo was hauled into court by April twenty-second. He protested. He fought. His defenses were overwhelmed eventually by that tidal wave of witnesses.

His own attitude assisted in maintaining the spectacular newspaper display, extending all over the nation and as far as Europe. With few relapses, ordinarily he was cool and calm, steadfastly proclaiming he had not killed the two girls. Most of the time, such was the progress of his dementia due to the collision of all the circumstances, it is highly probable he did believe he was blameless. In those days his unshaken assurance was taken with more weight by the general public than we hope it would be in these enlightened times. During the course of the trial appeared the usual assortment of trivia and oddments, meat for the newspaper. Women flocked to the jail. A "Sweet Pea" girl was steadily present, giving Theo bunches of sweet peas. Crank messages poured in. Possibly the only interest all this now has for us, expected in these days, is that histor-

ically Theo Durrant's case was one of the very first to be dra-
matically handled all the way by the press: streamers, headlines
daily, special reporters, all the pyrotechnics of what we are
accustomed to consider modern times. He was tried, convicted,
sentenced to be hanged. At the end he made a good brave
speech, of the kind we might anticipate from a man who had
little if any exact and conscious understanding of what he had
done. It so affected two of the men detailed to supervise the
hanging that they became convinced he was innocent.

Theodore Durrant had the trap pulled from under him
on January 7, 1898, something less than three years after that
windy morning in April when he met Blanche Lamont at the
corner of Mission Street and Twenty-first.

His death bequeaths us at least one great mystery.

The mystery is why Minnie decided to meet Theo and
then go with him to the deserted church when she believed he
was involved in Blanche's disappearance. Minnie is dead these
fifty years; she can never tell anyone the answer. But enough
pieces of the puzzle have lain around, gathering dust in court
records and newspaper morgues all these years, to allow a
very good semblance of an answer to be put together. Here are
the pieces:

Minnie liked to spy. (Videlicet: her father, etc.)

A few days after April third, Theo ran into the same
medical student who had ridden with him on the street car
that morning he met Blanche; they discussed the case; Theo
said he thought Blanche might have been induced into a house
of ill fame; that Blanche "was a very innocent young lady"—
this from her murderer—and she could be easily led.

April twelfth, when Theo met Frank Sademan at the
Ferry Building, he told Sademan "his purpose in being there at
the time was to see what truth there was in a clue which he
claimed he had obtained in regard to Blanche Lamont."

We know that between the hours of five o'clock
April third and the evening of April fourth, before Minnie

saw her baker friend in Alameda, Theo managed somehow to convey to her that he knew something about the disappearance of Blanche.

From his own actions during these intervening days, Theo's own mental state was so tortured he was steadily impelled to confide at least outside fragments of facts to someone—a common phenomenon, the urge to assuage guilt by confession.

Minnie liked to "tell stories," to gossip. (Videlicet: Her comments about the startling relationship between Blanche and Theo.)

Her own status was that of a servant. She found escape from that status by her schemes, her connivings, by associating in the church with people much better off; she had adventures with mysterious men; in short, having made a somewhat lurid life of her own she was ready to believe in any lurid escapade of someone else.

Cannot these pieces be put together into something like this: From hints given to her by Theo she assumed that Blanche, if not actually in a house of ill fame, had vanished in some equal descent to wickedness. Probably she assumed Theo had a hand in it. Her avid curiosity was aroused. It would be a great thing for her own esteem if she had in her hands information that the haughty Miss Blanche Lamont had now become a tarnished woman. Minnie was quite willing to follow Theo anywhere to obtain the facts; and so envious and jealous was she of Blanche and all that Blanche represented, prepared to concede a great deal to Theo if he would only tell her.

Furthermore, under no consideration could it ever have occurred to her that Theo, the assistant Sunday School superintendent, the bungling emotional young man who had taken her home from Fruitvale, had killed Blanche. You see, and it is hard to say this with sufficient force, Theo *was* good. He was true. He was an upstanding young Sunday School executive—for most of the time. Even after he stood trial and all the facts in the matter were clear as daylight, so substantial and real was this part of Theo that few of his friends even then forsook him. They simply refused to believe Theo had ever killed anyone.

The solution, then, of that second sad episode seems rather plain if we accept Dr. Barrett's statements on time sequence, as I think we must. His statements confirm the last piece to the puzzle, a piece which locks into the pattern.

Having given Theo substantial proof of her affection, afterwards Minnie must have allowed her prying and spying instincts to take over. She would have asked him what he knew about Blanche—or asked a question bearing upon Blanche. We can conjecture that far with reasonable assurance, basing our conjecture upon established facts. The next we know is that he killed her. What set him off? What released the demon? What happened within that interval opaque to all others except Minnie and Theo? Remember, her entire previous attitude was not one of a girl having any suspicion Theo had murdered Blanche. Did Theo reveal the full truth? Did the horror open so suddenly for Minnie that Theo lost control of himself? We simply don't know.

That Theo had to rip pieces from her dress and force them so deeply into her mouth that they were later found lodged within her throat is evidence of the manner in which unhappy, obsessed little Minnie Williams attempted to shriek and shout when all her smartly concocted plans came tumbling about her. . . .

Theo was unstable, to be sure. If heredity plays any part in these matters, he must have derived some of his emotional imbalance from both his parents, whose behavior during and after the trial was something other than that of normal people. Nor did his sister have a prosaic career. Fourteen years later it was learned that she had changed her name to "Maude Allan" and was a sensation in Europe with her dance "The Vision of Salome." Evidently, Theo was not the only Durrant who felt the need of removing clothes.

The Second Coming

Joe Gores

"But fix thy eyes upon the valley: for the river of blood
draws nigh, in which boils every one who by violence
injures another."
CANTO XII, 46-48
THE INFERNO OF DANTE ALIGHIERI

I'VE THOUGHT ABOUT it a lot, man; like why Victor and I made that terrible scene out there at San Quentin, putting ourselves on that it was just for kicks. Victor was hung up on kicks; they were a thing with him. He was a sharp dark-haired cat with bright eyes, built lean and hard like a French skin-diver. His old man dug only money, so he'd always had plenty of bread. We got this idea out at his pad on Potrero Hill—a penthouse, of course—one afternoon when we were lying around on the sunporch in swim trunks and drinking gin.

A former private detective, JOE GORES is the author of dozens of novels and short stories, including the popular DKA series and the screenplay to Francis Ford Coppola's *Hammett*. Published in 1966, his story "The Second Coming" affords a glimpse into Gores's early career.

"You know, man," he said, "I have made about every scene in the world. I have balled all the chicks, red and yellow and black and white, and I have gotten high on muggles, blue-jays, redbirds, and mescaline. I have even tried the white stuff a time or two. But—"

"You're a goddam tiger, dad."

"—but there is one kick I've never had, man."

When he didn't go on I rolled my head off the quart gin bottle I was using for a pillow and looked at him. He was giving me a shot with those hot, wild eyes of his.

"So like what is it?"

"I've never watched an execution."

I thought about it a minute, drowsily. The sun was so hot it was like nailing me right to the air mattress. Watching an execution. Seeing a man go through the wall. A groovy idea for an artist.

"Too much," I murmured. "I'm with you, dad."

The next day, of course, I was back at work on some abstracts for my first one-man show and had forgotten all about it; but that night Victor called me up.

"Did you write to the warden up at San Quentin today, man? He has to contact the San Francisco police chief and make sure you don't have a record and aren't a psycho and are useful to the community."

So I went ahead and wrote the letter, because even sober it still seemed a cool idea for some kicks; I knew they always need twelve witnesses to make sure that the accused isn't sneaked out the back door or something at the last minute like an old Jimmy Cagney movie. Even so, I lay dead for two months before the letter came. The star of our show would be a stud who'd broken into a house trailer near Fort Ord to rape this Army lieutenant's wife, only right in the middle of it she'd started screaming so he'd put a pillow over her face to keep her quiet until he could finish. But she'd quit breathing. There were eight chicks on the jury and I think like three of them got broken ankles in the rush to send him to the gas chamber. Not that I cared. Kicks, man.

Victor picked me up at seven-thirty in the morning, an hour before we were supposed to report to San Quentin. He was wearing this really hip Italian import, and fifty-dollar shoes, and a narrow-brim hat with a little feather in it, so all he needed was a briefcase to be Chairman of the Board. The top was down on the Mercedes, cold as it was, and when he saw my black suit and hand-knit tie he flashed this crazy white-toothed grin you'd never see in any Director's meeting.

"*Too much*, killer! If you'd like to comb your hair you could pass for an undertaker coming after the body."

Since I am a very long, thin cat with black hair always hanging in my eyes, who fully dressed weighs as much as a medium-size collie, I guess he wasn't too far off. I put a pint of Jose Cuervo in the side pocket of the car and we split. We were both really turned on: I mean this senseless, breathless hilarity as if we'd just heard the world's funniest joke. Or were just going to.

It was one of those chilly California brights with blue sky and cold sunshine and here and there a cloud like Mr. Big was popping Himself a cap down beyond the horizon. I dug it all: the sail of a lone early yacht out in the Bay like a tossed-away paper cup; the whitecaps flipping around out by Angel Island like they were stoned out of their minds; the top down on the 300-SL so we could smell salt and feel the icy bite of the wind. But beyond the tunnel on U.S. 101, coming down towards Marin City, I felt a sudden sharp chill as if a cloud had passed between me and the sun, but none had; and then I dug for the first time what I was actually doing.

Victor felt it, too, for he turned to me and said, "Must maintain cool, dad."

"I'm with it."

San Quentin Prison, out on the end of its peninsula, looked like a sprawled ugly dragon sunning itself on a rock; we pulled up near the East Gate and there were not even any birds singing. Just a bunch of quiet cats in black, Quakers or Mennonites or something, protesting capital punishment by their silent presence as they'd done ever since Chessman had gotten his out there. I felt dark frightened things move around inside me when I saw them.

"Let's fall out right here, dad," I said in a momentary sort of panic, "and catch the matinee next week."

But Victor was in kicksville, like desperate to put on all those squares in the black suits. When they looked over at us he jumped up on the back of the bucket seat and spread his arms wide like the Sermon on the Mount. With his tortoise-shell shades and his flashing teeth and that suit which had cost three yards, he looked like Christ on his way to Hollywood.

"Whatsoever ye do unto the least of these, my brethren, ye do unto me," he cried in this ringing apocalyptic voice.

I grabbed his arm and dragged him back down off the seat. "For Christ sake, man, cool it!"

But he went into high laughter and punched my arm with feverish exuberance, and then jerked a tiny American flag from his inside jacket pocket and began waving it around above the windshield. I could see the sweat on his forehead.

"It's worth it to live in this country!" he yelled at them.

He put the car in gear and we went on. I looked back and saw one of those cats crossing himself. It put things back in perspective: they were from nowhere. The Middle Ages. Not that I judged them: that was their scene, man. Unto every cat what he digs the most.

The guard on the gate directed us to a small wooden building set against the outside wall, where we found five other witnesses. Three of them were reporters, one was a fat cat smoking a .45-calibre stogy like a politician from Sacramento, and the last was an Army type in lieutenant's bars, his belt buckle and insignia looking as if he'd been up all night with a can of *Brasso*.

A guard came in and told us to surrender everything in our pockets and get a receipt for it. We had to remove our shoes, too; they were too heavy for the fluoroscope. Then they put us through this groovy little room one-by-one to x-ray us for cameras and so on; they don't want anyone making the Kodak scene while they're busy dropping the pellets. We ended up inside the prison with our shoes back on and with our noses full of that old prison detergent-disinfectant stink.

The politician type, who had these cold slitted eyes like a Sherman tank, started coming on with rank jokes: but everyone put him down, hard, even the reporters. I guess nobody but fuzz ever gets used to executions. The Army stud was at parade rest with a face so pale his freckles looked like a charge of shot. He had reddish hair.

After a while five guards came in to make up the twelve required witnesses. They looked rank, as fuzz always do, and got off in a corner in a little huddle, laughing and gassing together like a bunch of kids kicking a dog. Victor and I sidled over to hear what they were saying.

"Who's sniffing the eggs this morning?" asked one.

"I don't know, I haven't been reading the papers." He yawned when he answered.

"Don't you remember?" urged another, "it's the guy who smothered the woman in the house trailer. Down in the Valley by Salinas."

"Yeah. Soldier's wife; he was raping her and . . ."

Like dogs hearing the plate-rattle, they turned in unison toward the Army lieutenant; but just then more fuzz came in to march us to the observation room. We went in a column of twos with a guard beside each one, everyone unconsciously in step as if following a cadence call. I caught myself listening for measured mournful drum rolls.

The observation room was built right around the gas chamber, with rising tiers of benches for extras in case business was brisk. The chamber itself was hexagonal; the three walls in our room were of plate glass with a waist-high brass rail around the outside like the rail in an old-time saloon. The other three walls were steel plate, with a heavy door, rivet-studded, in the center one, and a small observation window in each of the others.

Inside the chamber were just these two massive chairs, probably oak, facing the rear walls side-by-side; their backs were high enough to come to the nape of the neck of anyone sitting in them. Under each was like a bucket that I knew contained hydrochloric acid. At a signal the executioner would drop sodium cyanide pellets into a chute; the pellets would roll down into the bucket; hydrocyanic acid gas would form; and the cat in the chair would be wasted.

The politician type, who had this rich fruity baritone like Burl Ives, asked why they had two chairs.

"That's in case there's a double-header, dad," I said.

"You're kidding." But by his voice the idea pleased him. Then he wheezed plaintively: "I don't see why they turn the chairs away—we can't even watch his face while it's happening to him."

He was a true rank genuine creep, right out from under a rock with the slime barely dry on his scales; but I wouldn't have wanted his dreams. I think he was one of those guys who tastes the big draught many times before he swallows it.

We milled around like cattle around the chute, when they smell the blood from inside and know they're somehow involved; then we heard sounds and saw the door in the back of the chamber swing open. A uniformed guard appeared to stand at attention, followed by a priest dressed all in black like Zorro, with his face hanging down to his belly button. He must have been a new man, because he had trouble maintaining his cool: just standing there beside the guard he dropped his little black book on the floor like three times in a row.

The Army cat said to me, as if he'd wig out unless he broke the silence: "They . . . have it arranged like a stage play, don't they?"

"But no encores," said Victor hollowly.

Another guard showed up in the doorway and they walked in the condemned man. He was like sort of a shock. You expect a stud to *act* like a murderer: I mean, cringe at the sight of the chair because he knows this is it, there's finally no place to go, no appeal to make, or else bound in there full of cheap bravado and go-to-hell. But he just seemed mildly interested, nothing more.

He wore a white shirt with the sleeves rolled up, suntans that looked Army issue, and no tie. Under thirty, brown crewcut hair—the terrible thing is that I cannot even remember the features on his face, man. The closest I could come to a description would be that he resembled the Army cat right there beside me with his nose to the glass.

The one thing I'll never forget is that stud's hands. He'd been on Death Row all these months, and here his hands were still red and chapped and knobby, as if he'd still been out picking turnips in the San Joaquin Valley. Then I realized: I was thinking of him in the past tense.

Two fuzz began strapping him down in the chair. A broad leather strap across the chest, narrower belts on the arms and legs. God they were careful about strapping him in. I mean they wanted to make sure he was comfortable. And all the time he was talking with them. Not that we could hear it, but I suppose it went *that's fine, fellows, no, that strap isn't too tight, gee, I hope I'm not making you late for lunch.*

That's what bugged me, he was so damned *apologetic!* While they were fastening him down over that little bucket of oblivion, that poor dead lonely son of a bitch twisted around to look over his shoulder at us, and he *smiled.* I mean if he'd had an arm free he might have *waved!* One of the fuzz, who had white hair and these sad gentle eyes like he was wearing a hair shirt, patted him on the head on the way out. No personal animosity, son, just doing my job.

After that the tempo increased, like your heart beat when you're on a black street at three A.M. and the echo of your own footsteps begins to sound like someone following you. The warden was at one observation window, the priest and the doctor at the other. The blackrobe made the sign of the cross, having a last go at the condemned, but he was digging only Ben Casey. Here was this M.D. cat who'd taken the Hippocratean Oath to preserve life, waving his arms around like a tv director to show that stud the easiest way to die.

Hold your breath, then breathe deeply: you won't feel a thing. Of course hydrocyanic acid gas melts your guts into a red-hot soup and burns out every fiber in the lining of your lungs, but you won't be really feeling it as you jerk around: that'll just be raw nerve endings.

Like they should have called his the Hypocritical Oath.

So there we were, three yards and half an inch of plate glass apart, with us staring at him and him by just turning his head able to stare right back: but there were a million light years between the two sides of the glass. He didn't turn. He was shrived and strapped in and briefed on how to die, and he was ready for the fumes. I found out afterwards that he had even willed his body to medical research.

I did a quick take around.

Victor was sweating profusely, his eyes glued to the window.

The politician was pop-eyed, nose pressed flat and belly indented by the brass rail, pudgy fingers like plump garlic sausages smearing the glass on either side of his head. A look on his face, already, like that of a stud making it with a chick.

The reporters seemed ashamed, as if someone had caught them peeking over the transom into the ladies' john.

The Army cat just looked sick.

Only the fuzz were unchanged, expending no more emotion on this than on their targets after rapid-fire exercises at the range.

On no face was there hatred.

Suddenly, for the first time in my life, I was part of it. I wanted to yell out STOP! We were about to gas this stud and *none of us wanted him to die!* We've created this society and we're all responsible for what it does, but none of us as individuals is willing to take that responsibility. We're like that Nazi cat at Nuremberg who said that everything would have been all right if they'd only given him more ovens.

The warden signalled. I heard gas whoosh up around the chair.

The condemned man didn't move. He was following doctor's orders. Then he took the huge gulping breath the M.D. had pantomimed. All of a sudden he threw this tremendous convulsion, his body straining up against the straps, his head slewed around so I could see his eyes were tight shut and his lips were pulled back from his teeth. Then he started panting like a baby in an oxygen tent, swiftly and shallowly. Only it wasn't oxygen his lungs were trying to work on.

The lieutenant stepped back smartly from the window, blinked, and puked on the glass. His vomit hung there for an instant like a phosphorus bomb burst in a bunker; then two fuzz were supporting him from the room and we were all jerking back from the mess. All except the politician. He hadn't even noticed: he was in Henry Millerville, getting his sex kicks the easy way.

I guess the stud in there had never dug that he was supposed to be gone in two seconds without pain, because his body was still arched in that terrible bow, and his hands were still claws. I could see the muscles standing out along the sides of his jaws like marbles. Finally he flopped back and just hung there in his straps like a machine-gunned paratrooper.

But that wasn't the end. He took another huge gasp, so I could see his ribs pressing out against his white shirt. After that one, twenty seconds. We decided that he had cut out.

Then another gasp. Then nothing. Half a minute nothing.

Another of there final terrible shuddering racking gasps. At last: all through. All used up. Making it with the angels.

But then he did it *again*. Every fiber of that dead wasted comic thrown-away body strained for air on this one. No air: only hydrocyanic acid gas. Just nerves, like the fish twitching after you whack it on the skull with the back edge of the skinning knife. Except that it wasn't a fish we were seeing die.

His head flopped sideways and his tongue came out slyly like the tongue of a dead deer. Then this gunk ran out of his mouth. It was just saliva—they said it couldn't be anything else—but it reminded me of the residue after light-line resistors have been melted in an electrical fire. That kind of black. That kind of scorched.

Very softly, almost to himself, Victor murmured: "Later, dad."

That was it. Dig you in the hereafter, dad. Ten little minutes and you're through the wall. Mistah Kurtz, he dead. Mistah Kurtz, he very very goddamn dead.

I believed it. Looking at what was left of that cat was like looking at a chick who's gotten herself bombed on the heavy, so when you hold a match in front of her eyes the pupils don't react and there's no one home, man. No one. Nowhere. End of the lineville.

We split.

But on the way out I kept thinking of that Army stud, and wondering what had made him sick. Was it because the cat in the chair had been the last to enter, no matter how violently, the body of his beloved, and now even that febrile connection had been severed? Whatever the reason, his body had known

what perhaps his mind had refused to accept: this ending was no
new beginning, this death would not restore his dead chick to
him. This death, no matter how just in his eyes, had generated
only nausea.

Victor and I sat in the Mercedes for a long time with the
top down, looking out over that bright beautiful empty peninsula, not named, as you might think, after a saint, but after some
poor dumb Indian they had hanged there a hundred years or so
before. Trees and clouds and blue water, and still no birds making
the scene. Even the cats in the black suits had vanished, but now
I understood why they'd been there. In their silent censure, they
had been sounding the right gong, man. We were the ones from
the Middle Ages.

Victor took a deep shuddering breath as if he could
never get enough air. Then he said in a barely audible voice:
"How did you dig that action, man?"

I gave a little shrug and, being myself, said the only
thing I could say. "It was a gas, dad."

"I dig, man. I'm hip. A gas."

Something was wrong with the way he said it, but I
broke the seal on the tequila and we killed it in fifteen minutes, without even a lime to suck in between. Then he started
the car and we cut out, and I realized what was wrong.
Watching that cat in the gas chamber, Victor had realized for
the very first time that life is far, far more than just kicks. We
were both partially responsible for what had happened in
there, and we had been ineluctably diminished by it.

On U.S. 101 he coked the Mercedes up to 104
m.p.h. through the traffic, and held it there. It was wild: it
was the end: but I didn't sound. I was alone without my
Guide by the boiling river of blood. When the Highway
Patrol finally got us stopped, Victor was coming on so
strong and I was coming on so mild that they surrounded us
with their holsters' flaps unbuckled, and checked our veins
for needle marks.

I didn't say a word to them, man, not one. Not even my name. Like they had to look in my wallet to see who I was. And while they were doing that, Victor blew his cool entirely. You know, biting, foaming at the mouth, the whole bit—he gave a very good show until they hit him on the back of the head with a gun butt. I just watched.

They lifted his license for a year, nothing else, because his old man spent a lot of bread on a shrinker who testified that Victor had temporarily wigged out, and who had him put away in the zoo for a time. He's back now, but he still sees that wig picker, three times a week at forty clams a shot.

He needs it. A few days ago I saw him on Upper Grant, stalking lithely through a gray raw February day with the fog in, wearing just a t-shirt and jeans—and no shoes. He seemed agitated, pressed, confined within his own concerns, but I stopped him for a minute.

"Ah . . . how you making it, man? Like, ah, what's the gig?"

He shook his head cautiously. "They will not let us get away with it, you know. Like to them, man, just living is a crime."

"Why no strollers, dad?"

"I cannot wear shoes." He moved closer and glanced up and down the street, and said with tragic earnestness: "I can hear only with the soles of my feet, man."

Then he nodded and padded away through the crowds on silent naked soles like a puzzled panther, drifting through the fruiters and drunken teenagers and fuzz trying to bust some cat for possession who have inherited North Beach from the true swingers. I guess all Victor wants to listen to now is Mother Earth: all he wants to hear is the comforting sound of the worms, chewing away.

Chewing away, and waiting for Victor; and maybe for the Second Coming.

Ironside

Jim Thompson

IT WAS THE kind of a place where if you didn't
spit on the floor at home you could go down there
and do it. The smell was thick enough to write your
name on (if you were still using your own name)—the aroma of
stale beer and cheap wine and cloying sweat, colored and
given body by the gut-like strands of cigarette smoke. In the
nearly opaque nightfog of San Francisco, the place could
hardly be seen from the outside. But the smell from the interior pointed an invisible finger at it. And even in the distance
of the bay, the ferries and tugs seemed to acknowledge it with
sickish and shuddery hoots.

From somewhere in the smoke and stench, an unrea-
sonable facsimile of a piano player was doing his own arrangement of "Goofus." It had to be his own; no one else would have
claimed it. At the bar, a rail-thin man sipped muscatel and sur-
reptitiously counted the cigarettes in his package. At one of the
small, smeared tables, which seemed splattered rather than
scattered around the sawdust-covered floor, a bloated-faced
woman made an apparently endless appeal to a thin-lipped
young man who apparently rejected her endlessly.

At his death in 1977, all of JIM THOMPSON's novels were out of
print. With the success of such films as *The Grifters* and
After Dark, My Sweet, nearly all of Thompson's thirty novels
have now been reissued, with the exception of *Ironside.*

The Killer sat at the rear of the room, facing the door. He was drinking coffee—coffee which had been especially and carefully brewed for him. Although the fact was somehow not noticeable—the Killer had a quality of unnoticeability—the hand which held the coffee cup was gloved. Also gloved was the hand which occasionally lifted a cigarette to his mouth. Both gloves were drawn skintight, flexing and shifting easily with the movements of the flesh and bone which they covered.

Tolerantly, which is not to say approvingly, the Killer effortlessly absorbed the sights and sounds of the saloon. The unforgivable stench. The unmusical music. The irredeemable people. He understood such places—the reason for their being. He understood their habitués—the myriad dark byways which had brought them here. He understood so he did not condemn, just as he would not have condemned a hole or the poisonous snakes which populated it. Just as God would not have condemned his own creations.

The Killer's condemnation was reserved for creatures of free will. For those who might have done very well and had, perversely, done very badly. As with God (reputedly), the Killer had tolerance and understanding for the hapless evil of predestination. But for the wickedness which need not have been, for the willful doer of evil, the Killer had nothing but death.

What did the Killer look like? Well, what does God look like? Presumably, having been made in God's image, the Killer looked about like anyone else. A grocery clerk. An accountant. An installment collector. A doctor, lawyer, merchant, thief—no, strike that last! Definitely, strike it.

The Killer did not look like a thief or any other kind of criminal. On the contrary, having been chosen as the instrument of God's wrath (in his own mind), perhaps even *being* God (in his own mind), the Killer wore a protective cloak of innocuousness. What he looked like was anything but what he was.

Probably the denizens of this place he was in tonight— one which he patronized frequently—surmised the truth about him. But it was a matter of sensing rather than knowing. Throughout their shoddy lives they had lived in death's shadow, so they sensed its physical embodiment in the Killer. More than that, they were grateful for his tolerant abiding of them, and were venomously pleased that another outsider was to be struck down tonight.

Why not, anyway? What gave with this brother's-keeper gig? Maybe they'd look into it when it became a two-way street. In the meantime, however, their concern was only for Mr. Jones or Mr. Smith or Mr. Brown or whatever he chose to call himself, a guy who was fast with the big buck and who always made it easy for you to swallow.

The Killer came out of his reverie. He caught the bartender's eye and nodded imperceptibly. The bartender promptly became active, moving up and down the bar and around the room, and within minutes a miracle had taken place. The piano player became expert. The muscatel drinker ceased to count his cigarettes. The thin-lipped young man nodded and smiled to the bloated-faced woman. God taketh away, but he also giveth—money and all the good things which money buys—white powder and young flesh and booze, and all else desirable. And Mr. Jones or Mr. Brown or Mr. Smith—the Killer, the God, had given unto them once again.

They did not openly express their gratitude, of course. The Killer would not have liked that, nor was it necessary. For, having been aware of their need, he would also be aware of their gratitude. Besides which there were better ways of showing their appreciation. Ways which they were on the point of having to demonstrate, for the Killer's victim had just entered the place.

She was twenty-four years old. As a human being, she wasn't worth a plugged nickel. But the bank and tax authorities assayed her at approximately 16 million dollars. Her maiden name, reacquired after each of her five divorces, was a very distinguished one—Eleanor McNesmith Chisholm. But it was not the name which the habitués of the bar would have applied to her. They had never seen her before, but they had met all her sisters and cousins and other kindred. So they knew her name well.

They spelled it t-r-a-m-p.

Penetrating the smoke, her eyes swept over them contemptuously, then settled on the Killer. He struck a match, lighted a cigarette with it, then very carefully blew it out. Eleanor McNesmith Chisholm tightened her savagely imperious mouth, and crossed swiftly to his table. She sat down opposite him and leaned across the table, careless of any soiling of her five-hundred-dollar slack suit or her one-hundred-fifty-dollar sweater. And then she began to talk. She talked steadily for almost five minutes.

Nothing that she said was printable. At least, it is seldom seen in print except on toilet walls. The substance of her discourse (to put it in the politest terms) was that anyone who thought she would hold still for blackmail was too stupid to know pea soup from pineapple juice, and that she personally was able and willing to kick his butt through his brains.

The Killer listened to her with a deepening frown. When she had finished, he said he didn't have the slightest idea what she was talking about.

"I just dropped in here for a drink, and you make these outrageous charges against me. Just why—"

"You signaled me, that's why! When you lighted your cigarette!"

"Signaled you by lighting a cigarette? Now, really, miss."

"Well . . ." Miss Chisholm hesitated a moment. "Don't kid me, buster! You came here to meet me! To collect a payoff! What else would you be doing here?"

The Killer shrugged idly. What was anyone doing here? he asked. What was she doing here? Miss Chisholm snorted that he knew damned well what she was doing there.

And taking a folded sheet of paper from her purse, she slammed it down in front of him.

"Look." She smoothed it out for him to read. "Now, tell me you didn't send me that!"

The Killer studied the paper, its message composed of words and letters cut from newsprint. When he had finished, he looked up puzzledly.

"This says you starred in some kind of movie."

"Yeah, doesn't it, though!"

"Well? I'm afraid I don't see . . ."

Miss Chisholm leaned closer to him. "Now, listen," she said harshly, lowering her voice a little, "I don't know how you found out . . . how you guessed. . . . I was wearing a mask, and—" She broke off, her tone becoming harsher still. "But I'm not paying, get me? Once I start paying, I'll be paying forever!"

The Killer remarked that he saw nothing in the note about a demand for money. Miss Chisholm said that he thought he was pretty damned cute, didn't he?

"You let me worry a few days! Then you put the bite on me over the phone! Well, all I've got to say—"

"I called you? You're saying that I called you?"

"Well . . . well, all right! Maybe I can't prove it. But I'm warning you—"

"Don't," the Killer said. "Just go to the police. That's what you should have done in the first place."

Miss Chisholm said nuts to the police (or words to that effect). She was plenty able to handle any blackmailer by herself, and he'd better believe it.

"How?" the Killer asked.

"Never you mind how! You try pulling something like this again—"

"I really don't know what you're talking about, miss. I honestly don't." The Killer grinned at her. "Now, why don't you let me call the police for you, and we'll get this settled right now."

Miss Chisholm stared at him. She started to say some-thing, and changed her mind. She made a second start at saying something, and again changed her mind.

He continued to grin at her. Her gaze moved uneasily around the room, and met with other knowing grins. A sense of helplessness seeped into her body. The all-gone feeling of one who has bet everything on a bluff, and had the bluff called. At the same time, she was intrigued, her satiated emotions tit-illated for the first time in years.

So? So! But it was kind of a kick, wasn't it? And a gal had to pay for her kicks, didn't she?

That stag movie had seemed safe enough. Everyone con-nected with it had had as much to lose from discovery as she. And thinking about it, thinking about the thousands upon thousands of men who would sit popeyed and slavering as they watched . . .

A kick. The kind of kick that would set you tingling delightfully each time you thought about it. A real kick—and that was what life was all about, wasn't it? A search for bigger and better kicks?

Eleanor McNesmith Chisholm looked at the Killer, and suggested that he put it on the line for her. "It's the only way I can play, right? Unless you admit you're putting the squeeze on me . . ."

"You've made a mistake," the Killer said mildly. "I think you'd better leave."

"Huh? But—"

"By the way. I believe you dropped something there on the floor. A key, isn't it?"

It was a key. A key with a room tag on it. She picked it up, and examined it, then followed the direction of the Killer's gaze. He was glancing over his shoulder at a small neon sign with the single word ROOMS. Beneath it was an arrow pointing toward a rear door.

"Yes," the Killer intoned. "You'd better leave imme-diately. And don't forget to take your package with you."

A small sack flipped under the table, and landed in Miss Chisholm's lap. She glanced inside it briefly, and a sudden flush flooded her patrician features.

But, wow! This promised to be something else again!

She stood up, her breasts rising and falling with excitement. "You're right," she said. "I'll leave now." And she went past the sign and out the back door.

The Killer took his time about joining her, first finishing his coffee and making a telephone call. When he finally entered the rickety cabin—one of several behind the saloon—she was already out of her clothes and dressed in the tiny bikini he had given her.

Grinning lewdly, she looked down at herself, then raised sultry eyes to his. She came toward him a step, arms outstretched. The Killer shook his head and pointed toward the bathroom.

Miss Chisholm frowned; pouted. Then, hips swinging, she entered the bathroom.

The Killer took off his shoes, socks and outer garments. After primly buttoning each button of his long, old-fashioned underwear, he also went into the bathroom. He turned on the water in the shower, turning it on full blast. Pushing Miss Chisholm ahead of him, he stepped under it with her.

They talked above the roar of the water.

"You were afraid I might be bugged? Carrying some kind of transmitter."

"I can't take any chances."

"I've got the ten thousand in my bag. The bills aren't marked, either."

"Naturally. There'd be no point in marking them unless you'd called in the police."

"How did you recognize me in the picture? With a mask on, I mean?"

"You're in the newspapers a lot. I've studied countless pictures of you through a magnifying glass."

"Yes?"

"You've moved from one thrill to another, on a descending scale. It was only a matter of time until you hit bottom. I was on the lookout for you when you finally landed."

"But the mask . . ."

"It didn't cover your ears. Something as distinctive as fingerprints. It didn't cover this or this or that." The Killer pointed to various small blemishes on her face and body. "I've made people like you my business, Miss Chisholm. It's hard work, but I almost never have a failure."

"I'd say it paid pretty well."

"The money is only incidental. I use it all for carrying on my work."

"Mmm? Then maybe you're entitled to a little bonus." Miss Chisholm leaned toward him invitingly. "Well?"

"Certainly not! Do you think I'm as filthy as you are?"

"Wha—" She drew herself up, glaring, then suddenly laughed hoarsely. "You're cute, you know it? A real kick in the head. When do I make the next payoff?"

The Killer said there would be no next one. The ten thousand was not only the first but final payment. "We won't be seeing each other again, Miss Chisholm. Now, if you'd like to get out and get dressed, I'll fix us a drink."

"But—but, I just don't get it. You mean, this is all? The whole ball of wax?"

"This is all. Unless," the Killer added politely, "you'd like me to wash your back."

THE TRUCK HAD a high-speed engine, and a custom-built van body. I rolled noiselessly into the police garage and came to a gentle stop. The young Negro driver hopped down from his seat and trotted around to the rear doors. He opened them. Lights went on, revealing the interior of the van—a surprising contrast to the vehicle's humble-looking exterior.

There was a radio telephone, a desk, a small laboratory.

There was a sink with hot and cold running water, and a two-burner stove. Concealed behind a sliding panel, there was even a bar of sorts, with a nice assortment of bottles, and a miniscule refrigerator. Last but by no means least was the van's most important fixture—a huskily handsome giant of a man, whose great bulk overflowed the wheelchair to which he was confined and would always be confined.

He was Robert T. Ironside, formerly chief of detectives of the San Francisco Police Department. Now, since the criminal act which had crippled him, he served as consultant to the city's police commissioner and worked on special assignment from the commissioner. He was also solely responsible to that official.

The young Negro's name was Sanger, Mark Sanger. Once a suspect in the sniping which had permanently crippled Ironside, he now served as the latter's chauffeur, companion and all-around helper. Life had treated Mark Sanger badly up until the time of his meeting with Robert Ironside. A juvenile delinquent from a broken home, he might easily have ended his days behind bars or the small green door of the gas chamber. But the gruff-talking, rough-mannered detective had intervened; giving him a job, seeing to it that he attended school. Thus, a new life had opened up for Mark, and he could now hold up his head with any man. Ironside had made life worth living for Mark. In his gratitude, the young Negro returned the favor insofar as he could: doing everything possible to mitigate and lessen his employer's handicap, unobtrusively easing the burdens of the crippled man's life.

Naturally, a deep bond of affection existed between the two men. But it was *between* them, a private thing, never for a moment to be worn on the surface. Any hint of their true feelings would have been unbearably embarrassing to either man. Their surface attitude was one of mere tolerance—of almost incessant jeering and bantering and grumbling at one another.

Now, as Mark raised and lowered the elevator-step of the van, bringing the wheelchair and its occupant down to the garage floor, Chief Ironside assured the young man that the latter was out of his flamin' mind.

"Flamin' engine's runnin' perfectly," he scolded. "What d'you mean draggin' me out to listen to it right at dinnertime?"

"Dinner, humph!" Mark grunted. "Better off without none, the way you eat."

"Better off without *any!* Can't you ever learn any flamin' grammar?"

"That's what I said—better off without none." Mark wheeled him onto the elevator and pressed the UP button. "Honest, boss, don't you ever eat *anything* but chili?"

Ironside roundly declared that chili was a perfect diet. It contained all the nutriments necessary for a healthful existence. "And what about that engine?" he demanded, suddenly remembering the reason for their recent excursion. "What do you mean tellin' me it was making a lot of noise?"

"You just couldn't hear it," Mark said. "All that chili's eaten out your eardrums."

Chief Ironside's apartment was above the police garage, a former storeroom which had been converted into living quarters after his crippling by the sniper. Its main room served in several capacities—as an office, a living room, a dining room and kitchen. From an aesthetic standpoint, it left much to be desired; a vast, barnlike area which would have given an interior decorator nightmares. But for a man living without legs, a man who had to be wheeled or otherwise conveyed wherever he went, it was well-nigh perfect. Uncrowded, plenty of room to move about without bumping into things. As close to transportation as the elevator. Convenience and privacy: being able to get around without a lot of flamin' fools gawking at him. What more could a man ask of an apartment?

The elevator door rolled open, and Mark wheeled him out into the main room. And Chief Ironside immediately found something to ask for.

"The lights," he demanded of the darkness. "What's wrong with the flamin' lights?"

"You just hush," Mark's voice came to him from several feet away. "Be some light in a minute."

"Huh? Where you goin', anyway? What's goin' on here?"

"Take it easy," Mark cautioned from an even greater distance. "Try seein' how it feels with your jaws closed for a change."

Chief Ironside tried to raise himself from his chair; he let out an angry bellow. "Now, by all the flamin' saints—"

There was a flick of a match, then the lights went on. A light, rather. It came from an enormous candle in the dining-room area. The candle sat atop a gallonsize can of chili. Ranged around the table were his three best friends—his three trusted co-workers: Mark Sanger, Detective Sergeant Ed Brown and Policewoman Eve Whitfield. They spoke in unison, beaming at him out of their fresh, young faces:

"Happy birthday, Chief."

Chief Ironside blinked. He swallowed heavily and managed a ferocious scowl; did some throaty mumbling and grumbling about flamin' nonsense and people who should be old enough to have good sense. Finally, having established that he was not a man to be touched by sentiment, he allowed himself to take note of the bottle which stood beside the chili can.

"Well, open it up!" he roared. "Did you just bring it here to look at it? Can't a man get anyone to drink with him on his own birthday?"

"How about me?" Mark said. "I get a drink, too?"

"You do not. You have to go to school tonight."

"Humph. But I get some chili, huh?"

"Why, certainly," Robert Ironside declared generously. "You can even have extra helpings."

THE BIRTHDAY PARTY was over. Mark Sanger had taken his books, and gone off to night school. Eve Whitfield was in the kitchen area, cleaning up the last of the dishes. Sergeant Ed Brown was having a final drink with Chief Ironside. As they talked, Ironside's eyes and his thoughts strayed frequently to Eve—only to be yanked away from her just as frequently, their owner cursing them silently for their misbehavior.

It wasn't to be thought of. Never, ever, for even a moment. She was his protégée, as was Mark Sanger and Ed Brown. Like them, she was part of his "family," the only family he had or wanted. He had brought them all together, pulling them out of their own lives and making them part of his. And it was his sacred obligation to see that none of them suffered for it.

Eve was a member of one of San Francisco's first families, a society girl who had been taking a fling at police reporting when she first caught Ironside's attention. He had pointed out, not unreasonably, that there was no point in wading when she could be swimming. He had asked, not unreasonably, why a smart girl should be writing about what people did when she could be doing it herself. So, after some similarly blunt questionings and promptings, Eve Whitfield had come into the department—his department. And it was unthinkable that she should ever leave it. As unthinkable as it was that he should ever give her any cause to do so—any cause for embarrassment or discomfort. Such as, for example, amorous advances from a man who was ten-plus years older than she and permanently crippled besides.

There had been hints that she might not mind such advances. That she would even welcome them. There had been hints that she had joined the department with such an end in mind. Which mattered not a flaming damn to Bob Ironside.

Eve, like the others, was his responsibility. He was obligated to see that she got nothing but the best from life, and the best was certainly not marriage to the likes of him.

She finished the dishes and came out to them, murmuring that she guessed she'd better say good-night.

"Unless I can do something for you, Chief. Like me to fix you another drink?"

"Got plenty," he grunted, not looking at her. "You run along, an'—an', uh, thanks, Eve. Nice party."

"I could stay and talk a while, if you like. I'm supposed to go to a wedding, the younger sister of a girl I went to Vassar with. But—"

"Spare us the flamin' details," Ironside said. "We'll read about it in the newspapers."

"Well . . . if you're sure. I don't have to be there until nine, and—"

"Will this woman never leave?" Ironside groaned. "First she plies me with drink, and now she tries to talk me to death."

Eve laughed and departed. Ed Brown fixed drinks for himself and his chief.

"Now, you were saying . . ." Ironside prompted him, ". . . about that hit-and-run case the commissioner assigned us . . ."

"Chisholm," Brown nodded. "Eleanor McNesmith Chisholm. I'd say we were about wrapped up on our end of it."

"Took you long enough. What'd you do—take a trip to Bermuda or somethin'?"

"You'd gripe if they hung you with a new rope," Ed chuckled. "It's approximately twenty hours since she was killed, and we've practically got it in the bag. Nothing much left to do but turn it over to the lab boys, and let them finger our hit-and-runner."

"Well . . ." Ironside hesitated grudgingly. "Guess that's not too bad—for a beginner."

Brown slapped his forehead in mock despair. The phone rang and he started toward it, then brought himself up short with an effort. Chief Ironside was already rolling his chair toward the phone. Touchy about his disability, he resented help in doing things that he could do for himself.

Ironside picked up the phone, spoke into it. Brown heard him grunt with surprise and displeasure.

"Huh? . . . Well, what for? . . . Not workin' hours, y'know. Hardly the time of night to . . . Yes."—very sharply. "Well, that's for me to say, isn't it? . . . Well, all right. . . . All right. . . . In fifteen minutes."

Ironside slammed down the receiver, spun the chair around and came back to Brown.

"Got some company comin'," he announced. "The DA, and one of his oldest and dearest friends—it says here."

"Yeah?"

"Yes. Coleman Duke—ever hear of him?"

It was a rhetorical question. Coleman Duke was one of the big names of the shipping industry. "I've heard of his son, too," said Sergeant Brown, "in case you were going to ask me."

"Babe Duke!" Ironside snorted disgustedly. "Lummox is almost thirty years old, and they call him Babe! Manslaughter drunk driving, right?"

"Reduced to misdemeanor. Driving while under the influence. Then there was a case before that—"

"Fleeing the scene of an accident. Flight to avoid arrest. Felony—reduced to misdemeanor."

"Well," Brown shrugged, "he seems to have been behaving himself recently."

"Has he? With the DA coming up here, and bringing Papa Duke along?"

"Well, I don't know of anything that—" Ed Brown broke off, glanced sharply at Ironside. "Eleanor Chisholm! He fits the pattern to a T!"

Ironside nodded grimly. "Hit-and-run and Babe Duke. Go together like ham and eggs. You'd better get out of here, Ed."

"Yeah?"

"Yes. The DA and Coleman are due here in fifteen minutes, and I've got things to do before they arrive."

Sergeant Brown departed.

Robert Ironside freshened his drink and reached for the telephone.

COLEMAN DUKE HAD an incredibly tanned face, a lustrous headful of iron-gray hair and a crisp military mustache. His teeth (his own) were beautifully white and even. His eyes were deceptively soft, and his voice seemed filtered through some amusing secret. Warm, good-humored—serious, of course, when seriousness was called for, but generally tuned to the happy things in life.

District Attorney Wayne Billington, on the other hand, might have posed as front man for a mortuary. A professional consoler of the bereaved. Newspaper reporters and other unkindly people had dubbed him "Crying Billie" and "Wayne the Weeper," and charged him with mourning his way into a long string of convictions. Once Billington turned on the tears, they said, a defendant was halfway to San Quentin.

Such statements and their authors deeply saddened the district attorney. He said that they were patently the words of twisted and evil men, and it wrenched his heart to think of the wretched fate which must inevitably be theirs.

Now, after introducing Coleman Duke, he again shook Ironside's hand, clinging to it as he assured the Chief that he would never forgive himself for his shocking lapse of memory.

"I'm mortified, Bob! *Heartsick!* How could I possibly have forgotten that today was your birthday?"

"How could you possibly have remembered it?" Ironside asked dryly, "when you couldn't possibly have known when it was?"

The district attorney didn't seem to hear him. "I'm ashamed of myself, Bob. I wish I could do something to make up for it. Coleman,"—he slid a meaningful glance at the shipping magnate, "couldn't we do something about a birthday remembrance, even now? Better late than never, wouldn't you say?"

Duke's deceptively warm eyes flicked over Ironside's face and made an immediate and accurate appraisal. "I'm afraid not," he smiled. "I suspect Chief Ironside wouldn't accept it in the spirit in which it was offered."

"What?" The DA blinked. "Oh, now, I'm sure Bob wouldn't think that—"

"Bob just might think that," Ironside said. "So why don't we drop the subject?"

"Right," Duke said heartily. "Chief Ironside doesn't accept bribes—or anything that might remotely be construed as such. And I never give bribes."

Ironside grinned, then laughed openly. "What, never?" he asked.

"Well . . ." Again that lightning-quick, unerringly accurate appraisal. "Well, *hardly* ever."

And then Duke's own warm laughter joined in with Ironside's. "You too, hmm? You know, *Pinafore* has always been one of my favorites, Chief."

"When it comes to Gilbert and Sullivan," Ironside said, "I'm afraid I have no favorites."

"Spoken like a true Savoyard! Wayne,"—Duke sidled a mock-reproachful glance at the district attorney—"you've been keeping things from me! Chief Ironside is a man of parts, not just another police detective."

Ironside murmured deprecatingly, urged his guests to help themselves to drinks. Beaming, Coleman Duke poured a drink for himself and Billington. Things were going just as he wanted. They were also—as a point of fact—going just as Ironside wanted. There was a margin of time to be dealt with, a margin which had to be of a certain wideness. As it would be, in a few more minutes.

The district attorney beamed happily from one man to the other. "Didn't I tell you, Coleman?" he demanded eagerly. "Didn't I tell you that Bob was one hell of a guy?"

"Well, I insist on a final bit of proof," Duke smiled. "I

insist that he share my box the next time we have the D'Oyly Carte company in San Francisco."

"A pleasure," Ironside said. "Unfortunately, I have a box of my own where I'm host to several friends."

Duke's expression changed ever so slightly; he said he hadn't meant to be patronizing. "Guess I'm a little over anxious to please," he apologized. "Perhaps you've had the same experience in meeting someone for the first time?"

"Frequently. I usually overcome it with booze."

"A word to the wise." Duke's warm laughter again filled the room. "And I think I'll just act on it!"

He added more whiskey to his glass; made a gesture of toasting Ironside with it. "Your very good health—uh—Look, do we have to be so formal? I mean, why don't I call you Bob or Robert, if you prefer?"

"Bob is fine," Ironside said.

"And, of course, you'll call me Cole or Coleman."

Ironside shook his head. The safety margin had widened sufficiently. There was no longer need to stall.

"No," he said bluntly. "I'll call you Mr. Duke, or Duke, if you prefer."

"B-But—but I thought—"

"I admire you, Mr. Duke. I can understand how you started in as a water boy fifty years ago, and got to where you are today. But I can't and don't like you. I've seen too much misery and crime derive from men like you."

"Bob—!" Wayne Billington was aghast. "How can you—"

"Quiet," Coleman Duke said. "Go on, Chief."

"I intend to," Ironside said. "To be quite frank, Mr. Duke, I think you'd tie your mother to a hot stove if she had something you wanted. I think that anyone who gets in your way had better never turn his back on you again. I think that with you as a model, a man he could neither accept nor reject— your son just about had to be the complete mess that he is."

District Attorney Billington appeared on the point of bursting into tears. "Bob!" he wailed. "You've given grievous and gratuitous offense—"

Duke gestured, cutting him off again; then nodded evenly to Ironside.

"We seem to understand each other, Chief. Suppose you tell me just where you stand in the present case."

"The hit-and-run death of Eleanor Chisholm?"

"Of course."

Ironside held up a hand, "Item: the high-speed skid marks of special-type racing tires; relatively few of them sold. Item: paint samples from the car; one of the two ultraexpensive foreign makes. Item: part of a broken lens from the headlight of the same car. Item . . . yes?"

"Suppose I told you that the car was stolen the day before yesterday. What would you say to that?"

"Something I'd hate to say. That you were a liar."

Billington's face sagged. Duke sighed.

"I'll tell you the truth," he said. "Or what my son tells me is the truth. I don't suppose I can blame you if you don't believe it."

"No," said Ironside. "I don't suppose you can."

"He was at a bachelor party for a friend. Someone phoned him that Miss Chisholm had to see him immediately. He doesn't know who the person was—some servant, he supposes. At any rate, he wasn't able to leave the party right away, so he had to hurry pretty fast when he did leave."

"Very fast," Ironside agreed. "A fast driver with a bellyful of booze."

"He'd been to a party," Duke shrugged. "Naturally, he'd been drinking. But getting on with the story: He'd been instructed to meet Miss Chisholm near the intersection of Crensmore and Antioch streets. A rather disreputable neighborhood, as you know, but Miss Chisholm was, uh—"

"Let's put it euphemistically and say she was a somewhat unconventional young woman. Your son wasn't surprised by the fact that she'd be in such a neighborhood."

"She was no good, Bob," Billington put in earnestly. "A wicked, wanton woman. A degenerate wastrel. A—Well, you know what she was."

Ironside said he knew what she was *now*. A corpse with its back broken in three places, its brains smeared over a block of pavement, its torso literally burst open from the terrific force of the car's impact.

Duke paled a little under his tan.

"All right, Chief," he continued quietly. "All right. Babe—my son—was on a one-way street. He was traveling almost seventy miles an hour. He'd been drinking. Things couldn't look worse for him if they'd been deliberately planned that way! That's why he was so frightened, you see. Why he failed to stop and report to the police, even though it hadn't been his fault."

"It *hadn't* been? Really, Mr. Duke."

"Let me tell you. He was supposed to meet Miss Chisholm at the intersection of Crensmore and Antioch. But he was three blocks away from there—*three blocks,* mind you— when she suddenly jumped out in front of him. Right into the path of his car. He couldn't stop. He couldn't have stopped if he'd been dead sober and traveling at the legal speed limit."

"But she wouldn't have been killed *if* he'd been traveling at the legal speed limit."

"Well, that's open to debate. But—"

"And the story you've told me is the one he told you. Which hardly makes it synonymous with the truth."

"Maybe it was suicide, Bob," the DA interjected. "Certainly sounds like it, doesn't it? She set up a set of circumstances which would compel poor Babe to, uh, well . . ."

His voice trailed away as the two men stared at him, wordlessly. There was a moment of heavy silence, and then Duke spoke again.

"You're right, Chief. However you look at it and regard-less of the circumstances, Babe is guilty. That's a fact and it can't be changed. The only thing to do now, as I see it, is to make the best of a bad situation."

"Which is?"

"You have certain evidence. It all points to Babe, and it would only be a matter of hours before you caught up with him. You were sure he was guilty even before I came in here and admitted it."

Ironside nodded. "So?"

"So this." Coleman Duke leaned forward. "Pretend to be stalled. Temporarily at a dead end in your investigation. After all, it could happen that way, couldn't it? Investigations don't always go smoothly. Evidence is seldom as clear-cut as it is in this case. I'm not asking you to drop it, understand. Wayne would no more agree to that than you would."

"I'm sure he wouldn't," Ironside agreed. "Wayne's an honest man, a good prosecutor. He's also very much a human being, however, and human beings—which office holders are not—can't possibly be completely objective about their friends."

"Now, Bob. . . ." Billington hesitated. "I hope you're not implying that I would misuse the law to favor a friend."

"Not in your own viewpoint, no. But the law allows you a great deal of discretion. You can prosecute virtually the same crime very severely or very lightly—or not prosecute it at all. Decide that the so-called crime was not actually one, and call for a dismissal of the charge. I think this is as it should be. I think it's one of the great virtues of our legal system. I also think, however, that Wayne has abused that discretion in his ultralenient handling of your son."

"I'm sorry to hear you say that!" Billington snapped. "Very sorry!"

"And I'm sorry to have to say it. But getting back to you, Mr. Duke. I anticipated the reason for this visit before Wayne brought you up here. My answer is no."

"But why?" Duke frowned. "I'll give you my word, Chief. Within three hours of the time you announce that you're at a dead end in the case, my son will give himself up. Nothing will be changed. He'll still face trial and certain conviction. What possible difference can it make if—"

Ironside cut him off with an angry snort. It would make all the difference in the world, he said, and Duke flamin' well knew it!

"Your son is an irresponsible slob. Now that he feels the hot breath of the law on his neck, he wants to play the responsible citizen. An honest man, coming forward freely to admit his mistake. By so doing, he would give Wayne justification for handling his case leniently, and he'd probably get off with a fine and a suspended sentence."

Billington shook his head mournfully. "You've accused me of being unfair, Bob. Aren't you being unfair yourself? You've confessed to disliking Mr. Duke. Can you honestly say that your attitude isn't colored by that dislike?"

"I don't think so, no. Not, at any rate, to the extent that your liking for him has colored your attitude." Ironside turned to the shipping man. "Mr. Duke, I mentioned that I anticipated the reason for your coming here. So I called your son before you arrived. He made a full confession to me. By now, thanks to your extended efforts to be ingratiating, the police have had plenty of time to get him in jail."

A muscle rippled in Coleman Duke's face. In his bronzed forehead, a blue vein swelled and throbbed. Then, with perfectly steady hands, he took out a flat, gold case, selected a cigarette from it and carefully held a lighter-flame to its tip.

"I don't imagine you stopped with that, did you?" he asked. "You didn't leave any way open to make him look good?"

"Not a one. Newspapers, radio, television—they've all been informed. The truth is out, and it can't be colored or covered up."

Wayne Billington gave him a stricken look, let his gaze shift nervously to Duke. "A rotten shame, Coleman. Babe is such a fine young man, I—"

"He's a bum," Duke said flatly. "A stinker from the word go. But he's my son, and any disgrace to him is one to me. I don't like being disgraced, Chief. There doesn't appear to be anything I can do about it at the moment. But . . ." He stood up, and held out his hand. "I had to try. No hard feelings?"

"None on my part," Ironside said, and took the extended hand. "I'm sorry to—"

Fire burned his palm. Burned into it. He suppressed a wince, the impulse to jerk free from the iron grip of the other man. Instead, he shifted and tightened his own grasp, forcing Duke to share the pain which the latter had tried to inflict on him.

When they at last released each other, he glanced down at his palm in apparent surprise. "I hope I didn't burn you, Mr. Duke," he apologized. "Strange that I didn't feel it, but I must have been holding a lighted cigarette."

"Quite all right," Duke smiled at him handsomely. "I didn't feel anything either. Well,"—he turned to the district attorney—"shall we be going, Wayne?"

Billington arose, giving Ironside a bitterly tragic look. "I'm afraid I'm not going to be able to forget this, Bob. I'm afraid I'll always remember it."

"Good," Ironside said.

"We're all going to remember," Duke said. "I'll guarantee it."

"Would you like to shake hands on it?" Ironside said.

Duke's smile suddenly wiped out. He whirled and strode off toward the elevator, the DA tagging after him.

EVE TUGGED OPEN the door of the place and stepped hesitantly inside. Then, as the incredible stench struck her like a blow—the thick smog of stale smoke and stale bodies and stale drinks—she almost fell back. Held herself where she was only by tremendous exertion of willpower.

She stood blinking, trying to penetrate the stinking and clouded dimness. Gradually, her eyes accustomed themselves to the dimness, and she was able to see a little. And that little brought a gasp of horror to her lips. Why it looked like . . . *like Hell!* A madman's concept of Hell!

She, Eve Whitfield, had come off a twisting San Francisco street and stepped into Hell.

She couldn't see what she was looking for. The rear table with a magazine lying open on it and a cigarette tray sitting on top of the magazine. The smog was too thick; there were too many monstrously masked and garbed figures in the way. Staggering and swaying in lunatic simulation of a dance.

Gingerly, she started to make her way through them toward the rear. Cringing a little as they brushed against her. Then, an apelike figure suddenly grabbed her and drew her close to him, grinning into her face as he violently jigged her up and down. She jerked away from him, taking a half-stumbling step backward. She bumped into a Devil, and he, the Devil, twirled her around with drunken gracefulness, and brought her face to face with a Frog. The Frog grasped her other wrist. Dipping and swaying, dragging Eve up and down with them, they began to dance.

A dance like no other had ever been. A quadrille, a waltz, a tango, rock'n'roll—everything and nothing. A dance to fit the preposterous music of the piano.

There was beauty in the music, or, more accurately, the memory of beauty, now as lost as a lost love; something that lay buried in an unknown dimension like the final decimal of pi. Now, as though avenging itself upon an evil and uncaring world, it had sprouted into hideousness—a seed gone mad. And its terrible blossoms of sound hinted at a greater terror to come. Here, said the music, was a taste of Armageddon. Here, the Ultima Thule. Here the inevitable destination of a planet whose mass of six sextillion, four hundred and fifty quintillion short tons was turned into a slaughterhouse instead of a garden. Here, the fruit of neglect, that socially approved form of murder. Here, the basic lie in its final extension.

A whole *was* greater than its parts . . . or was there no Bomb, no minute amalgam of neutrons and protons? Add three billion to the planet's mass, and subtract kindness and caring, and you were left not with an unkindly, uncaring three billion, but death. So said the seed, the music, now sunk in the morass of a wilderness from which it had vainly cried out. There would be no refuge from the coming terror. No place to hide. No familiar thing to cling to. Something would become nothing, robbed of its intrinsic beauty and safety, and all else. There would be only a smoking, steaming, blown-apart, crushed-together, mishmash where brother was himself eaten by brother while eating brother, ad nauseam, ad infinitum. Even so:

"*Deutschland Uber*" "*Mississippi Mud*" "*Internationale Funeral March*" "*Stars Fell on*" "*The Star-spangled*" "*Shiek of Araby*" "*I Left My Heart in*" "*Black Bottom*" "*Rhapsody in*" "*Saber Dance*" "*Spring Song*" "*At Sundown*" "*How You Gonna Keep 'Em*" "*Down on the Levee*" "*Boo-Hoo*" "*Mammy*" "*Fire Dance*" "*Over There*" "*Toot, toot, Tootsie*" "*Good-bye, Forever*" . . .

A Witch with thick ankles motioned curtly to the Devil and the Frog. They released their grasp on Eve Whitfield, and the Witch took her by the arm, guided her through the crowd to a rear table with an opened magazine on it and an ashtray on top of the magazine.

Eve sank gratefully down at the table, nearly breathless, a little weak from her enforced dancing. The Witch sat down near her, informed her that the party she wished to see would be along shortly.

"Now, what'll you have to drink, dear?"

"Nothing," Eve said. "I don't care for a thing, thanks."

"Got to have something. House rule," the Witch said

firmly. Then, leaning closer for confidential speech, "Know how y'feel, honey. Tell you what I always do in this place. Order somethin' that ain't dolled up, y'know? Somethin' clear that you can see through, like vodka an' soda."

"But I—"

"I'll have one with you, if you'll buy. About all I got these days is the habit."

"Oh, well, of course," said Eve, and she put money into the Witch's gloved hand.

The latter went away, returned shortly with the drinks. Eve stalled, fumbling with a cigarette, until the Witch had taken a long, thirsty drink. Then, she took a tiny sip of her own drink.

It seemed all right—chloral hydrate is colorless, tasteless, odorless. Eve told herself that it would have to be all right. As Belle Larabee, she represented money to the blackmailer. He would have no reason to harm her, at least until he had collected.

So, as the Witch greedily drained her glass, Eve took a long drink from hers. She needed one after what she had been through, and with the ordeal she had still to face.

The Witch mumbled a "Drink hearty," and arose from the table. She said she would just find Eve's party herself, see to it he came to the table right away. Eve nodded her thanks, and the Witch disappeared in the crowd. But she did not immediately summon the Killer.

She meant to. More importantly, she had been ordered to by none other than the Skeleton, the Deity, himself. But even as she hurried to obey the order, she collided with a rail-thin Demon. So she stopped to talk to him, to plead with him, for what was to be only a moment. But the Demon shook his head, shaking it more and more firmly the more urgently she pleaded. And the intended moment became a minute. Minutes.

IN THE WEED-GROWN patio behind the place, the Killer paced back and forth, occasionally smacking one gloved fist into the palm of his other hand, occasionally swinging his arm in a gesture of emphasis, or snorting out a curt laugh of triumph, as he scored in the debate within himself.

In the darkness, against the black background of the shroud, the phosphorous Skeleton moved eerily to and fro, every move exaggeratedly jerky, seeming to flop and fling itself about like a thing animated by a string.

Tonight was a very special night for the Killer. So special that he had worked himself into a fever pitch of excitement, at last crashing through the hard shell of reserve and inhibition in which he had always been contained. For tonight—the woman who was to die tonight was someone he knew. Knew as he had known no other woman. And his other victims had been strangers to him.

He knew them, naturally. He had watched them, studied them over a considerable period of time. Taking note of each of their transgressions, carefully keeping score on them, withholding his awful judgment until the score reached a certain total and they had proved themselves in need of recalling to the Factory. For he, the Killer, was a just and forbearing Deity.

They had not known him, but he had known them. Finally and regretfully (or so he told himself) weighing them on his scales and finding them wanting. Even as he had finally and regretfully (or so he told himself) been forced to do in the case of Belle Larabee, the woman he knew well and who knew him well.

Because he knew her, he had been more forbearing than with any of the others. Because she had exhausted his forbearance, willfully throwing away each new chance she was given, his ultimate attitude toward her was unusually severe. She had a good husband. (None of the other victims had been married.) So it was only just that she should suffer some of the torture he had suffered before she was struck down.

Hence, his deliberate delay in meeting her—a delay that would be a fearsome, worry-filled eternity for her. Thus, his demand for a sum which she could not possibly pay—something which had to be done, yet could not be, and must agonizingly tear her apart as her husband had been torn.

She would come tonight, of course, to beg. He, the Killer would take her back to one of the cabins, and there tell her the price she was to pay. And the dope would be working on her by then, and while she could listen and understand, that would be all she could do. Only listen in paralyzed horror as he pronounced sentence and carried it out:

The loss of the loveliness that she had misused. The loss, insofar as possible, of everything that identified her as a woman. So that she would go to her deserved death as something so hideous that even the sharks would pause before—

The Skeleton jerked fantastically, as it made a sudden start. Part of the bones of its left arm disappeared, as the sleeve of the shroud was pulled up.

A watch glowed in the darkness. The Killer looked at it, grunted in dismayed surprise. Could he have been wrong? Would Belle Larabee fail to come and beg?

No—the skeleton head moved in a firm negative. No, that couldn't be. He knew Belle too well, knew exactly how she would think and act. She would come, all right. In fact, she would have had to be here by now. And that being the case—

The Killer yanked down his sleeve. Angrily, he strode across the patio, stepped through the rear door of the place. His table was obscured by a mass of masqueraders. But he saw the Witch and the rail-thin Demon. Almost at the same time, the Demon saw him, and he interrupted the Witch's pleading with an urgent nudge—a hasty nod toward the rear door.

The Witch turned around, stood fear-frozen for a moment. Then, at a faltering but anxious pace, she hurried up to the Killer.

"Got her," she mumbled. "Fixed her good, just like you said."

"Did you?" said the Killer. "How long ago?"

"Well, I . . . not very long. Honest, not very long."

"What does that mean?" the Killer asked. "Ten minutes, fifteen, thirty?"

"N-not very long, h-honest. H-honest, n-not v-v-very—"

The Killer looked at her. His hand closed over her arm in a steely grip. "Come," he said coldly. "Come."

Pulling her along with him, he started toward his table, the masqueraders almost frantically falling back to make way for him. At last they were out of the throng, the Killer and the Witch, and into a relatively open space. And there they stopped short. The Witch looking fearfully up at the Killer. The Killer staring incredulously at Eve Whitfield.

This woman? Not the woman who was to die. What in the—

Never mind! *Never mind!* The Killer, the Deity, was just. Always, always just. In punishing the wicked, he was—was he not?—protecting the righteous. Only with this knowledge, this rationalization, could he go about his self-appointed duties. Only thus—and only by permitting, admitting no error. For the hand of the Deity must always be sure, and an erring Deity is no Deity at all.

"You!" he told the Witch. "You get her out of here. *Now!*"

"B-but—but—"

"Say that her party can't see her! Tell her anything! Just get her out!"

The Witch nodded numbly, but she didn't move. She was bewildered, terrified by something in his tone. Incapable of speech or movement.

"Didn't you hear me? If I have to—"

There was a soft thud, the clatter of shattering glass. The Killer's eyes swerved toward the table.

Eve had pitched forward in her chair. Her face half-turned toward him, her arms limply outspread, she lay crumpled across the smeared top of the table.

The Witch had found her voice at last. What was wrong she didn't know, but she knew the Killer, knew that he did not tolerate wrong. And mumbling incoherently, she pleaded for mercy. And almost sobbed with relief at the evidence of his forgiveness.

He wasn't sore at her, thank God. He couldn't be. For here in her hand was proof positive.

A small white disc. A precious cap, whose crystalline whiteness testified to its purity.

"Have it now," the Killer said gently. "You deserve it."

The
Phosphorescent
Bride

O s c a r   L e w i s

MONG THE SEVERAL hundred physicians practicing in San Francisco in the year 1885 was a pale,
bearded, stockily built man of forty-two; his name
was J. Milton Bowers. There was nothing at all remarkable
about him. To be sure, a few might have considered that in the
form of his name there was something mildly eccentric, for in
those days the fashion of hiding first names behind the semi-
anonymity of an initial was less common than it later became.
Aside from this singularity, however, there was little to set him
apart from scores of other hardworking doctors one daily
encountered on the streets of the hustling city. He was neither
successful nor unsuccessful, neither obscure nor conspicuous. He
spent his mornings, in horse and buggy, hurrying from one to
another of his bedridden patients, and his afternoons in office
consultations with those well enough to come downtown.
During his limited leisure he lived an active but rather narrow

San Francisco native OSCAR LEWIS penned this 1924 account
of the perils of matrimony. Lewis is the author of *A History of
San Francisco*.

social life, attending meetings of the half dozen fraternal organizations to which he belonged. He had a wife and twelveyearold stepdaughter. His income was ample for his unextravagant tastes, and it had been increasing from year to year; of late he had formed the habit of putting his surplus earnings into insurance on his own life and that of his wife. He was a moderately successful, moderately prosperous, moderately popular general practitioner. That he was about to become a very conspicuous figure indeed, his odd name familiar to uncounted thousands all over the coast, was a possibility few could have foreseen.

Dr. Bowers was born in Baltimore in 1843. In 1885, when he abruptly rose to prominence, he had been living and practicing in San Francisco for eleven years. Earlier he had practiced in Brooklyn and earlier still in Chicago. His parents had died when he was five and he had been reared by an uncle. The doctor himself once stated that his father had left him an estate of $50,000, but of that sum he had been able to collect only $20,000. In 1859 he had used part of his heritage to finance a trip to Germany, where for a few months he studied medicine. Returning to this country, he joined the staff of the Patterson Hospital at Washington, D. C., remaining throughout the Civil War. All that time he had no diploma; it was not until his graduation from the Bennett Eclectic Medical College at Chicago that he became a certified physician. That was in 1873 or 1874, when he was about thirty.

The doctor always maintained that he was a man of strong domestic attachments, and his statement was borne out by the facts: his current wife was his third. The first Mrs. Bowers was the former Miss Fannie Hammond, of Chicago, whom he married in the middle Sixties. She died in 1874 and, his home having burned at about the same time, he left Chicago and went to New York, intending to continue on to Europe. Instead, he there married wife number two, a young actress named Teresa Sherek, whom he had known in Chicago and who accompanied him to California in late 1874 or early 1875.

Much more is known of Teresa Sherek than of the shadowy Miss Hammond. She lived with the doctor six or seven years; then, on January 28, 1881, she too died. The obituary notices in local papers gave her age as twenty-four; she could therefore have been only seventeen or eighteen at the time of her marriage. She was said to have been beautiful and talented and it is known that she wielded a facile pen. In 1877, at the age of twenty, she blossomed forth as the author of *The Dance of Life,* a little book extolling the innocent virtues of the waltz. It was written as an "answer" to another San Francisco publication called *The Dance of Death,* which took an opposite view of waltzing and was then having a wide reading. *The Dance of Death* was a hoax perpetrated by three young San Franciscans, one of whom was Ambrose Bierce. The public took their tongue-in-cheek attack on the evils of ballroom dancing so seriously that 18,000 copies were said (on Bierce's authority) to have been sold in a few months, and it received the endorsement of a number of dignified organizations, among them the Methodist Church Conference. Mrs. Bowers' "answer" was less scandalous and less popular, but it too was widely read. Bierce helped the controversy along by reviewing both volumes in his column in the *Argonaut* and pronouncing them equally worthless. It has been suggested that Bierce may have had a hand in writing both books, and it is pleasant to imagine the journalist and Teresa Bowers in the role of collaborators; but there is, unfortunately, no good evidence to support that theory. In any case *The Dance of Life* adds a curious literary note to the story of Dr. Bowers' career, which has otherwise but few connections with belles lettres.

Wife number three was Cecelia Benhayon Levy, whom he married in June 1881, four months after the death of the authoress of *The Dance of Life.* Cecelia was twenty-nine. Her friendship with the doctor began, as had Teresa's, when she consulted him professionally. She was described as short, plump and full of high spirits, but prone to frequent and violent outbursts of jealousy. This last, it must be supposed, was an unhappy trait in the wife of a young physician whose patients were mostly women. She had a daughter, the child of the first of her two former husbands, and she had besides a mother and a brother. She lived with Bowers a little more than four years; then, like the doctor's other wives, she too sickened and died.

When Cecelia Bowers' death became known it must have occurred to many that the home-loving doctor was having singularly bad luck with his helpmates. He had married three wives in fifteen years and all three had come to untimely ends. Dr. Bowers' behavior during his latest bereavement indicated that these successive blows were almost more than he could bear: he was the picture of manly grief, candid and unashamed. It is recorded that a few minutes before Cecelia died he turned a stricken face to the attending physician and cried, "Baby's going, doctor—is there nothing we can do for her?" At the funeral he sat with bowed head, his small step-daughter beside him: a touching picture of a little family tragically disrupted. And beside the grave, robust man though he was and professionally inured to the mystery of death, his grief so overcame him that he fainted dead away.

But while this was going on events of another nature were taking shape. On the morning following Cecelia's death the coroner received in the mail an unsigned letter which hinted broadly that the passing of young Mrs. Bowers might bear a bit of looking into. Coroner O'Donnell sensibly gave small credence to such anonymous warnings, but he was a conscientious official and, in order that there might be no doubt in anyone's mind, he ordered an inquest. When the widower was told of the order he interposed no objection; indeed he pronounced himself eager to cooperate in every way possible.

The inquest was held on November 3, 1885 (Mrs. Bowers had died on the first), in the second-floor parlor of the Arcade House, the family hotel on upper Market Street where the doctor had both his office and his living quarters. A large number of witnesses were called and the hearing consumed the greater part of the day, further evidence of Coroner O'Donnell's admirable thoroughness.

Nothing of a suspicious nature was uncovered. The dead woman had fallen ill about two months earlier and she had been bedridden for five weeks. During most of that time she had had the services of two physicians of her own selection, for Dr. Bowers, like many another doctor, preferred not to treat members of his own household. One or another of her physicians had visited her daily, and between times Dr. Bowers or his nurse was always available: his office was just down the hall from the sickroom. Later, after her condition became grave, the nurse, Mrs. Zeissing, spent all day with the patient, and the doctor himself took over nights, sleeping on a cot in their bedroom and administering medicine as it was required.

All this came out at the inquest. Bowers himself and the two attending physicians were agreed on the diagnosis: the deceased had succumbed to an abscess of the liver. All this professional testimony must have sounded convincing to the reporter from the *Alta California*, for he ended his story of the hearing with this pronouncement: "None of the evidence introduced could by any possibility be construed to support the theory that the deceased had come to her death otherwise than by natural causes."

The investigation into the death of Cecelia Bowers might have ended there. It unquestionably would have so ended but for the presence at the inquest of several strangers. They presently identified themselves as agents for certain fraternal organizations with which the deceased had carried life insurance. The amount of insurance was substantial, totalling approximately $17,000. They had listened with skepticism to the testimony of the medical men and when the hearing was about to close one of them expressed dissatisfaction with the diagnosis and asked that an autopsy be performed.

Again Dr. Bowers offered no strong objection. He pointed out, however, that plans for the funeral had been completed and that to change them at so late a date would inconvenience both the family and friends of the deceased. But that difficulty was easily surmounted. It was agreed that the services would be held as scheduled, and that the body, instead of being buried, would be placed in the receiving vault at the cemetery, from which on the following morning it would be returned to the undertaking parlors; the autopsy would be performed there. This arrangement being acceptable to all the interested parties, the inquest was recessed until the report of the autopsy surgeon could be presented.

Following this program, the funeral was held the next morning in lodge rooms on O'Farrell Street; at their conclusion the body was placed in a hearse and taken to a cemetery in the Mission district. This was on Tuesday. Shortly before four o'clock Wednesday Coroner O'Donnell received a phone message from Dr. Balch, the city physician. Dr. Balch was calling from the undertaking parlors, where he and his assistants had gone to perform the autopsy.

He reported that the body was not there.

The coroner, a man of action, summoned the city dead wagon and drove to the cemetery, intending to pick up the corpse at the receiving vault. When he arrived he learned that the body was not there either; indeed the cemetery superintendent informed him that it had been buried immediately after the funeral procession had reached the burial ground the previous day. The coroner ordered the cemetery official to exhume the corpse. He waited while his instructions were carried out, whereupon the body was placed in the dead wagon and O'Donnell took it to the city morgue. The delayed autopsy was performed the following morning, which was Thursday.

By then the case was beginning to attract general attention. On the morning of the fifth, the *Alta*, no longer convinced that Mrs. Bowers had died from natural causes, headed its story: "A Queer Proceeding: The Body of Mrs. Bowers Hurriedly Buried." The next day preliminary findings of the autopsy reached the public. The body was that of a well-nourished woman, exhibiting none of the emaciation usually associated with a long illness; its weight was 125 pounds and its height just under five feet; an ulcer had been found on the stomach wall, and there was evidence that an abortion had recently been performed on the deceased. Additional findings were promised on completion of a chemical analysis of the stomach contents and a microscopic examination of the vital organs.

There was no further news for three days; when it came it was sensational. On November 9th the autopsy surgeon reported to the coroner's jury that death had been due to phosphorus poisoning, and the jury promptly named Bowers as a suspect. The doctor was arrested that afternoon and lodged in the county jail. Two days later he was formally charged with murder.

DR. BOWERS ACCEPTED these developments with little outward show of concern. To reporters who gathered outside his cell he stated his belief that within a few hours his name would be cleared and his freedom restored. The theory that he had administered lethal doses of phosphorus to his wife he dismissed as preposterous. "People who know me know I'm not such a fool," he stated. "Phosphorus permeates the entire system. . . ." Reminded that he was facing a serious charge, he held out his arm and invited his visitors to see how steady it was. "See," he observed, "I'm not a bit nervous. My hand doesn't tremble in the slightest." Some of his remarks were mildly humorous. Asked if it was true that he had married three times, he cheerfully admitted the charge and smilingly added, "I'd get married twenty times if I chose." Interviewers came away convinced that, guilty or not, the prisoner was a remarkably cool individual.

Meantime the police had been delving into his past, and certain details of his activities since he had come west were brought to light; not all of them were to his credit. One official stated that his practice, while lucrative, was "not very high class," and another, less circumspect, charged bluntly that he was an abortionist. It was recalled that once, five years earlier, he had been briefly involved with the authorities. The charge was a minor one, petty larceny: the theft of some medical books from a Market Street store. He was tried, found guilty, and fined $150, with the alternative of spending seventy-five days in jail. Bowers' attorney appealed the case and three months later he was re-tried, this time by a jury. The jury disagreed and the charge was dropped. So far as was ever learned this was his one previous brush with the law.

The trial opened before Superior Court Judge D. J. Murphy on March 9, 1886, four months after his arrest. The opposing legal staffs were headed by two noted trial lawyers, Eugene Duprey for the people and Colin Campbell representing Bowers; both were veterans of some of the Coast's most celebrated criminal trials. The proceedings were long, involved and, to the layman, not very interesting. Weeks were devoted to the highly technical dissertations of physicians and chemists, for it was soon evident that the case would turn on the opinion of experts as to the nature and characteristics of phosphorus poisoning. The prosecution maintained that the symptoms of the deceased and the findings of the autopsy were such as could have been produced only by phosphorus, while the defense claimed that like symptoms and findings might be present in persons who had died from natural causes. Both sides brought in authorities of high professional standing who, after the habit of expert witnesses, reached exactly opposite conclusions.

The papers daily printed columns of this involved testimony; readers skimmed it (or skipped it entirely) and concentrated on more understandable evidence. Much of the latter was damaging to Bowers. He was pictured as an accomplished ladies' man, not averse to boasting of his conquests to friends and acquaintances and even to his wife. Witnesses testified that the pair had frequently quarrelled in public, that he had kicked her, blackened her eye, threatened her with a riding whip and offered her $10,000 if she would give him his freedom. The state made much too of the insurance Bowers had taken out on his wife's life, and of the fact that he had rejected pleas of his mother-in-law (with whom he was on bad terms) that his stepdaughter be named the beneficiary of some of the policies. Henry Benhayon, the dead woman's brother, bitterly assailed the prisoner for his conduct during Cecelia's illness, charging that members of her family were usually excluded from the sick-chamber and that on the rare occasions when they were admitted, Bowers himself or his nurse, Charlotte Zeissing, were pointedly present.

The prosecution bent every effort to prove that Bowers had possessed a supply of the fatal drug, but here the testimony was inconclusive. No clear evidence of his ever having purchased phosphorus was presented, although the prisoner admitted that preparations containing the substance might have been sent him as samples by pharmacopoeial manufacturers or wholesalers. His gaunt and close-mouthed nurse, Mrs. Zeissing, had been in possession of the keys to his office for two days after his arrest; the state's attorneys did not fail to point out that she thus had ample opportunity to get rid of incriminating evidence.

The accused man had two ardent champions: Mrs. Zeissing and a comely young woman known as Theresa Farrell. The latter had once been a maid in the Bowers household; when the doctor and his wife moved to the Arcade House they got her a position there as a waitress. Both stoutly denied charges that the married life of the Bowers had been stormy, picturing it instead as singularly tranquil and happy. Nurse Zeissing testified that the order banning visitors from the sickroom had been at the patient's own request, adding that the sick woman had asked only that she be allowed to die in her husband's arms. Miss Farrell (on the stand she admitted that she was married and that her true name was Mrs. Wilson) stated that Mrs. Bowers was of an uncontrollably jealous disposition and that despite this annoying trait the doctor treated her with uniform kindness and forbearance. She added that, unknown to her husband, Mrs. Bowers had twice taken measures to bring on a miscarriage.

The doctor himself spent a day on the stand; he proved a cool and resourceful witness. He entered a comprehensive denial that he had been an errant or abusive husband, that he had administered injurious drugs to his wife, or that his conduct had ever been other than that of a considerate and loving mate. He adroitly answered every charge the prosecution brought against him. He had loved his wife and they had been congenial and happy. Why should he have wanted to poison her? The insurance? In his profession he earned an income adequate for his needs; besides his own life was insured for the same sum he carried on his wife, and she was the beneficiary. He smiled at the idea that had he been inclined to homicide he would have followed so clumsy a method as that charged against him. Phosphorus was one of the easiest of all drugs to detect in the human system. He was a medical man, familiar with the properties of dozens of poisons; he would surely have chosen a more subtle drug, one that would have been virtually impossible to detect. Besides, he had forbidden the undertaker to embalm the body; had this been done neither autopsy nor chemical analysis would have revealed anything incriminating.

He had an explanation for every damaging statement, important or trivial. A prosecution witness had testified that once, when Cecelia had been involved in a buggy accident, Bowers had shouted, "I wish you had broken your damned neck!" The doctor smilingly stated that what he had really said was, "Darn the buggy, so long as your neck is not broken." Nor had he ever remarked to his stepdaughter, "Go to hell, you

brat." He was sure of that because he never used profanity; his most outspoken expletive, he explained, was "darn it." He accounted for the premature burial by saying that he had no knowledge that the coroner would object to such a proceeding, since it would be easy to dig the body up again, and he denounced the city physician's failure to invite him to witness the autopsy. Only once during his hours on the stand did his self-possession seemingly desert him. While he was describing Cecelia's death his voice broke and he stopped for a few moments and wiped his eyes before proceeding.

The trial lasted from March 11th to late April, 1886. At the end of six weeks 130 witnesses had been examined; twenty-five days had been given over to hearing testimony, and the shorthand notes filled seventeen large volumes. It was the longest murder trial in the city's history. Final arguments were concluded on April 23rd; the judge took another half day to instruct the jury, whereupon the jurors retired.

They were out only thirty-five minutes. Bowers, who had been killing time by "animatedly discussing the subject of hanging . . . with a group in the courtroom," broke off his monologue as the jurors filed into the box. He seemed the least interested person in the room as the foreman announced the verdict: "We the jury find the defendant guilty of murder in the first degree."

The prisoner was returned to jail while his attorneys prepared an appeal. On June 3rd he was again brought into court. Judge Murphy denied the motion for a new trial, then asked the prisoner if he had anything to say before sentence was passed. Bowers stood up, faced the court and in a composed tone proclaimed his innocence and his willingness to die. Then he added:

> "Since I must make my exit I ask that you . . . grant me this boon, and fully knowing that my late dear wife did not die of phosphorus poisoning I ask this: That I

should be placed somewhere with the same surrounding conditions, etc., and a crowd of medical men be around and administer to me as the prosecution has claimed has been administered to my late dear wife. I am willing to show that she did not die of phosphorus poisoning."

Ignoring this unorthodox proposal, the judge there-upon sentenced the prisoner to death by hanging. He was returned to his cell to await execution. He remained there for many months, pending a hearing by the State Supreme Court of an appeal from the judgment of the Superior Court. Not until June 1, 1889, three years after his conviction, did the higher court pass on this matter.

Meantime there had been curious new developments.

▲

ON TUESDAY, OCTOBER 18, 1887, a young man climbed the steps of a rooming house at 22 Geary Street, just off Market, and rang the bell. When the proprietress, Mrs. Higson, answered, the stranger made known his wish to rent a room. His was shown several that chanced to be vacant; he was pleased with none of them, but expressed an interest in room 21. Mrs. Higson informed him that number 21 was occupied but that the tenant was moving out the following Saturday. The visitor thanked her and left. The next day, Wednesday, another young man appeared and stated that he had heard room 21 would be vacant Saturday. On being told that this was so he paid a five-dollar deposit and was given a key.

On Sunday, October 23rd, a Chinese servant entered room 21 for the purpose of tidying up. He emerged very promptly. The figure of a man was lying on the floor, fully clothed and with his arms resting neatly at his side; he was dead.

Summoned by the servant, Mrs. Higson entered and bent over the corpse. It was not that of the young man who had rented the room or of the other young man who had made preliminary inquiries concerning it. Mrs. Higson had never laid eyes on this young man before. She observed that the following articles had been laid out on a bedside table: a flask of whisky, partly empty; a bottle of chloroform liniment; and a bottle, not quite full, containing a liquid that was subsequently found to be cyanide of potassium. The bottles were tightly corked. There were also pen, ink, paper and three letters. One was addressed to a local newspaper and one to Coroner O'Donnell.

The third was addressed to Dr. J. Milton Bowers. All three were signed H. Benhayon—the name of the dead woman's brother.

Identification of the corpse quickly followed; it was indeed that of Henry Benhayon. The contents of the bedside letters was made public. That to the newspaper requested the insertion of an advertisement for the return of a lost memorandum book. The message to Bowers cautioned the latter against some of his supposed friends, informed him that Cecelia had lost money in stock speculations, and that certain diamonds the doctor had bought for his wife were paste. This letter began: "I only ask that you do not molest my mother as she is not responsible, and also Tilly is not responsible for my acts. I made all the reparation in my power. . . ."

The letter to the coroner, made public a day or two later, proved to be no less than a confession that Benhayon himself had murdered his sister. This is its text:

"The history of the tragedy commenced after my sister married Dr. Bowers. I had reasons to believe that he would leave her soon, as they always quarrelled and on one occasion she told me that she would poison him before she would permit him to leave her. I said in jest, Have him insured. She said, All right. But Bowers objected for a long time, but finally said, If it will keep you out of mischief, go ahead. They both joined several lodges and I got the stuff ready to dispose of him, but my sister would not listen to the proposition and threatened to expose me. After my sister got sick I felt an irresistible impulse to use the stuff on her and finish him afterward. I would then become administrator for my little niece, Tilly, and would have the benefit of the insurance. I think it was Friday, November 24, 1885, that I took one capsule out of her pill box and filled it with two kinds of poison. I didn't think Bowers would get into any kind of trouble, as the person who gave me the poison told me it would leave no trace in the stomach. This person committed suicide before the trial, and as it might implicate others if I mention his name I will close the tragedy."

These disclosures set the town in an uproar. Reporters who hurried to the jail to get the reaction of Dr. Bowers observed a pronounced change in the latter's demeanor. His dull and apathetic expression had been succeeded by animation and his voice had a confident ring. As always, he proved eager to air his opinions in the press. He expressed his belief that Benhayon had been insane; he did not believe that his wife had ever planned to murder him; he thought there must be something in Benhayon's story about the diamonds; he had suspected that they were not genuine.

The attorneys who had conducted the trial were also interviewed. Those who had represented the defendant were naturally jubilant: now that the real murderer had confessed they were confident that their client would be released. But the prosecutor, Eugene Duprey, took a different view. He hinted broadly that Benhayon's death might not have been suicide at all, but part of a plot to enable the wily doctor to escape the gallows.

There was a great deal that seemed to support that view. The town's newspapers (most of which had long been

convinced of the doctor's guilt) expounded at length the theory
that Bowers had engineered from his cell this scheme by which
Benhayon had been lured to his death and made the central figure in a carefully staged suicide hoax. Captain of Detectives I.
W. Lees and his assistant Robert Hogan had no sooner started
their investigation than they adopted that theory.

There were many suspicious angles to the case: it
did not look like suicide. The composed position in which
the body was found aroused natural doubts, as did the fact
that the bottle containing the quick-acting poison was
securely corked and that the pen with which the confession
letters had purportedly been written appeared never to have
been used. These were all suspicious circumstances, but not
more so than the visits of the two strangers who had rented
the room, and the fact that the persons most familiar with
the dead man's handwriting unhesitatingly pronounced the
confession letters forgeries. Decidedly it had the appearance
of murder, and the investigation turned to the man who
stood to benefit most.

But how could Bowers, who had been locked in jail
for more than two years, have accomplished this second murder? Pondering that question, detectives began to examine
those who had been in the habit of visiting the doctor in his
cell. The trail led to the two women who had all along been
his warmest supporters, Mrs. Zeissing and Theresa Farrell:
both had been almost daily callers during the many months of
his incarceration. From there it presently led to a third person,
a stocky, blonde young man named John Dimmig. Dimmig was
the husband of Theresa Farrell; he had married her, under the
name of Wilson, three or four years earlier. Dimmig was
arrested on suspicion of complicity and brought before the
rooming-house keeper, Mrs. Higson. She promptly identified
him as the man who, on October 19th, had rented room 21
and handed over the five-dollar deposit.

DIMMIG, THIRTY-THREE, ex-drug clerk, ex-cab driver
and currently a house-to-house peddler of "art books," was a
singular character. He was glib and cocksure (as becomes a
subscription book salesman) and an elegant dresser, affecting a
high silk hat and "a waxed attachment at either end of his
mustache." Vain and self-assertive, he proved a puzzle to the
detectives, who could not make up their minds whether he
was as scatter-brained as he seemed or if this was merely a
pose to conceal a devious and crafty nature. Here is one example of his absurd behavior: On his arrest he was taken to
police headquarters and photographed. At once he lost interest in the serious situation in which he found himself and
repeatedly asked if the picture had yet been developed and
how it had "turned out."

At the inquest Dimmig admitted that he had rented
room 21, explaining blandly, "I am a married man. . . . I
have got a woman. . . ." He identified this lady, whom he
referred to slyly as a "side issue," as a Miss Timkins, of San
Jose. It developed that renting rooms in which to entertain
"side issues" was a frequent occurrence in his life. He maintained a room on Market Street in which he had installed
another young woman whose last name he professed not to
know; she appears on the record only as "Dimples." Theresa
Farrell Wilson Dimmig, testifying in the suspect's behalf,
stated that she knew about "Dimples" and the other "side
issues" but that she loved her husband and proposed to stand
by him. The coroner's jury considered the evidence strong
enough to warrant holding the prisoner; a day or two later
Dimmig was charged with murder. That bumptious young
man promptly changed his tune and thereafter posed as a
model husband and father. He announced that he did not
care what happened to him but that he was determined to
clear his name because of his wife and children. During the
trial he frequently took his small daughter on his knee,
"holding her so that she would not be entirely hidden from

the jury." Altogether, John Dimmig was unique, a puzzle alike to the police, the jury and the public.

The evidence against him, although it was largely circumstantial, was detailed and reasonably complete. He admitted that he had known the dead man well and that he had often visited Dr. Bowers in his cell. The autopsy revealed that Benhayon had died of cyanide poisoning. Dimmig denied ever having purchased cyanide but when the prosecution produced a druggist who testified that he had given some of the poison to the prisoner, Dimmig cheerfully admitted that this was so; he had used it for a "skin ailment." It was brought out that Dimmig had recently hired Benhayon to do some copying for him; the state contended that this had been a ruse to obtain samples of Benhayon's handwriting in order to forge the confession letters.

The authenticity of the letters became a major factor in the case. Both sides brought in handwriting experts and again the experts disagreed. The unpredictable defendant changed his story about his reason for renting room 21; he had not wanted it for a "side issue" after all; he had engaged the room merely to obtain entrance and sell his art books. He presently added to the confusion by producing yet another Benhayon letter, this time addressed to Dimmig himself. It was a short note written from 22 Geary Street and stating that he (Benhayon) was in trouble and wished Dimmig to call at once. The letter had been mailed, special delivery, not to Dimmig's residence, but to a Market Street business firm where he sometimes worked. Although Dimmig rarely received mail at that address, he appeared there only an hour or two after the letter was delivered and asked if any mail had come for him. When the letter was handed him he stuffed it unopened into his pocket, betraying no curiosity as to its contents. He had, he said, ignored Benhayon's request to call.

There was a great deal of argument over the question of how Benhayon had met his end. It was hard to believe that he had taken his own life. He was of a cheerful disposition and had always enjoyed good health. He had recently begun the study of dentistry and was looking forward to a professional career. He had been fond of his sister and bitter toward Bowers, of whose guilt he seems never to have had any doubt. There was no record of insanity in his family and he was not given to dissipation; on the contrary, he was a singularly sedate young man. He rarely drank anything stronger than beer, he was seldom seen in the company of women, he liked to act in amateur theatricals and he had once written a play. It could not have been a very good play, for everyone agreed that, although he was a friendly and genial young man, he was not very bright. Decidedly he was not the sort who might reasonably be expected to plot a double murder or to end by taking his own life.

Dimmig's trial began in mid-December, 1887, and lasted three months, whereupon the jury retired to consider the verdict. At the end of sixteen hours it reported itself hopelessly deadlocked. The judge recalled the jurors to the courtroom and dismissed them. Throughout their deliberations the vote had stood seven for acquittal and five for conviction. An editorial in the Call commented: "It appears almost impossible that Benhayon could have committed suicide. But all murder theories are confused and the evidence is circumstantial." Dimmig was returned to jail (the same jail in which Bowers was by now a semipermanent guest) to await a new trial.

Meantime the slow-moving wheels of justice had again brought the doctor's own case to the fore. On June 15, 1888, the State Supreme Court rejected his appeal for a new trial. The prisoner seemed undisturbed by this reverse; he pointed out that the higher court had not considered Benhayon's "suicide" in reaching its decision, and expressed confidence that when this new evidence was presented the case would be returned to the county courts for retrial. This proved to be an accurate forecast. Only a month later the Supreme Court reversed its earlier ruling and granted the condemned man a new trial. The doctor commented triumphantly, "What I look for is exoneration. No jury will be found to convict me."

Dimmig's second trial began on December 10, 1888, and lasted until the fourth of the following January. Again the jury disagreed, but this time the judge insisted on a decision. The result was that the jurors brought in a verdict of not guilty, and Dimmig was turned loose.

There were no new developments for more than eight months. Bowers remained in the cell that had now been his home for nearly four years; the small chamber was so packed with books and papers as to leave little room for its occupant to move about. He was described as a model prisoner, making few demands on his keepers and ever willing to prescribe for ailing fellow inmates. He was still faithfully attended by Mrs. Zeissing who daily visited him with home-cooked delicacies designed to vary the prison fare.

The final move came on August 16, 1889. On that date the district attorney agreed to a dismissal of the charge, taking the stand that in view of the Benhayon episode and its outcome, it would be impossible to obtain a conviction. Bowers was given his unconditional release. This news too he took calmly. "At last," was his only remark. Mrs. Zeissing shed tears. The town's newspapers and the public were divided. Some protested that his release was a scandalous miscarriage of justice; other contended that, because of Benhayon's purported confession, to attempt to convict the physician of the murder of his wife would be a futile waste of the taxpayers' money.

Bowers resumed his practice, first in Oakland, then once more in San Francisco. In 1891 he maintained offices at 110 Powell Street and advertised that he was a specialist in the treatment of women. Upon his release he had announced that he planned to write a book about his case and to work for the passage of a law requiring a state chemist to be present at all autopsies where it was suspected that poison had been the cause of death. Neither the book nor the law ever materialized. Nor did he make any attempt to collect the insurance he had taken out on his wife's life. To do so would have brought on yet another lawsuit; besides, during his long imprisonment two of the companies had gone broke. From time to time his name appeared briefly in the newspapers. In 1894 he sued the estate of a former patient for a $55 bill. Late in 1901, during an argument over the material and fit of a suit of clothes, he seized a pair of shears and threatened to kill the tailor. Some time later he moved to San Jose. There he presently married for a fourth time and there, on March 7, 1904, he died. He was sixty-one. The *Chronicle* ended its account of his death by stating, with perhaps unconscious irony, that his widow, the former Mary Bird, "fortunately survives him."

THE BOWERS CASE was the longest and most compli-cated in the criminal annals of the city. For nearly four years it had occupied a large share of public attention all over the Coast. Cecelia Bowers and her brother were dead. There had been three long trials (one for Bowers, two for Dimmig) and any number of lesser skirmishes. Yet the main question at issue was left in doubt and remains so today.

Did Bowers murder his wife? It was widely believed that he did. In the public mind the fact that his three wives had all died within a few years after he married them counted heavily against him. Henry Benhayon's death was another highly suspi-cious circumstance. Few believed that Benhayon had committed suicide, and the authenticity of the letters found at his bedside was, to say the least, doubtful. The buffoon, Dimmig, who had rented the room in which the body was found, was shown to have procured a supply of the drug from which Benhayon had died; Dimmig was the husband of one of the doctor's two women disciples and a frequent visitor to Bowers in his cell.

The inferences to be drawn from all this are obvious. Had the doctor in truth, while he was under sentence of death, engineered from the city jail the murder of his brother-in-law and the fabrication of letters purporting to confess the crime of which he himself stood convicted? Many thought so. If it was so, does it not rank among the boldest devices ever employed by a murderer to escape the consequences of his act?

But the case bristles with unanswered questions. It has none of the tidy completeness of the mystery stories of fiction, where in the end the loose threads are gathered up one by one and woven neatly into place. In considering the question of Bowers' guilt one should like to know much more about the circumstances surrounding the deaths of his first two wives. All that was ever learned was that both had died young and that nothing about their passing aroused the suspicions of the authorities. Again, it would be helpful to know who sent the anonymous letter that advised the coroner to look into the death of the third Mrs. Bowers, and so brought about his arrest. Was it Henry Benhayon, or the dead woman's mother, or perhaps some skeptic from one of the lodges in which she was insured? What of the waitress, Theresa Farrell, and Mrs. Zeissing, the dour and close-mouthed nurse? What was the reason for their unwavering devotion to the doctor through all his troubles? Were they in love with him, and did they have guilty knowledge of the crime, if there was a crime? Assuming that the murder of Henry Benhayon was plotted by Bowers and carried out by Dimmig, what influences were brought to bear on that crass young man? Who persuaded him to risk his neck in so desperate an enterprise? Did he act because Bowers threatened to confess the murder of his wife and to name Theresa Farrell Dimmig as an accomplice? Or did the doctor offer him money, or play skillfully on his colossal vanity?

What of Bowers himself? Did he murder one—or all three—of his wives, and if so how good a craftsman was he? What place should posterity assign him in the difficult and exacting profession of his choice? One would not, at first thought, be inclined to rank him very high. He was a far from romantic figure and his methods lacked finesse. For a physician to use phosphorus to dispose of an unwanted wife was, as he himself was first to point out, an inexcusable piece of bad judgment, as was also his failure to permit the undertaker to embalm his victim's body. Moreover, the murder of Benhayon (though boldly planned) was badly mishandled; it was strictly an amateur job and bungled from beginning to end. Surely a man who would permit such crudities to mar the practice of his trade can hardly qualify even as a competent journeyman.

And yet—One can imagine the doctor himself pronouncing the final word. Bowers went free and Dimmig went free. The methods were crude, yes; they were inexpert, they were even bungling—but they worked. That is the unanswerable argument, and it leaves us exactly where we started, posing the same question: Was Bowers one of the boldest (and luckiest) operators in the history of homicide, or was he, as he stoutly maintained, a fond and doting husband whose wives had the deplorable habit of dying young? The question remains unanswered.

In the more than half century since Bowers regained his freedom the case has entered the realm of folklore and a variety of picturesque details have been added. In the preparation of this factual record it has been necessary to reject the story, several times published, that Benhayon's body was discovered only a few hours before the time set for Bowers' execution, and that while reporters were telling him of Benhayon's confession, a gang of carpenters were building a gallows in the courtyard outside his cell. Nor has it been possible to substantiate a still more dramatic story: that when Cecelia Bowers' body was disinterred and brought to the city morgue an attendant, entering the darkened room that night, found the corpse so impregnated with phosphorus that it gave off "a weird and ghostly light." Possibly the latter tale was the inspiration for a topical song said to have been written by a local wag and sung to applause at one of the theatres; its title was "The Phosphorescent Bride of Dr. Bowers."

Vertigo

Alfred   Hitchcock

XT. SAN FRANCISCO ROOF TOPS - (DUSK) - CLOSE SHOT. We see a close view of a roof parapet and the curved rail of a fire escape. In the b.g., are large skyscrapers with all their windows fully lit in the late win-ter afternoon. This background is used for the CREDIT TITLES of the picture. After the last card has FADED OUT, we HOLD on to the empty parapet, when suddenly a man's hand reaches and grips the top of the rail. It is followed by another hand and, after a beat, we see the face of a man in his early 30's. He is an Italian type, with rough features. He turns quickly and looks below him and then turning back, springs up over the empty parapet and is lost from view. We STAY on the EMPTY SCENE for a second or two as we HEAR the scraping of boots on the iron ladder. Someone else is coming up. Presently, two more hands and the head of a uniformed policeman with cap and badge starts to climb over the para-pet. The CAMERA PULLS BACK so that by the time he has com-pleted his climb, he is in full figure. He dashes out of the picture drawing his gun. Immediately following him over the

ALEC COPPEL and SAMUEL TAYLOR penned the screenplay to ALFRED HITCHCOCK's 1958 release, Vertigo. In the scenes excerpted here, you can appreciate the combination of straightforward writing and cinematic genius, particularly in the famous opening sequence.

parapet, a detective in plain clothes climbs over. This is JOHN
FERGUSON, known as SCOTTIE. He too pulls a gun and dashes
out of the picture.

EXT. SAN FRANCISCO ROOF TOPS - (DUSK) - LONG SHOT.
A vast panorama of the San Francisco skyline. Nearer to us are
three tiny figures running and jumping over the roof tops. The
man on the run, whom we first saw climb over the parapet, is
dressed in a white shirt and light tan linen slacks, and wearing
sneakers. The uniformed man is shooting at him. Scottie is
dressed in medium gray clothes. The CAMERA SLOWLY PANS the
group across the roof tops.

EXT. SAN FRANCISCO ROOF TOPS - (DUSK) - MED. SHOT
We now see a short gap between rooftops, with a drop
below. The pursued man makes the leap successfully followed
by the uniformed policeman. Scottie makes the same leap, but
almost trips in taking off and is thrown off balance. He tries
to recover, lands awkwardly on the opposite roof, and falls
forward, prone, with a heavy impact that hurts and drives
the breath from his body. He tries to rise but raises his head
with a look of pain—one leg is doubled up under the other.
The tiles give way, and he slides backwards, and his legs go
over the edge of the roof, then his body. In his daze he grasps
at the loose tiles, and as he goes over the edge he clutches on
to the gutter, which gives way, and he swings off into space,
looking down.

EXT. SAN FRANCISCO ROOF TOPS - (DUSK) - LONG SHOT
Scottie looking down.

EXT. SAN FRANCISCO ROOF TOPS - (DUSK) - LONG SHOT
From Scottie's viewpoint, the gap beneath the building and
the ground below. It seems to treble its depth.

EXT. SAN FRANCISCO ROOF TOPS - (DUSK) - CLOSEUP
Scottie looking down with horror. His eyes close as a wave of
nausea overcomes him.

EXT. SAN FRANCISCO ROOF TOPS - (DUSK) - MEDIUM SHOT
In the distance the fleeing criminal. The policeman, seeing
what has happened to Scottie, returns to the slope of the roof
and strains to reach down to Scottie.

POLICEMAN
Give me your hand!

EXT. SAN FRANCISCO ROOF TOPS - (DUSK) - CLOSE UP
SCOTTIE'S HEAD. His hands grip the edge of the guttering. The
tips of the fingers of the policeman straining to reach Scottie,
are at the top of screen. Scottie begins to open his grip but
stares down, he quickly resumes his grip looking up hopelessly
towards the helping hand. He looks down again.

FROM SCOTTIE'S VIEWPOINT - the ground below still a long
way away.

EXT. SAN FRANCISCO ROOF TOPS - (DUSK) - MEDIUM SHOT
The policeman's hand in foreground, his face beyond.

POLICEMAN
What's the matter with you? Give me your hand!

Policeman endeavors to stretch out his hand further.

EXT. SAN FRANCISCO ROOF TOPS - (DUSK)
The tiles beneath the policeman's heel begin to give. The
Policeman starts to slide. He claws desperately at the surface of
the roof.

EXT. SAN FRANCISCO ROOF TOPS - (DUSK) - CLOSEUP
Scottie, his eyes closed. He opens them as he hears a wild cry.

EXT. SAN FRANCISCO ROOF TOPS - (DUSK) - LONG SHOT
The policeman falling through space.

EXT. SAN FRANCISCO ROOF TOPS - (DUSK) - CLOSEUP
Scottie stares down in horror.

EXT. SAN FRANCISCO ROOF TOPS - (DUSK) - LONG SHOT
The body of the policeman sprawled on the ground below. People are running into the alleyway; they stare at the body, look up to where Scottie is hanging. We see the light on their upturned faces. And now we hear a police whistle blown shrilly, again and again.

EXT. PALACE OF THE LEGION OF HONOR- (LATE AFTERNOON)
Madeleine approaches the green Jaguar, gets in, and the car starts away. Scottie's car moves into the scene, following.

DISSOLVE TO:
EXT. SEA CLIFF DRIVE - (LATE AFTERNOON)
We see the green Jaguar proceeding, the gray sedan at a careful distance behind. Beyond, looking northeast, we see the Golden Gate Bridge in the late afternoon sun, and Richmond and Berkeley in the distance.

DISSOLVE TO:
INT. SCOTTIE'S CAR - (SUNSET)
Scottie carefully looking ahead.

EXT. PRESIDIO DRIVE - (SUNSET)
Madeleine's car approaches along the drive to the gates of the Presidio, and passes through the gates and is swallowed by the trees. Scottie's car follows, and it, too, disappears.

DISSOLVE TO:

EXT. PRESIDIO - (SUNSET)

The two cars driving along the wooded road.

INT. SCOTTIE'S CAR - (SUNSET)

Scottie looking ahead.

DISSOLVE TO:

EXT. FORT POINT - (SUNSET)

Scottie's car is traveling down the slope toward the jutting point of old Fort Winfield Scott. It comes to a stop in the level clearing. The green Jaguar stands there, empty.

EXT. BRIDGE - (SUNSET) - MEDIUM SHOT

Scottie gets out of his car and looks off out of picture.

EXT. BRIDGE - (SUNSET) - LONG SHOT

Madeleine walking away round the dockside. The vast bridge towers above her. She carries the nosegay. Scottie moves into the f.g., and makes off in the same direction. Madeleine disappears round the corner of the old fort wall. Now she is out of sight, we see Scottie quicken his pace as he approaches the corner of the fort wall.

EXT. BRIDGE - (SUNSET) - MEDIUM SHOT

SHOOTING back, we see Scottie approach the wall and peer cautiously around.

EXT. BRIDGE - (SUNSET) - SEMI-LONG SHOT

From his viewpoint, we see Madeleine standing at the water's edge. She is mechanically tearing off the lace-edged paper from the nosegay.

EXT. BRIDGE - (SUNSET) - CLOSEUP

Scottie watching her curiously.

EXT. BRIDGE - (SUNSET) - SEMI-CLOSEUP

Madeleine lets the paper drift away down to the water. She proceeds to unwind the wire around the flowers and begins to scatter them on the water.

CLOSE SHOT OF FLOWERS FLOATING ON THE WATER

EXT. BRIDGE - (SUNSET) - CLOSEUP

Scottie watching Madeleine.

EXT. DOCKSIDE - (SUNSET) - SEMI-LONG SHOT

The full figure of Madeleine, scattering the rest of the flowers. Then she raises her head and stares up at the sky. A moment in which her body seems poised, and then she is gone, lost to view in the water.

EXT. DOCKSIDE - (SUNSET) - LONG SHOT

Scottie dashes around the wall and the CAMERA PANS him to the water's edge. He is throwing his coat off.

EXT. DOCKSIDE - (SUNSET) - SEMI-LONG SHOT

SHOOTING down into the water, we see Madeleine's upturned face as she floats away. She disappears now and again.

EXT. DOCKSIDE - (SUNSET) - MEDIUM SHOT

SCOTTIE, running down the few stone steps towards the water. When the water is up to his knees, he swims out towards her.

EXT. DOCKSIDE - (SUNSET) - CLOSEUP MADELEINE

Her eyes staring, sinks beneath the water. She is surrounded by the scattered flowers. Scottie swims in and grabs her.

EXT. DOCKSIDE - (SUNSET) - CLOSEUP

As he holds her, the two heads are pressed together. He turns and starts to swim back with her. The screen is filled with their two heads. Madeleine's staring eyes begin to close as she is moved away.

LAP DISSOLVE

EXT. DOCKSIDE - (SUNSET) - MEDIUM SHOT
We see Scottie coming up some stone steps. He is staggering with the weight of Madeleine's water-soaked body and clothes. He carries her over towards the green Jaguar.

EXT. DOCKSIDE - (SUNSET) - MEDIUM SHOT
Resting her for a moment, he throws open the door on the passenger's side.

EXT. DOCKSIDE - (SUNSET)
Scottie's head is close to hers. She is now breathing heavily.

SCOTTIE (Whispering) Are you all right?

Her eyes open slowly.

SCOTTIE (Calling softly) Madeleine. . . .

Her eyes show no sign of recognition or response: they move past his face and stare out. The CAMERA SLOWLY MOVES IN until her head fills the screen. She stares out as though in a trance.

EXT. CYPRESS POINT OR POINT LOBOS - (DAY) Same day.
Below the point of land, the sea pounds against the rocks. Madeleine stands alone, silhouetted against the sky. Scottie sits in the car, watching her. She does not move. Then slowly she starts to walk toward the sea, and as he watches he senses, without being sure, that her pace is increasing, and suddenly he opens the car door and jumps out and slams the door and begins to run. But then he sees something, and slows down

quickly and walks, for Madeleine has stopped and turned and is waiting for him. There is a gentle, apologetic smile in her eyes. She waits, and he comes to a stop before her.

MADELEINE Why did you run?

He looks down at her searchingly.

SCOTTIE (Finally, quietly) I'm responsible for you now, you know. The Chinese say that once you have saved someone's life, you are responsible for it forever. And so I'm committed. And I have to know.

MADELEINE And you'll go on saving me? Again and again?

He waits. She looks down.

MADELEINE There is so little I know. It is as though I were walking down a long corridor that once was mirrored, and fragments of mirror still hang there, dark and shadowy, reflecting a dark image of me . . . and yet not me . . . someone else, in other clothes, of another time, doing things I have never done . . . but still me. . . . And I can't stop to ask why, I must keep on walking. At the end of the corridor there is nothing but darkness, and I know when I walk into the darkness, I'll die.
 (Pause; she looks up)
But I've never come to the end; I've always come back, before then. Except once.

SCOTTIE Yesterday.

She nods.

SCOTTIE And you didn't know. You didn't know what happened. Until you found yourself there with me.

She shakes her head.

SCOTTIE You don't know where you were.

She shakes her head.

SCOTTIE But the small scenes, the fragments in the mirror: you remember them.

MADELEINE Vaguely. . . .

SCOTTIE What do you remember?

MADELEINE (Searching) A room . . . there is a room, and I sit there alone . . . always alone. . . .

SCOTTIE Would you know the room?

MADELEINE No . . . it's in shadow.

SCOTTIE What else?

MADELEINE A grave . . .

SCOTTIE Where?

MADELEINE I don't know. An open grave. I stand by the grave-stone looking down into it. And it's my grave.

SCOTTIE How do you know?

MADELEINE I know.

SCOTTIE There's a name on the gravestone.

MADELEINE No. It's new and clean, and waiting.

SCOTTIE (Beginning to feel lost) What else?

MADELEINE (Searching) This part is dream, I think. There is a tower . . . and a bell . . . and a garden below . . . but it seems to be in Spain . . . a village in Spain. And then it clicks off, and is gone.

SCOTTIE A portrait? Do you ever see a portrait?

MADELEINE No.

SCOTTIE Of the woman in the mirror. Would you know her if you saw her?

MADELEINE But I'm the woman in the mirror!

SCOTTIE (Desperately) No!

She looks up at him, rebuffed, desperately lost, and her eyes well with tears. Scottie is looking away, lost in thought.

SCOTTIE (To himself) If I could find the key . . . find the beginning . . . put it together. . . .

MADELEINE (Quietly, lost) And so explain it away? But there is a way to explain it, you see. If I'm mad? That would explain it, wouldn't it?

Scottie looks at her, and her eyes are big with fright and despair and a plea for denial, and suddenly she breaks, and the tears flow, and she turns her head away sharply and turns and runs toward the edge of the land.

SCOTTIE Madeleine!!

He races after her and catches her and holds her, and she is against him, clinging tightly, deep in his embrace, and sobbing fiercely.

MADELEINE (Muffled, against his breast) I'm not mad. I'm not mad. And I don't want to die, but there's someone inside me, there's somebody else, and she says I must die. . . . Scottie, don't let me go!

SCOTTIE I'm here, I've got you. . . .

MADELEINE I'm so afraid. . . . (She looks up) you won't let it happen. . . .

Her face is close to his and they are clinging tightly together. He shakes his head, and then suddenly his mouth is on hers, and they are deep in a kiss. Their lips part, but remain close together.

MADELEINE (Whispering) Don't leave me . . . stay with me. . . .

SCOTTIE All the time.

They kiss again, passionately. And the wind blows, and the waves dash against the rocks, throwing up a curtain of spray.

EXT. THE HIGHWAY: A ROAD JUNCTION - (DAY)
Side angle SHOT of the Jaguar as it turns off the highway onto a side road. The CAMERA PANS the car, then loses it as it goes out of the SHOT, and HOLDS on a road sign that reads:

MISSION SAN JUAN BAUTISTA, 3 MILES

EXT. MISSION SAN JUAN BAUTISTA - (DAY)

We are looking along the cloisters, down the long corridor of arches. In the foreground a small sign on a standard reads:

EL CAMINO REAL, MISSION SAN JUAN BAUTISTA

FOUNDED JUNE 24, 1797

The music of the Mission theme, mingled with Carlotta's theme, begins to drift in, an evocation of the past; a sighing that grows and seems to have behind it the echo of lost voices calling. The CAMERA MOVES AND EASES AROUND A BIT to look through the arches across the green toward the open side and the valley and the hills beyond. A lone nun is crossing the green to the church. A clock strikes the half hour. The CAMERA PANS to look at the large wooden two-story house on the far side of the green, then the little garden, then the Plaza Livery Stable, and the road alongside. The Jaguar stands there empty. The CAMERA CONTIN-UES TO PAN along the whitewashed stone Castro House, sees the pepper tree, MOVES along the Plaza Hotel, and comes to REST SHOOTING at the saloon that forms the far corner of the hotel. Three tourists exit from the main entrance of the hotel, get into their car. The car moves toward the CAMERA, and goes past, and out of the SHOT. The CAMERA DOLLIES IN to the front door of the saloon. Over the door is a sign: PLAZA HOTEL BAR ROOM. On either side of the door are posters proclaiming rewards for the apprehension of bandits who have held up Wells Fargo Express Wagons. The CAMERA SHOOTS THROUGH the open door.

INT. PLAZA HOTEL BAR ROOM - (DAY)

Empty, silent; old pool tables in the foreground, the bar in the background. As the CAMERA SCANS the room:

DISSOLVE TO:

INT. PLAZA HOTEL FRONT PARLOR - (DAY)

It too is silent and deserted. In the far wall, a fireplace, with an old clock on the mantel. In one corner, a small old organ, with a hymnal open on the rack; in the other corner, a Victorian sofa. The flowered rug is faded, the furniture is shabby.

DISSOLVE TO:

EXT. PLAZA HOTEL - (DAY) Looking toward the lovely pepper tree and the whitewashed stone Castro House, and the tall eucalyptus tree beyond. The CAMERA PANS SLOWLY past the empty Jaguar and comes to REST on the dark opening of the Livery Stable and MOVES SLOWLY toward it.

DISSOLVE TO:

INT. LIVERY STABLE - (DAY) The dark interior of the Livery Stable. The figures of Scottie and Madeleine are seen a little way in. Madeleine is seated in a surrey, while Scottie stands by her.

INT. LIVERY STABLE - (DAY) Madeleine's eyes are closed. Scottie, leaning against the surrey, looks up at her intently. After a moment he calls to her softly.

SCOTTIE Madeleine . . .

She opens her eyes and looks down at him.

SCOTTIE Where are you now?

She smiles at him gently.

MADELEINE (Softly) Here with you.

SCOTTIE And it's all real.

MADELEINE Yes.

SCOTTIE (Firmly) Not merely as it was a hundred years ago. As it was a year ago, or six months ago, whenever you were here to see it. (Pressing) Madeleine, think of when you were here!

She looks down at him with a worried, regretful smile, wishing she could help him. Then she looks away into the distance, and speaks almost irrelevantly.

MADELEINE (Dreamily) There were not so many carriages, then. And there were horses in the stalls; a bay, two black, and a grey. It was our favorite place, but we were forbidden to play here, and Sister Teresa would scold us. . . .

Scottie looks up at her in desperation, then looks about the stable for help. His look scans the carriages and wagons lined against the wall, goes past the old fire truck on which there is a placard proclaiming the world's championship of 1884, and finally stops at a small buggy—a Bike Wagon—to which is hitched a full-size model of a handsome gray horse.

SCOTTIE Well, now, here!

He races to the horse. On it hangs a sign: "Greyhound World's Greatest Trotter."

SCOTTIE
Here's your grey horse! Course he'd have a tough time getting in and out of a stall without being pushed, but still. . . . You see? There's an answer for everything!

He looks across to Madeleine eagerly. She is staring ahead, lost in the past.

SCOTTIE Madeleine! Try!

No answer. The music is more insistent now, a pulling wind, and the faint voices call more clearly. Madeleine slowly rises to her feet as though sensing the call. Scottie moves back to her and stands there, looking up. He raises his arms, she puts her hands on his shoulders and slips to the ground with his help, and he is holding her. Their hands are close together.

SCOTTIE Madeleine, try . . . for me. . . .

With a small movement, their lips come together, and they kiss; not impulsively, as before, but with deep, sure love and hunger for each other. Their lips part, but he still holds her tightly, his head pressed down against hers, and she is looking past him, her eyes wide with anxiety. And a clock strikes the three-quarter hour.

SCOTTIE My love . . . because I love you. . . .

MADELEINE (Whispering) I love you, too . . . too late . . . too late. . . .

SCOTTIE No . . . we're together. . . .

MADELEINE Too late . . . there's something I must do. . . .

He holds her gently, now; brushes his lips along her hair, to her eyes, down to her mouth.

SCOTTIE (Murmuring) Nothing you must do . . . no one possesses you . . . you're safe with me . . . my love. . . .

And they kiss again. As they part:

MADELEINE Too late. . . .

She looks up at him with deep regret and wonder in her eyes, then suddenly breaks from him and runs out the door. He stands still, startled for a moment, then runs after her.

EXT. LIVERY STABLE - (DAY)
Madeleine is running across the grass toward the church. Scottie catches up with her.

EXT. LIVERY STABLE- (DAY) - REVERSE ANGLE
Scottie swings her around to face him.

SCOTTIE (Firmly) There are things I have to tell you, about how we met, and why we are together. But they can wait. The only important thing now is that I love you and I'm going to keep you safe.

MADELEINE (Trembling) You can't.

SCOTTIE Why?

MADELEINE Let me go.

SCOTTIE Where?

MADELEINE To the church. I must go there.

SCOTTIE Madeleine—

MADELEINE Please let me go.

She pulls away and turns and walks swiftly toward the church, her head bowed. CAMERA DOLLIES with her. She is frightened, and close to tears. Scottie follows her a half-step behind. The livery stable drops away out of the SHOT, and the two heads fill the screen with only the sky as background.

SCOTTIE Madeleine, don't fight me off, don't put me away. You've been fighting alone, and you're lost, but no more. Hold on to me. Be sure of me, always. And whatever it is, we'll lick it. I promise.

No answer. They keep walking, and then suddenly with head bowed, she begins to run again, and runs out of the SHOT. A moment, then he runs after her.

EXT. THE MISSION AND CLOISTERS - (DAY) - SEMI LONG SHOT
We see Madeleine running toward the Cloisters, Scottie after her. Finally he stops her once again.

EXT. THE CLOISTERS - (DAY) - MEDIUM SHOT
Scottie grabs her by the arm.

MADELEINE (Head low, brokenly) It's not fair, it's too late. It wasn't supposed to happen this way, it shouldn't have happened. . . !

SCOTTIE It had to. We're in love. That's all that counts. Madeleine—

MADELEINE (Frantic, struggling) Let me go! Let me go!!

SCOTTIE (Holding her; sharply) Madeleine!!

The struggle ceases. She remains limp in his grasp for a long moment, then slowly raises her head to look at him. Her eyes study his face searchingly.

MADELEINE You believe that I love you?

SCOTTIE Yes.

MADELEINE And if you lose me, you'll know that I loved you and wanted to go on loving you.

SCOTTIE I won't lose you.

PAUSE.

MADELEINE Let me go into the church alone.

SCOTTIE Why?

MADELEINE Please. Because I love you.

He stares at her, sees the pleading look in her eyes, and lets go. She turns and walks away toward the church, slowly, her head bowed. He watches her go and starts to move after her. Then slowly, as she goes, her head begins to go up until finally, as she walks, she is staring high above her. And then, suddenly, she breaks into a broken run.

EXT. CLOISTERS - (DAY)
Scottie jerks his head up to see what she was looking at.

EXT. CLOISTERS - (DAY)
From Scottie's viewpoint: the high church tower.

EXT. CLOISTERS - (DAY)
Scottie, immediately alarmed, brings his eyes down and looks toward the church entrance.

EXT. CLOISTERS - (DAY)
From Scottie's viewpoint: Madeleine runs through the open front door of the church, and vanishes.

EXT. CLOISTERS - (DAY)
Scottie starts to run toward the church.

SCOTTIE Madeleine!!!

He runs to the church door and runs in.

INT. CHURCH, SAN JUAN BAUTISTA - (DAY)

Scottie runs in and looks around frantically. The church is empty. A moment, then he hears the sound of footsteps running up wooden steps. He turns in the direction of the sound, sees a door standing open at the side of the church, and through the door the beginning of a flight of steps. He runs to the open door and goes through.

INT. CHURCH TOWER - (DAY)

Scottie runs in, stops at the foot of the steps, hears the running footsteps, and looks up. From his viewpoint we see Madeleine running up the open stairway that spirals up along the walls of the high tower. She is already well on her way. Scottie is immediately stricken by vertigo, and the tall tower seems to slide away from him. He makes an attempt to start up the stairs, flattens himself against the wall and struggles up. He claws his way up, crosses over to the hand-railing and uses it to pull his body up the steps, one by one, struggling for breath, unable to call, though he tries. And Madeleine keeps running.

Madeleine reaches the top, goes through a small wooden door. We see it slam, hear it locked.

Scottie, struggling up, reaches a landing next to a small open arch that looks out on the back garden, and has to stop to fight his nausea.

There is a scream from above. Through the arch he sees a body fall. He calls "Madeleine!" and looks down through the arch.

EXT. ROOF - (DAY) - LONG SHOT

Figure of the dead Madeleine. Her body is lying on the roof of the cloister.

INT. CHURCH TOWER - (DAY)

The vertigo hits Scottie again and the body and the roof of the cloister move and fall away into space, and this DISSOLVES THROUGH TO:

The body of the policeman falling from the rooftop, tumbling through space to the street below.

Scottie has to look away in desperate horror. He hears voices, looks through the arch again, and sees two nuns hurrying across the garden from the dormitory at the back, looking up at the roof of the cloister.

He turns and gazes down the great height he now has to descend, flattens himself against the wall, and with trancelike desperation tries to start moving.

FADE OUT

Follow That Car!

Mabel Maney

THE GOLDEN GATE Bridge glowed magnifi-
cently in the pink early-morning light. Cherry
nudged Midge awake. "We're here!" she squealed.

Midge sighed and covered her face with her hands.
"It's too early to get up, Mom," she groaned sleepily. "Are you
always so cheerful first thing in the morning?" she grumbled,
squinting at Cherry. "Gosh, I feel awful. Where are we?"

"We're exactly two hundred twenty feet above the
Pacific Ocean, Midge, on the Golden Gate Bridge," Cherry
answered.

Midge looked troubled. "How far up did you say we
were?" She gulped as she peered out her window at the blue
expanse of ocean below.

"Don't worry, Midge. There's enough steel wire supporting this bridge to circle the earth three times."

"If you ever give up nursing, you can become a tour

**MABEL MANEY's 1993 cult classic, *The Case of the Not-So-Nice
Nurse*, is a satiric romp through the girl detective genre. In
this chapter, devoted ingenue Nurse Cherry Aimless dashes
through the streets of 1950s San Francisco, looking for Nancy
Clue, the famous girl dick.**

guide," Midge laughed. She peered out the window at the giant steel structure, painted burnt orange. "So where's the gold?" she asked.

"You ask a lot of questions, young lady," Cherry said sternly, doing her best Nurse Marstad imitation.

Midge shook her head. "I've heard that before. I've always been like that. Drove my mom crazy." She fumbled through her jacket pockets for a cigarette, but found only empty packages. "Great. First Velma disappears. Now I run out of cigarettes. Could things get any worse?" she joked sourly.

Cherry had some news she hoped would cheer up Midge. "Guess what?" she chirped. "I have some exciting news. I heard on the radio that Nancy Clue is believed to be somewhere in San Francisco, and if the authorities can find her, they're going to call on her to solve the case of the missing nuns! Maybe she could help us, too!"

Midge made a face. "You mean that little rich goody-two-shoes who's always doing some good deed? The one who works with her famous attorney father, Carson Clue? Who solves every mystery without mussing her hair?"

"Haven't you heard, Midge? Don't you know what happened?" Cherry cried.

Cherry related everything she knew about the murder of Carson Clue. "The Clue's loyal housekeeper Hannah Gruel, who had been like a mother to Nancy since the death of her real mother twenty-one years ago, went berserk a few days ago while making a pie and shot Mr. Clue dead!"

Midge didn't seem too upset by the news. "If I had to clean somebody's house and cook his meals for twenty-one years, I'd kill him, too," she said gruffly.

"But Nancy and her father were very close," Cherry explained, a little put off by Midge's flip remark.

"Well that's too bad, then," Midge said, a softer tone creeping into her voice. "I guess I'm not much for family life, outside of me and Velma," she said. "Besides, even if we could find this Nancy Clue girl, we couldn't possibly afford her. Why, she's a rich society dame."

Cherry shook her head. Obviously, Midge wasn't much of a Nancy Clue fan! "She works for free, out of the goodness of her heart. I'm sure she'll help us, she's just got to!"

But Midge wasn't won over. "We'll just have to see about this girl dick," was all she would say.

Cherry smiled. She just knew that despite the tragedy of her own circumstances, Nancy Clue would help them. Her heart raced at the thought of meeting her beloved heroine.

"How about some breakfast," Cherry suggested. She was secretly hoping that if Midge got some food in her stomach, she'd be more agreeable to the idea of contacting Nancy Clue.

"Okay, but first I need to get to a phone and check in with Betty," Midge said anxiously. "I wonder if she's made any progress on the case? I wish they could put telephones in cars. That would sure save us a lot of time."

"I don't know, Midge. I can't see how it would be safe for people to drive and talk on the telephone at the same time," Cherry said. "Midge must be awfully tired to have such a strange idea," Cherry thought. By this time they were in a part of the city with hills so steep it felt like they were on a carnival ride.

"This area is called Russian Hill. Look, Midge, a cable car! Did you know that by the turn of the century San Francisco had six hundred cable cars traveling over one hundred miles of track?"

Cherry's command of details astonished her passenger. "How on earth did you know that?" Midge asked.

"After I decided to visit my Aunt Gertrude, I wrote to the San Francisco Chamber of Commerce and got pertinent information," Cherry replied. "In my glove box, I've got a notebook containing all kinds of information, like temperatures, average price of a meal, and things to see. And I know the safest parts of the city, just in case there's an earthquake."

If such an emergency did occur, Cherry was fully prepared, with fresh uniforms and a medical kit securely stowed in her trunk.

"Cherry, you're beginning to remind me of my favorite Girl Scout leader, Miss Mary Metz, a woman who could pull just about anything out of her purse," Midge chuckled.

That was high praise indeed, coming from Midge!

"In another few blocks, we'll be in the Castro area," Cherry said happily. "I stopped at a service station a few hours ago, filled the tank and purchased a map. You slept through the whole thing. Rather, you snored through the whole thing."

"No one's ever complained before," Midge said.

"Have a lot of girls had the opportunity to hear you snore?" Cherry teased.

Midge blushed, and changed the subject. "I think we're in the Castro," she announced. "Hey, look, there's the police station!"

They were lucky enough to find a parking spot right in front. "How convenient!" Cherry cried. "Maybe our luck is changing."

Midge slunk down in her seat and pulled her jacket collar high above her ears. "Cherry, why don't you go in and ask for Officer Jones? I'll stay out here with the car."

Cherry was frankly puzzled by Midge's strange behavior. She was just about to tease Midge about being shy, when she remembered her earlier reluctance to call the police. "There's something she's not telling me," Cherry decided. "I wonder what it is?"

She hopped out of the car, but not before taking a quick look in the rear view mirror to make sure she was presentable. "Golly, I look tired," she groaned when she saw the dark circles under her eyes. She reached for her compact.

"Cherry, let's make this a quick visit," Midge said nervously. "Didn't you say something about breakfast? And you still haven't gotten in touch with your aunt. Besides, you look fine. Really great. Never looked better."

Cherry knew she didn't look her best, but she didn't want to upset Midge any further. "I'll hurry," she said, racing out of the car and up the stairs. Once inside, Cherry looked around in confusion. The noise was deafening. Everywhere, people were talking and telephones were ringing. "Where do I go?" she wondered. She had never been in that kind of place before. "It's kind of scary in here," she thought. "I wish Midge had come with me. What if I run into a real live criminal?"

She walked up to a big, tall girl outfitted in a peach chiffon cocktail dress with a matching bolero jacket. "Excuse me, where would I go to find a particular officer?" she asked, adding, "By the way, I love your gown."

"Thanks. I made it myself," the girl replied, in a startlingly deep voice. "The front desk is right over there," she said, waving her cream-colored elbow-length gloves toward the back of the room.

Cherry thanked the friendly girl. "My, that was an unusually dressy outfit for this early in the morning," she thought, as she made her way to the front desk. "And, although she was very attractive, I'd do something about that mustache."

"Excuse me. I'm looking for Officer Jones," she said to the burly cop sitting behind the desk.

"Her shift doesn't begin for an hour. Come back then." He turned his back and began to type furiously.

"Do you know where I can find her now?" Cherry pressed. "It's really important," she added.

He stopped typing, and glared at Cherry. "I said, come back in an hour."

"Golly, he was uncooperative," she thought as she left, her face flushed with anger. "Why, if I weren't in such a hurry, I'd speak to his superior about his attitude!"

She spied a telephone booth in the corner of the lobby. "As long as I'm here, I might as well call Aunt Gert and tell her

I'm in town," Cherry decided. She let the telephone ring for a very long time, thinking that her aunt might be out in her back yard, pruning her fruit trees.

But Aunt Gert never came to the phone. "That's odd!" she cried. "This is the third time I've called and gotten no answer. Aunt Gert knows I'm scheduled to arrive today. She hasn't been home for days. How odd!"

She raced outside and found Midge leaning against the car, looking around frantically. "I'm so relieved to see you!" Midge cried. "I was afraid something happened in there. Did you find Officer Jones?"

Cherry shook her head. "Her shift doesn't start for another forty-five minutes. We'll have to come back then."

"We can't wait any longer!" Midge cried. "Velma's already been missing for twelve hours. We're losing valuable time. We need to find Officer Jones now!"

Someone tapped Cherry on the shoulder. Why, it was the big-boned girl in the beautiful chiffon dress Cherry had met inside.

"I hope you don't think I'm nosy, but I couldn't help overhearing your friend," the stranger said. "I know Officer Jones. She usually has coffee at Flora's Café in the mornings. You could try there.

"It's right around the corner," she added helpfully. "It's the place with all the dogs waiting out front."

"Thank you!" Cherry cried gratefully. "You've been a big help."

"Oh, sure, honey," the girl said, waving good-bye.

Midge grabbed Cherry's hand, and they raced to the coffee shop. The place was packed with people drinking coffee and chatting in a leisurely fashion. "They look like they have all the time in the world," said Cherry, thinking about her hectic life as a nurse in a big-city hospital. "Don't these people work?"

Midge suggested that since San Francisco was a drop-off point for the military after the war, there were probably a lot of retired soldiers with time on their hands. "And lots of WACs," she said, elbowing Cherry. "How do you feel about girls in uniform?"

"All that's on my mind right now is finding Officer Jones," Cherry replied, blushing nonetheless. Secretly, she did think girls in uniform looked *quite* dashing!

"That darn Midge can practically read my mind," Cherry thought.

Midge looked around. "I don't see any police officers," she said.

Cherry pointed out a stocky girl clad in blue serge slacks and shirt and heavy leather boots. What really caught Cherry's eye were the handcuffs hanging from the girl's belt. "That must be Officer Jones!" she exclaimed triumphantly. Before Midge could stop her, Cherry rushed up to the girl.

"I'm a friend of Betty's!" she cried.

The girl grinned and raised one eyebrow. "My, my my," she said, looking Cherry up and down and smiling. "I'm a friend of Betty's too. What's your name?"

Cherry felt a tug at her elbow. It was Midge. "Ixnay, Cherry. You've got the wrong girl," Midge whispered in her ear.

"But. . . but . . ." Cherry cried. Midge pulled her over to a table and deposited her in a chair.

"Don't talk to anyone. I'll be right back," she said.

A moment later, Midge returned carrying two cups of steaming coffee and a plate of breakfast rolls.

"I don't understand!" Cherry cried.

"I know, Cherry," Midge laughed.

A red-haired girl at the adjoining table shushed them. She went back to scribbling furiously in her notebook.

"Mind if we *sit* here?" Midge asked sarcastically.

The girl took a few seconds to answer. She did not appear to be in the best of moods, Cherry noticed.

"I don't care what you do, as long as you do it quietly," she hissed.

"Must be one of those nutty San Francisco writers you're always hearing about," Midge whispered to Cherry. "You know, they sit all day drinking coffee and writing. They don't work or anything. No one has any idea how they live."

"Shhh," Cherry whispered. "She might hear you. I'd feel more comfortable sitting outside. Besides, it's a lovely morning."

They took their coffee and rolls to the front stoop. Cherry settled near a gray and white Sheltie with sky-blue eyes. The dog put her head on Cherry's arm and sighed.

"What's wrong, sweetie?" asked Cherry, breaking off a piece of her roll for the dog. The dog daintily ate the offering and licked Cherry's hand in appreciation. Midge shared her roll with a Pekinese, who was doing tricks for her breakfast.

Midge sighed. "I miss my pets. I miss my girlfriend."

Suddenly someone appeared on the steps behind them. It was the crabby writer. "Too loud?" Midge asked, in a rude manner. Cherry hoped Midge wasn't going to start a fight! She held her breath.

The girl looked chagrined. "I'm a big grouch when I have a deadline," she said in a apologetic way.

Midge looked remorseful. The girl knelt and patted the little blue-eyed dog. "I see you've met Princess," she said.

"She's a beauty," chorused Midge and Cherry.

"Time to go home," the girl said, bending down to unleash her pet. The dog licked her on the nose and off they went.

"Well, there goes a happy couple," Midge said. "Too bad she was so grouchy. She was kind of cute, don't you think, Cherry?"

Cherry blushed and changed the subject quickly. "It must be time to go back to the police station," she said primly, making a big show of checking her watch. "In fact, we should have been there three whole minutes ago," she gasped.

"You go without me," Midge said. "I'll try to get in touch with Betty. Meet me back here."

Cherry raced to the police station and was sorely disappointed to learn that Officer Jones had already been sent out on assignment. "You're welcome to wait, lady," the sergeant said, pointing to a wooden bench already overflowing with impatient people. "But I don't know when she's going to be back."

"No, thanks," Cherry sighed. She persuaded the officer to let her leave a note and walked dejectedly back to the coffee shop. When she got there, Midge was sitting on the front steps, nursing her cup of coffee and looking pretty discouraged.

"Hey," Midge sighed upon spying Cherry. "I can tell you didn't find Officer Jones; it's written all over your face."

"I left a note telling her what we look like and where we're parked. Any luck getting in touch with Betty?" Cherry asked.

Midge shook her head. "I called, but she's out on a case. Our best chance of finding the men who have Velma is to find their car. To do that, we need a cop." Midge shuddered.

Cherry sat on the steps next to Midge. "I called my aunt, but she's not home either. What do we do next?" she asked, but stopped short when she realized she was talking to thin air.

For Midge was bounding up the block and yelling Velma's name!

Cherry panted as she raced up the steep hill behind her.

"I just saw a red convertible speed by," Midge yelled over her shoulder. "And Velma was in the back seat!"

Cherry was grateful she had selected flats as her travel shoes, otherwise she would have never been able to keep up with Midge as she raced up the steep Castro Street hill.

"Quick! Let's go back and get the car. If we hurry, we might be able to catch them!" Midge cried. She took off back down the hill with Cherry close behind her.

But when they reached Cherry's car, a police officer blocked their way. "What's going on?" Cherry cried.

"We're impounding a stolen car, miss," the officer replied in a peremptory manner.

"But that's *my* car," she asserted.

"Can you prove it?" asked the police officer.

Cherry went to the glove box and found it wide open. "That's odd," she said. "I distinctly remember having shut this." A closer inspection revealed that someone had tampered with it. Cherry's registration, title and pad of paper containing all her San Francisco information were gone!

Cherry looked under the floor mat and between the seats, but her search was futile. "Someone's stolen my registration!" she cried.

"Something's been stolen, all right, and I think I'm looking at the thieves!" said the police officer, glaring at Cherry and Midge. "Come with me, girls. You're under arrest!"

Midge, who was usually quick to fly off the handle, remained surprisingly calm. "But officer," she said, her voice as sweet as pie, "surely you don't think *we're* thieves." Was it Cherry's imagination, or did she just catch Midge batting her eyelashes?

"We're nurses. . . er, Girl Scout nurses, in San Francisco to attend a Girl Scout Jamboree and teach first-aid techniques."

Cherry was speechless at Midge's sudden fabrication.

"Well," said the cop, looking skeptical. "Can you prove it?"

"Er. . . ah . . ." Midge fudged for time. Cherry's mind raced. Suddenly, she had it.

"Our nurse's uniforms are in the trunk of our car—check for yourself!" she cried. Phew!

The police officer agreed to check the trunk. He first opened Midge's bag. Cherry puzzled over the pair of handcuffs he found.

"Oh, those are for a life-saving technique," said Midge, pocketing the cuffs. "We keep our uniforms in there," she said, pointing to Cherry's white leather suitcase.

Indeed, inside the bag were two fresh-starched nurse's

uniforms and two matching caps. Two pairs of freshly polished white shoes were tucked in a shoe bag in the bottom of the suitcase.

"Well, it certainly looks like you're nurses," said a cop, a grin breaking over his burly face. "Say, my daughter's a Girl Scout—where did you say your jamboree was?"

Cherry, who wasn't even sure what a jamboree was, kept her mouth shut. This time Midge groped for an answer.

"Uh. . . uh. . ."

"Causing more trouble, huh, girls?" It was the grouchy writer from the coffee shop, and her little dog, too.

"What's wrong, officer; what did these two do?" the girl asked.

"You know these girls?" he asked.

The writer grinned. "Sure I do; we're old pals."

"And they're Girl Scouts?"

"Absolutely."

Then the girl did a very queer thing. She put down her book bag and sang a song to the tune of "Frère-Jacques"; a little off-key but charming, nonetheless:

I'm a Girl Scout; I'm a Girl Scout.
Who are you? Who are you?
Can't you tell by looking? Can't you tell by looking?
I'm one, too. I'm one, too!

There was applause all around, even from passersby.

The police officer looked chagrined. "Well girls, I guess the stolen auto report was a prank. Sorry to have bothered you." He tipped his hat and strolled away.

"But wait!" Cherry cried. "Someone has stolen my car papers." But she was too late, for the police officer had already ducked into a nearby donut shop.

"Velma's kidnappers have a lot of nerve reporting us to the police as car thieves," Midge snarled. She clenched her fists. "If I could just get my hands on them! By now, I'm sure they're miles away from here. I guess we're stuck here until Officer Jones arrives. When we do find her, we'll insist she immediately run a check on the license number of that car!" Midge fumbled through her jacket pockets. "Jeez, I wish I had a cigarette."

She found a butt on the floor and lit it. Cherry examined herself in the car window. "I'm so rumpled," she wailed. She looked at her wrinkled outfit with dismay. "If only Aunt Gert were home, we could at least have a place to freshen up. I'd sure love to change my clothes," she wished aloud.

"Actually, Cherry, this *would* be a good time for you to change your clothes," Midge agreed. She crushed the cigarette under her black penny loafers. "Follow me!"

"What is she up to?" Cherry wondered. Midge didn't strike her as the type to worry about anyone's appearance, especially in the middle of a mystery!

"Where are we going?" Cherry asked as she walked behind Midge. "Does it involve running?" Cherry groaned. "It does, doesn't it?"

"WAIT A MINUTE," Cherry cried. "Nuns aren't allowed to date, are they?" Gert and Lana just laughed.

"How did you two meet?" Jackie wanted to know.

"We met ten years ago at a costume party at the What If Club," Gert replied. "It took Lana several days to convince me she was really a nun."

"Nuns go to bars?" Cherry asked in a shocked voice.

"Does the Pope know about this?" Lauren wondered.

"Oh, you young girls are such prudes," Aunt Gert giggled. "Nuns do a lot of things the Pope doesn't know about. The way I see it, if the Pope can wear a dress, I can wear these pants," she said.

They all had a good laugh. Lana continued her story.

"Gert and I met and knew instantly that we were

meant for each other. We were married nine years ago, not in the eyes of the church, but in the eyes of God."

"Or, whoever," Aunt Gert added, picking up the story. "We were happy here, until this land struggle started. I was in San Francisco the morning Lana disappeared with the evidence of the priest's wrongdoings. I was sitting down to my first cup of coffee when two armed deacons burst into my house, threw me in my car and brought me here. I was beside myself with worry; no one knew where Lana had gone! They trapped us down in that underground room, with no way out! We spent most of our time in the storage room, trying to fashion makeshift weapons. We were preparing for an attack when you girls showed up and saved us."

"I shudder to think what would have happened if you girls hadn't come along," Aunt Gert added.

"What really impressed me, Nancy, is how you tied up those deacons using only one short rope," Midge broke in.

Nancy explained that she had learned to tie fifty different knots in the Girl Scouts. "It's an old trick; with the right training anyone can do it," she said modestly. She agreed to give them all a little demonstration the next day.

Sister Kimi appeared at the door. "Telephone for Jackie," she announced.

When Jackie left the room, Midge leaned over and whispered something in Nurse Marstad's ear. Cherry couldn't make out what she was saying, but she could see that it made quite an impression on Nurse Marstad, who giggled and turned bright pink!

"What's going on?" Cherry cried. "There's still so much that's a mystery to me. I don't know why you're here, Nurse Marstad. Not that it's any of my business," she added hurriedly. She hadn't meant to sound so bossy!

Nurse Marstad grinned, showing off her darling dimples. "Call me Peg, Cherry. All my friends do."

Cherry gulped. Golly, friends with Nurse Marstad?

It was more than she could have hoped for!

"I left the hospital immediately after I spoke with you. I knew all along who our amnesia patient was. I followed the deacon's trail back here, but was caught sneaking around the outside of the convent."

Jackie returned as Nurse Marstad was finishing her story. She balanced on the arm of the head nurse's chair.

"Good news, Midge," she announced. "You are no longer a wanted criminal."

"Hip, hip, hooray!" The gang proclaimed.

"And I am no longer a patrol officer," Jackie added.

"What?" Cherry cried, stunned to hear the news. "Why, you put your life on the line saving all these people, while the boys at the station were busy laughing off possible leads. That can't be?"

Jackie's broad grin told her she was putting them on. "I'm no longer a patrol officer because I'm now the first black female detective in the SFPD!"

"Yes!" Midge exclaimed. Everyone broke out in wild cheering. Everyone except Nurse Marstad, who planted a big kiss on Jackie's cheek.

"There's still so much I want to know," Cherry cried. "Midge, you never told me why you carry those handcuffs. And, Velma, what about . . ." Cherry stifled a yawn. She hadn't gotten much sleep in the last few days.

Midge yawned, too. "I am *so* tired!" she exclaimed. She took Velma's hand. "Come on, honey, you look tired. Time for bed."

Velma, who frankly looked wide awake, yawned too.

Aunt Gert suggested they all get a good night's sleep and meet again in the morning for one of her famous brunches.

"Why, we've got a lot of time to get to know each other!" Lana declared, inviting them all to stay as long as they liked in the spacious and comfortable convent.

"Now that all the big mysteries are cleared up, I can

finally sleep," Cherry declared as she began neatly stacking the dessert plates and coffee cups.

All the girls pitched in and got the job done quickly. Suddenly Nancy, who had said very little all evening, spoke up.

"As long as we're telling the truth. . ." she started, her face turning red and her voice trailing off into a whisper.

"What is it, Nancy?" Aunt Gert went to the trembling girl and put an arm around her.

"This is very difficult to talk about," Nancy said. "But I must do it!" Everyone sat down and patiently waited for Nancy to have her say.

Nancy was in tears, unable to speak. Cherry rushed to her side.

"If it's about your father and his murder, we know all about it," she declared, squeezing her chum's hand.

Nancy shook her head.

"No, no!" she cried. "You don't know! Nobody knows!"

"Tell us what happened," Aunt Gert said gently.

After a few minutes, Nancy regained her composure. What she said next startled even the most hardened of the group.

"My father was not killed by Hannah Gruel! It was I who shot him!" she declared.

Cherry could scarcely believe what she was hearing. "Nancy Clue, *you* killed your own father? But why?"

"He was a monster!" Nancy cried. "To other people he was a civic leader and a respected attorney and even kind to animals. But in his own home he was a bully!"

She told them the whole horrible story.

"My mother died when I was three. Hannah Gruel was like a mother to me. For several years, things were good. Father was gone a lot on business and Hannah and I became the best of chums. But as I entered my teens, Father began spending more and more time around the house.

"The first time I got involved in a case with him, he was so pleased! I thought perhaps he had been lonely all those years without Mother. He seemed so happy to have someone to share in his interests.

"But pretty soon he wanted my help on all his cases, especially after all the publicity we received as a father-daughter team. After a while I barely had time for school and friends of my own! He frightened my best chums Bess and George so much they stopped coming to the house.

"He became obsessed with my appearance, insisting I wear grown-up dresses and stylish hair-dos. After we'd fight he'd always buy me something big and flashy, like a new car. The neighbors thought he was the greatest!"

She hung her head. Her voice dropped to a whisper.

"When I was thirteen I started maturing; I was becoming a woman. It was then he . . ." Her voice grew grim.

She took a deep breath. "From that time on until the day I shot him, my father . . . well, he forced me to do things."

She started to sob. "It was as if I were his wife!" she gasped. "The whole world thought he was the best dad ever. No one would have ever guessed what really went on in that tidy house in the exclusive neighborhood of River Depths.

"When he started bothering me, he told me that if I told anyone he'd harm Hannah," Nancy sobbed. "So I kept it a secret. No one else knows it, but Mother died in an asylum," she said, "and he used to say I was crazy, just like her! And he'd add, 'I could have you put away, just like I did her!'

"One day I couldn't stand it anymore! Hannah was going to visit her sister Hattie for a month, and I just knew it would get worse with her gone. I broke down and told her, and when my father came home, she confronted him.

"She said she was going to tell everyone what he really was, but he just laughed. 'Who'd believe you over me?' he said." Nancy put her hands over her ears. "Oh," she cried. "I can still hear his laughter.

"When Hannah picked up the phone to call the police, he pulled it out of the wall. I thought he was going to kill her, so I ran to the den and got one of his guns.

"'Father!' I screamed. He turned and faced me. I shot him right through the heart. He was dead before he hit the floor.

"Hannah begged me to let her say she did it, and I agreed. I was so scared and upset; I wasn't sure what I was doing. I packed some clothes, jumped in my car and headed west.

"She told me to forget and never tell anyone what happened. But I can't."

Nancy wiped her face on a clean handkerchief from Cherry.

"You're safe now; that's what matters," Aunt Gertrude said, putting her arms around the sobbing girl.

"Am I?" Nancy asked no one in particular. "Now I know what I've got to do," she said, rising from her chair looking very determined.

"I've got to go back to River Depths and free Hannah —no matter what it takes!"

"And we'll go with you!" Midge said.

"That's right!" cried Jackie. "There's got to be some way to prove what kind of man your father really was."

"There were letters he wrote to me," Nancy said. "Disgusting things that would prove his nature beyond a shadow of a doubt. Those and the diary I kept. I left them in my room; I was in such a panic that I forgot to take them."

"We'll go back and get that evidence!" Velma cried.

"You're not alone, Nancy!" Jackie added, already planning the investigation. "Why, with those letters and your diary, we're sure to get Hannah released, and clear you, too."

Lauren pulled a pencil from her overalls and grabbed some paper from the desk. "Gather round, girls," she cried. "We need a plan!"

Beyond the Wall

Ambrose Bierce

ANY YEARS AGO, on my way from Hongkong to New York, I passed a week in San Francisco. A long time had gone by since I had been in that city, during which my ventures in the Orient had prospered beyond my hope; I was rich and could afford to revisit my own country to renew my friendship with such of the companions of my youth as still lived and remembered me with the old affection. Chief of these, I hoped, was Mohun Dampier, an old schoolmate with whom I had held a desultory correspondence which had long ceased, as is the way of correspondence between men. You may have observed that the indisposition to write a merely social letter is in the ratio of the square of the distance between you and your correspondent. It is a law.

I remembered Dampier as a handsome, strong young fellow of scholarly tastes, with an aversion to work and a

---

Prior to his mysterious disappearance during the 1913 Mexican Civil War, AMBROSE BIERCE spent a number of years honing his writing skills at various newspapers in San Francisco. Considered one of the early masterpieces of the short story form, "Beyond the Wall" reflects the strong influence of Edgar Allan Poe.

marked indifference to many of the things that the world cares for, including wealth, of which, however, he had inherited enough to put him beyond the reach of want. In his family, one of the oldest and most aristocratic in the country, it was, I think, a matter of pride that no member of it had ever been in trade nor politics, nor suffered any kind of distinction. Mohun was a trifle sentimental, and had in him a singular element of superstition, which led him to the study of all manner of occult subjects, although his sane mental health safeguarded him against fantastic and perilous faiths. He made daring incursions into the realm of the unreal without renouncing his residence in the partly surveyed and charted region of what we are pleased to call certitude.

The night of my visit to him was stormy. The Californian winter was on, and the incessant rain plashed in the deserted streets, or, lifted by irregular gusts of wind, was hurled against the houses with incredible fury. With no small difficulty my cab-man found the right place, away out toward the ocean beach, in a sparsely populated suburb. The dwelling, a rather ugly one, apparently, stood in the center of its grounds, which as nearly as I could make out in the gloom were destitute of either flowers or grass. Three or four trees, writhing and moaning in the torment of the tempest, appeared to be trying to escape from their dismal environment and take the chance of finding a better one out at sea. The house was a two-story brick structure with a tower, a story higher, at one corner. In a window of that was the only visible light. Something in the appearance of the place made me shudder, a performance that may have been assisted by a rill of rain-water down my back as I scuttled to cover in the doorway.

In answer to my note apprising him of my wish to call, Dampier had written, "Don't ring—open the door and come up." I did so. The staircase was dimly lighted by a single gas-jet at the top of the second flight. I managed to reach the land-ing without disaster and entered by an open door into the lighted square room of the tower. Dampier came forward in gown and slippers to receive me, giving me the greeting that I wished, and if I had held a thought that it might more fitly have been accorded me at the front door the first look at him dispelled any sense of his inhospitality.

He was not the same. Hardly past middle age, he had gone gray and had acquired a pronounced stoop. His figure was thin and angular, his face deeply lined, his complexion dead-white, without a touch of color. His eyes, unnaturally large, glowed with a fire that was almost uncanny.

He seated me, proffered a cigar, and with grave and obvious sincerity assured me of the pleasure that it gave him to meet me. Some unimportant conversation followed, but all the while I was dominated by a melancholy sense of the great change in him. This he must have perceived, for he suddenly said with a bright enough smile, "You are disappointed in me—*non sum qualis eram.*"

I hardly knew what to reply, but managed to say: "Why, really, I don't know: your Latin is about the same."

He brightened again. "No," he said, "being a dead language, it grows in appropriateness. But please have the patience to wait: where I am going there is perhaps a better tongue. Will you care to have a message in it?"

The smile faded as he spoke, and as he concluded he was looking into my eyes with a gravity that distressed me. Yet I would not surrender myself to his mood, nor permit him to see how deeply his prescience of death affected me.

"I fancy that it will be long," I said, "before human speech will cease to serve our need; and then the need, with its possibilities of service, will have passed."

He made no reply, and I too was silent, for the talk had taken a dispiriting turn, yet I knew not how to give it a more agreeable character. Suddenly, in a pause of the storm, when the dead silence was almost startling by contrast with the previous uproar, I heard a gentle tapping, which appeared to come from the wall behind my chair. The sound was such as might have been made by a human hand, not as upon a door by one asking admittance, but rather, I thought, as an agreed sig-nal, an assurance of someone's presence in an adjoining room; most of us, I fancy, have had more experience of such communi-cation than we should care to relate. I glanced at Dampier. If possibly there was something of amusement in the look he did not observe it. He appeared to have forgotten my presence, and was staring at the wall behind me with an expression in his eyes that I am unable to name, although my memory of it is as vivid to-day as was my sense of it then. The situation was embarrassing; I rose to take my leave. At this he seemed to recover himself.

"Please be seated," he said; "it is nothing—no one is there."

But the tapping was repeated, and with the same gen-tle, slow insistence as before.

"Pardon me," I said, "it is late. May I call to-morrow?"

He smiled—a little mechanically, I thought. "It is very delicate of you," said he, "but quite needless. Really, this is the only room in the tower, and no one is there. At least—" He left the sentence incomplete, rose, and threw up a window, the only opening in the wall from which the sound seemed to come. "See."

Not clearly knowing what else to do I followed him to the window and looked out. A street-lamp some little distance away gave enough light through the murk of the rain that was again falling in torrents to make it entirely plain that "no one was there." In truth there was nothing but the sheer blank wall of the tower.

Dampier closed the window and signing me to my seat resumed his own.

The incident was not in itself particularly mysterious; any one of a dozen explanations was possible (though none has occurred to me), yet it impressed me strangely, the more, per-haps, from my friend's effort to reassure me, which seemed to dignify it with a certain significance and importance. He had

proved that no one was there, but in that fact lay all the interest; and he proffered no explanation. His silence was irritating
and made me resentful.

"My good friend," I said, somewhat ironically, I fear,
"I am not disposed to question your right to harbor as many
spooks as you find agreeable to your taste and consistent with
your notions of companionship; that is no business of mine. But
being just a plain man of affairs, mostly of this world, I find
spooks needless to my peace and comfort. I am going to my
hotel, where my fellow-guests are still in the flesh."

It was not a very civil speech, but he manifested no
feeling about it. "Kindly remain," he said. "I am grateful for
your presence here. What you have heard to-night I believe
myself to have heard twice before. Now I *know* it was no illusion. That is much to me—more than you know. Have a fresh
cigar and a good stock of patience while I tell you the story."

The rain was now falling more steadily, with a low,
monotonous susurration, interrupted at long intervals by the
sudden slashing of the boughs of the trees as the wind rose
and failed. The night was well advanced, but both sympathy
and curiosity held me a willing listener to my friend's monologue, which I did not interrupt by a single word from beginning to end.

"Ten years ago," he said, "I occupied a ground-floor
apartment in one of a row of houses, all alike, away at the
other end of this town, on what we call Rincon Hill. This had
been the best quarter of San Francisco, but had fallen into
neglect and decay, partly because the primitive character of its
domestic architecture no longer suited the maturing tastes of
our wealthy citizens, partly because certain public improve-
ments had made a wreck of it. The row of dwellings in one of
which I lived stood a little way back from the street, each having a miniature garden, separated from its neighbors by low
iron fences and bisected with mathematical precision by a box-
bordered gravel walk from gate to door.

"One morning as I was leaving my lodging I observed a young girl entering the adjoining garden on the left. It was a warm day in June, and she was lightly gowned in white. From her shoulders hung a broad straw hat profusely decorated with flowers and wonderfully beribboned in the fashion of the time. My attention was not long held by the exquisite simplicity of her costume, for no one could look at her face and think of any-thing earthly. Do not fear; I shall not profane it by description; it was beautiful exceedingly. All that I have ever seen or dreamed of loveliness was in that matchless living picture by the hand of the Divine Artist. So deeply did it move me that, without a thought of the impropriety of the act, I uncon-sciously bared my head, as a devout Catholic or well-bred Protestant uncovers before an image of the Blessed Virgin. The maiden showed no displeasure; she merely turned her glorious dark eyes upon me with a look that made me catch my breath, and without other recognition of my act passed into the house. For a moment I stood motionless, hat in hand, painfully con-scious of my rudeness, yet so dominated by the emotion inspired by that vision of incomparable beauty that my peni-tence was less poignant than it should have been. Then I went my way, leaving my heart behind. In the natural course of things I should probably have remained away until nightfall, but by the middle of the afternoon I was back in the little gar-den, affecting an interest in the few foolish flowers that I had never before observed. My hope was vain; she did not appear.

"To a night of unrest succeeded a day of expectation and disappointment, but on the day after, as I wandered aim-lessly about the neighborhood, I met her. Of course I did not repeat my folly of uncovering, nor venture by even so much as too long a look to manifest an interest in her; yet my heart was beating audibly. I trembled and consciously colored as she turned her big black eyes upon me with a look of obvious recognition entirely devoid of boldness or coquetry.

"I will not weary you with particulars; many times

afterward I met the maiden, yet never either addressed her or sought to fix her attention. Nor did I take any action toward making her acquaintance. Perhaps my forbearance, requiring so supreme an effort of self-denial, will not be entirely clear to you. That I was heels over head in love is true, but who can overcome his habit of thought, or reconstruct his character?

"I was what some foolish persons are pleased to call, and others, more foolish, are pleased to be called—an aristocrat; and despite her beauty, her charms and graces, the girl was not of my class. I had learned her name—which it is needless to speak—and something of her family. She was an orphan, a dependent niece of the impossible elderly fat woman in whose lodging-house she lived. My income was small and I lacked the talent for marrying; it is perhaps a gift. An alliance with that family would condemn me to its manner of life, part me from my books and studies, and in a social sense reduce me to the ranks. It is easy to deprecate such considerations as these and I have not retained myself for the defense. Let judgment be entered against me, but in strict justice all my ancestors for generations should be made co-defendants and I be permitted to plead in mitigation of punishment the imperious mandate of heredity. To a mésalliance of that kind in every globule of my ancestral blood spoke in opposition. In brief, my tastes, habits, instinct, with whatever of reason my love had left me—all fought against it. Moreover, I was an irreclaimable sentimentalist, and found a subtle charm in an impersonal and spiritual relation which acquaintance might vulgarize and marriage would certainly dispel. No woman, I argued, is what this lovely creature seems. Love is a delicious dream; why should I bring about my own awakening?

"The course dictated by all this sense and sentiment was obvious. Honor, pride, prudence, preservation of my ideals—all commanded me to go away, but for that I was too weak. The utmost that I could do by a mighty effort of will was to cease meeting the girl, and that I did. I even avoided the chance encounters of the garden, leaving my lodging only when I knew that she had gone to her music lessons, and returning after night-fall. Yet all the while I was as one in a trance, indulging the most fascinating fancies and ordering my entire intellectual life in accordance with my dream. Ah, my friend, as one whose actions have a traceable relation to reason, you cannot know the fool's paradise in which I lived.

"One evening the devil put it into my head to be an unspeakable idiot. By apparently careless and purposeless ques-tioning I learned from my gossipy landlady that the young woman's bedroom adjoined my own, a party-wall between. Yielding to a sudden and coarse impulse I gently rapped on the wall. There was no response, naturally, but I was in no mood to accept a rebuke. A madness was upon me and I repeated the folly, the offense, but again ineffectually, and I had the decency to desist.

"An hour later, while absorbed in some of my infernal studies, I heard, or thought I heard, my signal answered. Flinging down my books I sprang to the wall and as steadily as my beating heart would permit gave three slow taps upon it. This time the response was distinct, unmistakable: one, two, three—an exact repetition of my signal. That was all I could elicit, but it was enough—too much.

"The next evening, and for many evenings afterward, that folly went on, I always having 'the last word.' During the whole period I was deliriously happy, but with the perversity of my nature I persevered in my resolution not to see her. Then, as I should have expected, I got no further answers. 'She is dis-gusted,' I said to myself, 'with what she thinks my timidity in making no more definite advances'; and I resolved to seek her and make her acquaintance and—what? I did not know, nor do I now know, what might have come of it. I know only that I passed days and days trying to meet her, and all in vain; she was invisible as well as inaudible. I haunted the streets where we had met, but she did not come. From my window I watched the garden in front of her house, but she passed neither in nor out. I fell into the deepest dejection, believing that she had gone away, yet took no steps to resolve my doubt by inquiry of my landlady, to whom, indeed, I had taken an unconquerable aversion from her having once spoken of the girl with less of reverence than I thought befitting.

"There came a fateful night. Worn out with emotion, irresolution and despondency, I had retired early and fallen into such sleep as was still possible to me. In the middle of the night something—some malign power bent upon the wrecking of my peace forever—caused me to open my eyes and sit up, wide awake and listening intently for I knew not what. Then I thought I heard a faint tapping on the wall—the mere ghost of the familiar signal. In a few moments it was repeated: one, two, three—no louder than before, but addressing a sense alert and strained to receive it. I was about to reply when the Adversary of Peace again intervened in my affairs with a rascally suggestion of retaliation. She had long and cruelly ignored me; now I would ignore her. Incredible fatuity—may God forgive it! All the rest of the night I lay awake, fortifying my obstinacy with shameless justifications and—listening.

"Late the next morning, as I was leaving the house, I met my landlady entering.

" 'Good morning, Mr. Dampier,' she said. 'Have you heard the news?'

"I replied in words that I had heard no news; in manner, that I did not care to hear any. The manner escaped her observation.

" 'About the sick young lady next door,' she babbled on. 'What! you did not know? Why, she has been ill for weeks. And now——'

"I almost sprang upon her. 'And now,' I cried, 'now what?'

" 'She is dead.'

"That is not the whole story. In the middle of the

night, as I learned later, the patient, awakening from a long stupor after a week of delirium, had asked—it was her last utterance—that her bed be moved to the opposite side of the room. Those in attendance had thought the request a vagary of her delirium, but had complied. And there the poor passing soul had exerted its failing will to restore a broken connection—a golden thread of sentiment between its innocence and a monstrous baseness owning a blind, brutal allegiance to the Law of Self.

"What reparation could I make? Are there masses that can be said for the repose of souls that are abroad such nights as this—spirits 'blown about by the viewless winds'—coming in the storm and darkness with signs and portents, hints of memory and presages of doom?

"This is the third visitation. On the first occasion I was too skeptical to do more than verify by natural methods the character of the incident; on the second, I responded to the signal after it had been several times repeated, but without result. To-night's recurrence completes the 'fatal triad' expounded by Parapelius Necromantius. There is no more to tell."

When Dampier had finished his story I could think of nothing relevant that I cared to say, and to question him would have been a hideous impertinence. I rose and bade him good night in a way to convey to him a sense of my sympathy, which he silently acknowledged by a pressure of the hand. That night, alone with his sorrow and remorse, he passed into the Unknown.

Deceptions

Marcia Muller

S AN FRANCISCO'S GOLDEN Gate Bridge is deceptively fragile-looking, especially when fog swirls across its high span. But from where I was standing, almost underneath it at the south end, even the mist couldn't disguise the massiveness of its concrete piers and the taut strength of its cables. I tipped my head back and looked up the tower to where it disappeared into the drifting grayness, thinking about the other ways the bridge is deceptive.

For one thing, the color isn't gold, but rust red, reminiscent of dried blood. And though the bridge is a marvel of engineering, it is also plagued by maintenance problems that keep the Bridge District in constant danger of financial collapse. For a reputedly romantic structure, it has seen more than its fair share of tragedy: Some eight hundred-odd lost souls have jumped to their deaths from its deck.

Today I was there to try to find out if that figure should be raised by one. So far I'd met with little success.

I was standing next to my car in the parking lot of Fort Point, a historic fortification at the mouth of San

MARCIA MULLER's "Deceptions" first appeared in 1987, marking the fourth appearance of her series character, Sharon McCone. Muller has coedited nine mystery anthologies with her husband, Bill Pronzini, and was nominated for an Edgar Award in 1986.

Francisco Bay. Where the pavement stopped, the land fell away to jagged black rocks; waves smashed against them, sending up geysers of salty spray. Beyond the rocks the water was choppy, and Angel Island and Alcatraz were mere humpbacked shapes in the mist. I shivered, wishing I'd worn something heavier than my poplin jacket, and started toward the fort.

This was the last stop on a journey that had taken me from the toll booths and Bridge District offices to Vista Point at the Marin County end of the span, and back to the National Parks Services headquarters down the road from the fort. None of the Parks Service or bridge personnel—including a group of maintenance workers near the north tower—had seen the slender dark-haired woman in the picture I'd shown them, walking south on the pedestrian sidewalk at about four yesterday afternoon. None of them had seen her jump.

It was for that reason—plus the facts that her parents had revealed about twenty-two-year-old Vanessa DiCesare— that made me tend to doubt she actually had committed suicide, in spite of the note she'd left taped to the dashboard of the Honda she'd abandoned at Vista Point. Surely at four o'clock on a Monday afternoon *someone* would have noticed her. Still, I had to follow up every possibility, and the people at the Parks Service station had suggested I check with the rangers at Fort Point.

I entered the dark-brick structure through a long, low tunnel—called a sally port, the sign said—which was flanked at either end by massive wooden doors with iron studding. Years before I'd visited the fort, and now I recalled that it was more or less typical of harbor fortifications built in the Civil War era: a ground floor topped by two tiers of working and living quarters, encircling a central courtyard.

I emerged into the court and looked up at the west side; the tiers were a series of brick archways, their openings as black as empty eyesockets, each roped off by a narrow strip of yellow plastic strung across it at waist level. There was construction gear in the courtyard; the entire west side was under renovation and probably off limits to the public.

As I stood there trying to remember the layout of the place and wondering which way to go, I became aware of a hollow metallic clanking that echoed in the circular enclosure. The noise drew my eyes upward to the wooden watchtower atop the west tiers, and then to the red arch of the bridge's girders directly above it. The clanking seemed to have something to do with cars passing over the roadbed, and it was underlaid by a constant grumbling rush of tires on pavement. The sounds, coupled with the soaring height of the fog-laced girders, made me feel very small and insignificant. I shivered again and turned to my left, looking for one of the rangers.

The man who came out of a nearby doorway startled me, more because of his costume than the suddenness of his appearance. Instead of the Parks Service uniform I remembered the rangers wearing on my previous visit, he was clad in what looked like an old Union Army uniform: a dark blue frock coat, lighter blue trousers, and a wide-brimmed hat with a red plume. The long saber in a scabbard that was strapped to his waist made him look thoroughly authentic.

He smiled at my obvious surprise and came over to me, bushy eyebrows lifted inquiringly. "Can I help you, ma'am?"

I reached into my bag and took out my private investigator's license and showed it to him. "I'm Sharon McCone, from All Souls Legal Cooperative. Do you have a minute to answer some questions?"

He frowned, the way people often do when confronted by a private detective, probably trying to remember whether he'd done anything lately that would warrant investigation. Then he said, "Sure," and motioned for me to step into the shelter of the sally port.

"I'm investigating a disappearance, a possible suicide from the bridge," I said. "It would have happened about four yesterday afternoon. Were you on duty then?"

He shook his head. "Monday's my day off."

"Is there anyone else here who might have been working then?"

"You could check with Lee—Lee Gottschalk, the other ranger on this shift."

"Where can I find him?"

He moved back into the courtyard and looked around. "I saw him start taking a couple of tourists around just a few minutes ago. People are crazy; they'll come out in any kind of weather."

"Can you tell me which way he went?"

The ranger gestured to our right. "Along this side. When he's done down here, he'll take them up that iron stairway to the first tier, but I can't say how far he's gotten yet."

I thanked him and started off in the direction he'd indicated.

There were open doors in the cement wall between the sally port and the iron staircase. I glanced through the first and saw no one. The second led into a narrow dark hallway; when I was halfway down it, I saw that this was the fort's jail. One cell was set up as a display, complete with a mannequin prisoner; the other, beyond an archway that was not much taller than my own five-foot-six, was unrestored. Its waterstained walls were covered with graffiti, and a metal railing protected a two-foot-square iron grid on the floor in one corner. A sign said that it was a cistern with a forty-thousand-gallon capacity.

Well, I thought, that's interesting, but playing tourist isn't helping me catch up with Lee Gottschalk. Quickly I left the jail and hurried up the iron staircase the first ranger had indicated. At its top, I turned to my left and bumped into a chain link fence that blocked access to the area under renovation. Warning myself to watch where I was going, I went the other way, toward the east tier. The archways there were fenced off with similar chain link so no one could fall, and doors opened off the gallery into what I supposed had been the soldiers' living quarters. I pushed through the first one and stepped into a small museum.

The room was high-ceilinged, with tall, narrow windows in the outside wall. No ranger or tourists were in sight. I looked toward an interior door that led to the next room and saw a series of mirror images: one door within another leading off into the distance, each diminishing in size until the last seemed very tiny. I had the unpleasant sensation that if I walked along there, I would become progressively smaller and eventually disappear.

From somewhere down there came the sound of voices. I followed it, passing through more museum displays until I came to a room containing an old-fashioned bedstead and footlocker. A ranger, dressed the same as the man downstairs except that he was bearded and wore granny glasses, stood beyond the bedstead lecturing to a man and a woman who were bundled to their chins in bulky sweaters.

"You'll notice that the fireplaces are very small," he was saying, motioning to the one on the wall next to the bed, "and you can imagine how cold it could get for the soldiers garrisoned here. They didn't have a heated employees' lounge like we do." Smiling at his own little joke, he glanced at me. "Do you want to join the tour?"

I shook my head and stepped over by the footlocker. "Are you Lee Gottschalk?"

"Yes." He spoke the word a shade warily.

"I have a few questions I'd like to ask you. How long will the rest of the tour take?"

"At least half an hour. These folks want to see the unrestored rooms on the third floor."

I didn't want to wait around that long, so I said, "Could you take a couple of minutes and talk with me now?"

He moved his head so the light from the windows caught his granny glasses and I couldn't see the expression in his eyes, but his mouth tightened in a way that might have been annoyance. After a moment he said, "Well, the rest of the tour on this floor is pretty much self-guided." To the tourists, he added, "Why don't you go on ahead and I'll catch up after I talk with this lady."

They nodded agreeably and moved on into the next room. Lee Gottschalk folded his arms across his chest and leaned against the small fireplace. "Now what can I do for you?"

I introduced myself and showed him my license. His mouth twitched briefly in surprise, but he didn't comment. I said, "At about four yesterday afternoon, a young woman left her car at Vista Point with a suicide note in it. I'm trying to locate a witness who saw her jump." I took out the photograph I'd been showing to people and handed it to him. By now I had Vanessa DiCesare's features memorized: high forehead, straight nose, full lips, glossy wings of dark-brown hair curling inward at the jawbone. It was a strong face, not beautiful but strik-ing—and a face I'd recognize anywhere.

Gottschalk studied the photo, then handed it back to me. "I read about her in the morning paper. Why are you try-ing to find a witness?"

"Her parents have hired me to look into it."

"The paper said her father is some big politician here in the city."

I didn't see any harm in discussing what had already appeared in print. "Yes, Ernest DiCesare—he's on the Board of Supes and likely to be our next mayor."

"And she was a law student, engaged to some hotshot lawyer who ran her father's last political campaign."

"Right again."

He shook his head, lips pushing out in bewilderment. "Sounds like she had a lot going for her. Why would she kill herself? Did that note taped inside her car explain it?"

I'd seen the note, but its contents were confidential. "No. Did you happen to see anything unusual yesterday afternoon?"

"No. But if I'd seen anyone jump, I'd have reported it to the Coast Guard station so they could try to recover the body before the current carried it out to sea."

"What about someone standing by the bridge railing, acting strangely, perhaps?"

"If I'd noticed anyone like that, I'd have reported it to the bridge offices so they could send out a suicide prevention team." He stared almost combatively at me, as if I'd accused him of some kind of wrongdoing, then he seemed to relent a lit-tle. "Come outside," he said, "and I'll show you something."

We went through the door to the gallery, and he guided me to the chain link barrier in the archway and pointed up. "Look at the angle of the bridge, and the distance we are from it. You couldn't spot anyone standing at the rail from here, at least not well enough to tell if they were acting upset. And a jumper would have to hurl herself way out before she'd be noticeable."

"And there's nowhere else in the fort from where a jumper would be clearly visible?"

"Maybe from one of the watchtowers or the extreme west side. But they're off limits to the public, and we only give them one routine check at closing."

Satisfied now, I said, "Well, that about does it. I appreciate your taking the time."

He nodded and we started along the gallery. When we reached the other end, where an enclosed staircase spiraled up and down, I thanked him again and we parted company.

The way the facts looked to me now, Vanessa DiCesare had faked this suicide and just walked away—away from her wealthy old-line Italian family, from her up-and-coming liberal lawyer, from a life that either had become too much or just hadn't been enough. Vanessa was over twenty-one; she had a legal right to disappear if she wanted to. But her parents and her fiancé loved her, and they also had a right to know she was alive and well. If I could locate her and reassure them without ruining whatever new life she planned to create for herself, I would feel I'd performed the job I'd been hired to do. But right now I was weary, chilled to the bone, and out of leads. I decided to go back to All Souls and consider my next moves in warmth and comfort.

ALL SOULS LEGAL Cooperative is housed in a ramshackle Victorian on one of the steeply sloping side streets of Bernal Heights, a working-class district in the southern part of the city. The co-op caters mainly to clients who live in the area: people with low to middle incomes who don't have much extra money for expensive lawyers. The sliding fee scale allows them to obtain quality legal assistance at reasonable prices—a concept that is probably outdated in the self-centered 1980s, but is kept alive by the people who staff All Souls. It's a place where the lawyers care about their clients, and a good place to work.

I left my MG at the curb and hurried up the front steps through the blowing fog. The warmth inside was almost a shock after the chilliness at Fort Point; I unbuttoned my jacket and went down the long deserted hallway to the big country kitchen at the rear. There I found my boss, Hank Zahn, stirring up a mug of the Navy grog he often concocts on cold November nights like this one.

He looked at me, pointed to the rum bottle, and said, "Shall I make you one?" When I nodded, he reached for another mug.

I went to the round oak table under the windows, moved a pile of newspapers from one of the chairs, and sat down. Hank added lemon juice, hot water, and sugar syrup to the rum; dusted it artistically with nutmeg; and set it in front of me with a flourish. I sampled it as he sat down across from me, then nodded my approval.

He said, "How's it going with the DiCesare investigation?"

Hank had a personal interest in the case; Vanessa's fiancé, Gary Stornetta, was a long-time friend of his, which was why I, rather than one of the large investigative firms her father normally favored, had been asked to look into it. I said, "Everything I've come up with points to it being a disappearance, not a suicide."

"Just as Gary and her parents suspected."

"Yes. I've covered the entire area around the bridge. There are absolutely no witnesses, except for the tour bus driver who saw her park her car at four and got suspicious when it was still there at seven and reported it. But even he didn't see her walk off toward the bridge." I drank some more grog, felt its warmth, and began to relax.

Behind his thick horn-rimmed glasses, Hank's eyes became concerned. "Did the DiCesares or Gary give you any idea why she would have done such a thing?"

"When I talked with Ernest and Sylvia this morning, they said Vanessa had changed her mind about marrying Gary. He's not admitting to that, but he doesn't speak of Vanessa the way a happy husband-to-be would. And it seems like an unlikely match to me—he's close to twenty years older than she."

"More like fifteen," Hank said. "Gary's father was Ernest's best friend, and after Ron Stornetta died, Ernest more or less took him on as a protégé. Ernest was delighted that their families were finally going to be joined."

"Oh, he was delighted all right. He admitted to me that he'd practically arranged the marriage. 'Girl didn't know what was good for her,' he said. 'Needed a strong older man to guide her.' " I snorted.

Hank smiled faintly. He's a feminist, but over the years his sense of outrage has mellowed; mine still has a hair trigger.

"Anyway," I said, "when Vanessa first announced she was backing out of the engagement, Ernest told her he would cut off her funds for law school if she didn't go through with the wedding."

"Jesus, I had no idea he was capable of such . . . Neanderthal tactics."

"Well, he is. After that Vanessa went ahead and set the wedding date. But Sylvia said she suspected she wouldn't go through with it. Vanessa talked of quitting law school and moving out of their home. And she'd been seeing other men; she and her father had a bad quarrel about it just last week. Anyway, all of that, plus the fact that one of her suitcases and some clothing are missing, made them highly suspicious of the suicide."

Hank reached for my mug and went to get us more grog. I began thumbing through the copy of the morning paper that I'd moved off the chair, looking for the story on Vanessa. I found it on page three.

The daughter of Supervisor Ernest DiCesare apparently committed suicide by jumping from the Golden Gate Bridge late yesterday afternoon.

Vanessa DiCesare, 22, abandoned her 1985 Honda Civic at Vista Point at approximately four p.m., police said. There were no witnesses to her jump, and the body has not been recovered. The contents of a suicide note found in her car have not been disclosed.

Ms. DiCesare, a first-year student at Hastings College of Law, is the only child of the supervisor and his wife, Sylvia. She planned to be married next month to San Francisco attorney Gary R. Stornetta, a political associate of her father. . . .

Strange how routine it all sounded when reduced to journalistic language. And yet how mysterious—the "undisclosed contents" of the suicide note, for instance.

"You know," I said as Hank came back to the table and set down the fresh mugs of grog, "that note is another factor that makes me believe she staged this whole thing. It was so formal and controlled. If they had samples of suicide notes in etiquette books, I'd say she looked one up and copied it."

He ran his fingers through his wiry brown hair. "What I don't understand is why she didn't just break off the engagement and move out of the house. So what if her father cut off her money? There are lots worse things than working your way through law school."

"Oh, but this way she gets back at everyone, and has the advantage of actually being alive to gloat over it. Imagine her parents' and Gary's grief and guilt—it's the ultimate way of getting even."

"She must be a very angry young woman."

"Yes. After I talked with Ernest and Sylvia and Gary, I spoke briefly with Vanessa's best friend, a law student named Kathy Graves. Kathy told me that Vanessa was furious with her father for making her go through with the marriage. And she'd come to hate Gary because she'd decided he was only marrying her for her family's money and political power."

"Oh, come on. Gary's ambitious, sure. But you can't tell me he doesn't genuinely care for Vanessa."

"I'm only giving you her side of the story."

"So now what do you plan to do?"

"Talk with Gary and the DiCesares again. See if I can't come up with some bit of information that will help me find her."

"And then?"

"Then it's up to them to work it out."

THE DICESARE HOME was mock-Tudor, brick and half-timber, set on a corner knoll in the exclusive area of St. Francis Wood. When I'd first come there that morning, I'd been slightly awed; now the house had lost its power to impress me. After delving into the lives of the family who lived there, I knew that it was merely a pile of brick and mortar and wood that contained more than the usual amount of misery.

The DiCesares and Gary Stornetta were waiting for me in the living room, a strangely formal place with several groupings of furniture and expensive-looking knickknacks laid out in precise patterns on the tables. Vanessa's parents and fiancé—like the house—seemed diminished since my previous visit: Sylvia huddled in an armchair by the fireplace, her gray-blonde hair straggling from its elegant coiffure; Ernest stood behind her, haggard-faced, one hand protectively on her shoulder. Gary paced, smoking and clawing at his hair with his other hand. Occasionally he dropped ashes on the thick wall-to-wall carpeting, but no one called it to his attention.

They listened to what I had to report without interruption. When I finished, there was a long silence. Then Sylvia put a hand over her eyes and said, "How she must hate us to do a thing like this!"

Ernest tightened his grip on his wife's shoulder. His face was a conflict of anger, bewilderment, and sorrow.

There was no question of which emotion had hold of Gary; he smashed out his cigarette in an ashtray, lit another, and resumed pacing. But while his movements before had merely been nervous, now his tall, lean body was rigid with thinly controlled fury. "Damn her!" he said. "Damn her anyway!"

"Gary." There was a warning note in Ernest's voice.

Gary glanced at him, then at Sylvia. "Sorry."

I said, "The question now is, do you want me to continue looking for her?"

In shocked tones, Sylvia said, "Of course we do!" Then she tipped her head back and looked at her husband.

Ernest was silent, his fingers pressing hard against the black wool of her dress.

"Ernest?" Now Sylvia's voice held a note of panic.

"Of course we do," he said. But the words somehow lacked conviction.

I took out my notebook and pencil, glancing at Gary. He had stopped pacing and was watching the DiCesares. His craggy face was still mottled with anger, and I sensed he shared Ernest's uncertainty.

Opening the notebook, I said, "I need more details about Vanessa, what her life was like the past month or so. Perhaps something will occur to one of you that didn't this morning."

"Ms. McCone," Ernest said, "I don't think Sylvia's up to this right now. Why don't you and Gary talk, and then if there's anything else, I'll be glad to help you."

"Fine." Gary was the one I was primarily interested in questioning, anyway. I waited until Ernest and Sylvia had left the room, then turned to him.

When the door shut behind them, he hurled his cigarette into the empty fireplace. "Goddamn little bitch!" he said.

I said, "Why don't you sit down."

He looked at me for a few seconds, obviously wanting to keep on pacing, but then he flopped into the chair Sylvia had vacated. When I'd first met with Gary this morning, he'd been controlled and immaculately groomed, and he had seemed more solicitous of the DiCesares than concerned with his own feelings. Now his clothing was disheveled, his graying hair tousled, and he looked to be on the brink of a rage that would flatten anyone in its path.

Unfortunately, what I had to ask him would probably fan that rage. I braced myself and said, "Now tell me about Vanessa. And not all the stuff about her being a lovely young woman and a brilliant student. I heard all that this morning—but now we both know it isn't the whole truth, don't we?"

Surprisingly he reached for a cigarette and lit it slowly, using the time to calm himself. When he spoke, his voice was as level as my own. "All right, it's not the whole truth." Vanessa is lovely and brilliant. She'll make a top-notch lawyer. There's a hardness in her; she gets it from Ernest. It took guts to fake this suicide. . ."

"What do you think she hopes to gain from it?"

"Freedom. From me. From Ernest's domination. She's

probably taken off somewhere for a good time. When she's
ready she'll come back and make her demands."

"And what will they be?"

"Enough money to move into a place of her own and finish law school. And she'll get it, too. She's all her parents have."

"You don't think she's set out to make a new life for
herself?"

"Hell, no. That would mean giving up all this." The
sweep of his arm encompassed the house and all of the
DiCesares' privileged world.

But there was one factor that made me doubt his
assessment. I said, "What about the other men in her life?"

He tried to look surprised, but an angry muscle
twitched in his jaw.

"Come on, Gary," I said, "you know there were other
men. Even Ernest and Sylvia were aware of that."

"Ah, Christ!" He popped out of the chair and began
pacing again. "All right, there were other men. It started a few
months ago. I didn't understand it; things had been good with
us; they still *were* good physically. But I thought, okay, she's
young; this is only natural. So I decided to give her some rope,
let her get it out of her system. She didn't throw it in my face,
didn't embarrass me in front of my friends. Why shouldn't she
have a last fling?"

"And then?"

"She began making noises about breaking off the
engagement. And Ernest started that shit about not footing the
bill for law school. Like a fool I went along with it, and she
seemed to cave in from the pressure. But a few weeks later, it
all started up again—only this time it was purposeful, cruel."

"In what way?"

"She'd know I was meeting political associates for
lunch or dinner, and she'd show up at the restaurant with a
date. Later she'd claim he was just a friend, but you couldn't
prove it from the way they acted. We'd go to a party and she'd

flirt with every man there. She got sly and secretive about where she'd been, what she'd been doing."

I had pictured Vanessa as a very angry young woman; now I realized she was not a particularly nice one, either.

Gary was saying, ". . . the last straw was on Halloween. We went to a costume party given by one of her friends from Hastings. I didn't want to go—costumes, a young crowd, not my kind of thing—and so she was angry with me to begin with. Anyway, she walked out with another man, some jerk in a soldier outfit. They were dancing. . ."

I sat up straighter. "Describe the costume."

"An old-fashioned soldier outfit. Wide-brimmed hat with a plume, frock coat, sword."

"What did the man look like?"

"Youngish. He had a full beard and wore granny glasses."

Lee Gottschalk.

THE ADDRESS I got from the phone directory for Lee Gottschalk was on California Street not far from Twenty-fifth Avenue and only a couple of miles from where I'd first met the ranger at Fort Point. When I arrived there and parked at the opposite curb, I didn't need to check the mailboxes to see which apartment was his; the corner windows on the second floor were ablaze with light, and inside I could see Gottschalk, sitting in an armchair in what appeared to be his living room. He seemed to be alone but expecting company, because frequently he looked up from the book he was reading and checked his watch.

In case the company was Vanessa DiCesare, I didn't want to go barging in there. Gottschalk might find a way to warn her off, or simply not answer the door when she arrived. Besides, I didn't yet have a definite connection between the two of them; the "jerk in a soldier outfit" could have been someone else, someone in a rented costume that just happened to resemble the working uniform at the fort. But my suspicions were strong enough to keep me watching Gottschalk for well over an hour. The ranger *had* lied to me that afternoon.

The lies had been casual and convincing, except for two mistakes—such small mistakes that I hadn't caught them even when I'd read the newspaper account of Vanessa's purported suicide later. But now I recognized them for what they were: The paper had called Gary Stornetta a "political associate" of Vanessa's father, rather than his former campaign manager, as Lee had termed him. And while the paper mentioned the suicide note, it had not said it was *taped* inside the car. While Gottschalk conceivably could know about Gary managing Ernest's campaign for the Board of Supes from other newspaper accounts, there was no way he could have known how the note was secured—except from Vanessa herself.

Because of those mistakes, I continued watching Gottschalk, straining my eyes as the mist grew heavier, hoping Vanessa would show up or that he'd eventually lead me to her. The ranger appeared to be nervous: He got up a couple of times and turned on a TV, flipped through the channels, and turned it off again. For about ten minutes he paced back and forth. Finally, around twelve-thirty, he checked his watch again, then got up and drew the draperies shut. The lights went out behind them.

I tensed, staring through the blowing mist at the door of the apartment building. Somehow Gottschalk hadn't looked like a man who was going to bed. And my impression was correct: In a few minutes he came through the door onto the sidewalk carrying a suitcase—pale leather like the one of Vanessa's Sylvia had described to me—and got into a dark-colored Mustang parked on his side of the street. The car started up and he made a U-turn, then went right on Twenty-fifth Avenue. I followed. After a few minutes, it became apparent that he was heading for Fort Point.

When Gottschalk turned into the road to the fort, I kept going until I could pull over on the shoulder. The brake lights of the Mustang flared, and then Gottschalk got out and unlocked the low iron bar that blocked the road from sunset to sunrise; after he'd driven through he closed it again, and the car's lights disappeared down the road.

Had Vanessa been hiding at drafty, cold Fort Point? It seemed a strange choice of place, since she could have used a motel or Gottschalk's apartment. But perhaps she'd been afraid someone would recognize her in a public place, or connect her with Gottschalk and come looking, as I had. And while the fort would be a miserable place to hide during the hours it was open to the public—she'd have had to keep to one of the off-limits areas, such as the west side—at night she could probably avail herself of the heated employees' lounge.

Now I could reconstruct most of the scenario of what had gone on: Vanessa meets Lee; they talk about his work; she decides he is the person to help her fake her suicide. Maybe there's a romantic entanglement, maybe not; but for whatever reason, he agrees to go along with the plan. She leaves her car at Vista Point, walks across the bridge, and later he drives over there and picks up the suitcase. . . .

But then why hadn't he delivered it to her at the fort? And to go after the suitcase after she'd abandoned the car was too much of a risk; he might have been seen, or the people at the fort might have noticed him leaving for too long a break. Also, if she'd walked across the bridge, surely at least one of the people I'd talked with would have seen her—the maintenance crew near the north tower, for instance.

There was no point in speculating on it now, I decided. The thing to do was to follow Gottschalk down there and confront Vanessa before she disappeared again. For a moment I debated taking my gun out of the glovebox, but then decided against it. I don't like to carry it unless I'm going into a dangerous situation, and neither Gottschalk nor Vanessa posed any particular threat to me. I was merely here to deliver a message from Vanessa's parents asking her to come home. If she didn't care to respond to it, that was not my business—or my problem.

I got out of my car and locked it, then hurried across the road and down the narrow lane to the gate, ducking under it and continuing along toward the ranger station. On either side of me were tall, thick groves of eucalyptus; I could smell their acrid fragrance and hear the fog-laden wind rustle their brittle leaves. Their shadows turned the lane into a black winding alley, and the only sound besides distant traffic noises was my tennis shoes slapping on the broken pavement. The ranger station was dark, but ahead I could see Gottschalk's car parked next to the fort. The area was illuminated only by small security lights set at intervals on the walls of the structure. Above it the bridge arched, washed in fog-muted yellowish light; as I drew closer I became aware of the grumble and clank of traffic up there.

I ran across the parking area and checked Gottschalk's car. It was empty, but the suitcase rested on the passenger seat. I turned and started toward the sally port, noticing that its heavily studded door stood open a few inches. The low tunnel was completely dark. I felt my way along it toward the court-yard, one hand on its icy stone wall.

The doors to the courtyard also stood open. I peered through them into the gloom beyond. What light there was came from the bridge and more security beacons high up on the wooden watchtowers; I could barely make out the shapes of the construction equipment that stood near the west side. The clank-ing from the bridge was oppressive and eerie in the still night.

As I was about to step into the courtyard, there was a movement to my right. I drew back into the sally port as Lee Gottschalk came out of one of the ground-floor doorways. My first impulse was to confront him, but then I decided against it. He might shout, warn Vanessa, and she might escape before I could deliver her parents' message.

After a few seconds I looked out again, meaning to fol-low Gottschalk, but he was nowhere in sight. A faint shaft of

light fell through the door from which he had emerged and rippled over the cobblestone floor. I went that way, through the
door and along a narrow corridor to where an archway was
illuminated. Then, realizing the archway led to the unrestored
cell of the jail I'd seen earlier, I paused. Surely Vanessa wasn't
hiding in there. . . .

I crept forward and looked through the arch. The light
came from a heavy-duty flashlight that sat on the floor. It
threw macabre shadows on the waterstained walls, showing
their streaked and painted graffiti. My gaze followed its beams
upward and then down, to where the grating of the cistern lay
out of place on the floor beside the hole. Then I moved over to
the railing, leaned across it, and trained the flashlight down
into the well.

I saw, with a rush of shock and horror, the dark hair
and once-handsome features of Vanessa DiCesare.

She had been hacked to death. Stabbed and slashed,
as if in a frenzy. Her clothing was ripped; there were gashes
on her face and hands; she was covered with dark smears of
blood. Her eyes were open, staring with that horrible flatness
of death.

I came back on my heels, clutching the railing for support. A wave of dizziness swept over me, followed by an icy
coldness. I thought: He killed her. And then I pictured
Gottschalk in his Union Army uniform, the saber hanging from
his belt, and I knew what the weapon had been.

"God!" I said aloud.

Why had he murdered her? I had no way of knowing
yet. But the answer to why he'd thrown her into the cistern,
instead of just putting her into the bay, was clear: She was
supposed to have committed suicide; and while bodies that fall
from the Golden Gate Bridge sustain a great many injuries,
slash and stab wounds aren't among them. Gottschalk could
not count on the body being swept out to sea on the current; if
she washed up somewhere along the coast, it would be obvious

she had been murdered—and eventually an investigation might have led back to him. To him and his soldier's saber.

It also seemed clear that he'd come to the fort tonight to move the body. But why not last night, why leave her in the cistern all day? Probably he'd needed to plan, to secure keys to the gate and the fort, to check the schedule of the night patrols for the best time to remove her. Whatever his reason, I realized now that I'd walked into a very dangerous situation. Walked right in without bringing my gun. I turned quickly to get out of there . . .

And came face-to-face with Lee Gottschalk.

His eyes were wide, his mouth drawn back in a snarl of surprise. In one hand he held a bundle of heavy canvas. "You!" he said. "What the hell are you doing here?"

I jerked back from him, bumped into the railing, and dropped the flashlight. It clattered on the floor and began rolling toward the mouth of the cistern. Gottschalk lunged toward me, and as I dodged, the light fell into the hole and the cell went dark. I managed to push past him and ran down the hallway to the courtyard.

Stumbling on the cobblestones, I ran blindly for the sally port. Its doors were shut now—he'd probably taken that precaution when he'd returned from getting the tarp to wrap her body in. I grabbed the iron hasp and tugged, but couldn't get it open. Gottschalk's footsteps were coming through the courtyard after me now. I let go of the hasp and ran again.

When I came to the enclosed staircase at the other end of the court, I started up. The steps were wide at the outside, narrow at the inside. My toes banged into the risers of the steps; a couple of times I teetered and almost fell backwards. At the first tier I paused, then kept going. Gottschalk had said something about unrestored rooms on the second tier; they'd be a better place to hide than in the museum.

Down below I could hear him climbing after me. The sound of his feet—clattering and stumbling—echoed in the close space. I could hear him grunt and mumble: low, ugly sounds that I knew were curses.

I had absolutely no doubt that if he caught me, he would kill me. Maybe do to me what he had done to Vanessa. . . .

I rounded the spiral once again and came out on the top floor gallery, my heart beating wildly, my breath coming in pants. To my left were archways, black outlines filled with dark-gray sky. To my right was blackness. I went that way, hands out, feeling my way.

My hands touched the rough wood of a door. I pushed, and it opened. As I passed through it, my shoulder bag caught on something; I yanked it loose and kept going. Beyond the door I heard Gottschalk curse loudly, the sound filled with surprise and pain; he must have fallen on the stairway. And that gave me a little more time.

The tug at my shoulder bag had reminded me of the small flashlight I keep there. Flattening myself against the wall next to the door, I rummaged through the bag and brought out the flash. Its beam showed high walls and arching ceilings, plaster and lath pulled away to expose dark brick. I saw cubicles and cubbyholes opening into dead ends, but to my right was an arch. I made a small involuntary sound of relief, then thought *Quiet!* Gottschalk's footsteps started up the stairway again as I moved through the archway.

The crumbling plaster walls beyond the archway were set at odd angles—an interlocking funhouse maze connected by small doors. I slipped through one and found myself in an irregularly shaped room heaped with debris. There didn't seem to be an exit, so I ducked back into the first room and moved toward the outside wall, where gray outlines indicated small high-placed windows. I couldn't hear Gottschalk any more—couldn't hear anything but the roar and clank from the bridge directly overhead.

The front wall was brick and stone, and the windows had wide waist-high sills. I leaned across one, looked through the salt-caked glass, and saw the open sea. I was at the front of the fort, the part that faced beyond the Golden Gate; to my immediate right would be the unrestored portion. If I could slip over into that area, I might be able to hide until the other rangers came to work in the morning.

But Gottschalk could be anywhere. I couldn't hear his footsteps above the infernal noise from the bridge. He could be right here in the room with me, pinpointing me by the beam of my flashlight. . . .

Fighting down panic, I switched the light off and continued along the wall, my hands recoiling from its clammy stone surface. It was icy cold in the vast, echoing space, but my own flesh felt colder still. The air had a salt tang, underlaid by odors of rot and mildew. For a couple of minutes the darkness was unalleviated, but then I saw a lighter rectangular shape ahead of me.

When I reached it I found it was some sort of embrasure, about four feet tall, but only a little over a foot wide. Beyond it I could see the edge of the gallery where it curved and stopped at the chain link fence that barred entrance to the other side of the fort. The fence wasn't very high—only five feet or so. If I could get through this narrow opening, I could climb it and find refuge . . .

The sudden noise behind me was like a firecracker popping. I whirled, and saw a tall figure silhouetted against one of the seaward windows. He lurched forward, tripping over whatever he'd stepped on. Forcing back a cry, I hoisted myself up and began squeezing through the embrasure.

Its sides were rough brick. They scraped my flesh clear through my clothing. Behind me I heard the slap of Gottschalk's shoes on the wooden floor.

My hips wouldn't fit through the opening. I gasped, grunted, pulling with my arms on the outside wall. Then I turned on my side, sucking in my stomach. My bag caught again, and I let go of the wall long enough to rip its strap off my elbow. As my hips squeezed through the embrasure, I felt Gottschalk grab at my feet. I kicked out frantically, breaking his hold, and fell off the sill to the floor of the gallery.

Fighting for breath, I pushed off the floor, threw myself at the fence, and began climbing. The metal bit into my fingers, rattled and clashed with my weight. At the top, the leg of my jeans got hung up on the spiky wires. I tore it loose and jumped down the other side.

The door to the gallery burst open and Gottschalk came through it. I got up from a crouch and ran into the darkness ahead of me. The fence began to rattle as he started up it. I raced, half-stumbling, along the gallery, the open archways to my right. To my left was probably a warren of rooms similar to those on the east side. I could lose him in there . . .

Only I couldn't. The door I tried was locked. I ran to the next one and hurled my body against its wooden panels. It didn't give. I heard myself sob in fear and frustration.

Gottschalk was over the fence now, coming toward me, limping. His breath came in erratic gasps, loud enough to hear over the noise from the bridge. I twisted around, looking for shelter, and saw a pile of lumber lying across one of the open archways.

I dashed toward it and slipped behind, wedged between it and the pillar of the arch. The courtyard lay two dizzying stories below me. I grasped the end of the top two-by-four. It moved easily, as if on a fulcrum.

Gottschalk had seen me. He came on steadily, his right leg dragging behind him. When he reached the pile of lumber and started over it toward me, I yanked on the two-by-four. The other end moved and struck him on the knee.

He screamed and stumbled back. Then he came forward again, hands outstretched toward me. I pulled back further against the pillar. His clutching hands missed me, and when they did he lost his balance and toppled onto the pile of lumber. And then the boards began to slide toward the open archway.

He grabbed at the boards, yelling and flailing his arms.

I tried to reach for him, but the lumber was moving like an avalanche now, pitching over the side and crashing down into the courtyard two stories below. It carried Gottschalk's thrashing body with it, and his screams echoed in its wake. For an awful few seconds the boards continued to crash down on him, and then everything was terribly still. Even the thrumming of the bridge traffic seemed muted.

I straightened slowly and looked down into the courtyard. Gottschalk lay unmoving among the scattered pieces of lumber. For a moment I breathed deeply to control my vertigo; then I ran back to the chain link fence, climbed it, and rushed down the spiral staircase to the courtyard.

When I got to the ranger's body, I could hear him moaning. I said, "Lie still. I'll call an ambulance."

He moaned louder as I ran across the courtyard and found a phone in the gift shop, but by the time I returned, he was silent. His breathing was so shallow that I thought he'd passed out, but then I heard mumbled words coming from his lips. I bent closer to listen.

"Vanessa," he said. "Wouldn't take me with her. . . ."

I said, "Take you where?"

"Going away together. Left my car . . . over there so she could drive across the bridge. But when she . . . . brought it here she said she was going alone. . . ."

So you argued, I thought. And you lost your head and slashed her to death.

"Vanessa," he said again. "Never planned to take me . . . tricked me. . . ."

I started to put a hand on his arm, but found I couldn't touch him. "Don't talk any more. The ambulance'll be here soon."

"Vanessa," he said. "Oh God, what did you do to me?"

I looked up at the bridge, rust red through the darkness and the mist. In the distance, I could hear the wail of a siren.

Deceptions, I thought.

Deceptions. . . .

Francis Bruguière
1908

Heat
Lightning

John Lantigua

IT WAS JUST after noon when Cruz rode the elevator to the seventh floor of the Hall of Justice and let himself into the Homicide office. It was Sunday, the office was empty like all the other businesses downtown. At a glance it might have been any other business—insurance, stocks, marketing—with its scarred desks stacked with folders, old filing cabinets and a bulletin board full of notices and for-sale advisories. It was only when you looked closely that the nature of the business became clear. The bulletin board notice was from the chief and had to do with extradition proceedings, and a for-sale notice was for a bullet-proof vest. The folders were full of macabre photographs and the chalk outlines of bodies. The cabinets held the records of past "clients," all murderers. The business was homicide.

Closed since Friday, the place was like a steambath. Cruz pushed open a window, turned on a stand-up fan and

---

Chicano homicide detective David Cruz is the flawed hero of John Lantigua's *Heat Lightning.* While investigating the murder of an El Salvadoran woman, San Francisco Police Detective Cruz is torn between the tedium of his profession, and the diversity, energy, and allure of San Francisco's Mission District.

threw his suit jacket over a chair. He opened a folder waiting
on his blotter and found the coroner's report on Gloria Soto.
This report confirmed several of the medical examiner's obser-
vations made on the scene: According to tissue deterioration
and the stomach contents, the girl had died late Friday or in
the earliest hours Saturday; she had certainly died of a single
bullet to the brain; she had not engaged in sexual intercourse,
forced or otherwise, in the hours preceding her death. The
report also said there were several small contusions on the
body but those had been caused after the girl was dead, probably in the process of disposing of the body. In addition, a close
examination of the girl's thumbs and the cuts left by the waxed
string indicated the thumbs had been tied once Gloria Soto
was already dead. It was just as Cruz had told Bill Clarke,
somebody had probably tied the thumbs to throw the police
off. This last item indicated that Gloria Soto's body, at the
time of her death, contained a considerable amount of alcohol,
enough to mean she had been intoxicated. This thread of information made Cruz frown.

In a separate small envelope on the desk Cruz found
the ballistics report and the bullet in question. He shook it out
into his palm. The tip of the slug had been blunted, possibly
from hitting the skull. The ballistics reports identified it as .38
caliber, the same kind of slug that would have come in one of
the boxes he had found in the Hernandez house.

Cruz took out blank, official-sized paper, opened his
notebook and began to type his report, covering the lot where
the body had been found and his interviews with Victor Soto,
Elvira Hernandez, Dennis and Elaine Miranda, Stacy Stoner,
and Bill Clarke.

Lieutenant Weintraub, chief of Homicide, was a stick-
ler for written reports. He wanted one at least every other day
on cases under investigation. He wanted names, places, days,
times and bloody details. But Weintraub was an amateur soci-
ologist and he also expected what he called the inside story:

He wanted evaluations of the people involved, where they came from, how much money they had, how they lived. He wanted to see reasons beneath the surface. Cruz listed the times and places of his interviews and the basic information gathered on each one. Then he looked out the window for a while before continuing.

"El Salvador is in a war and these two families, the Sotos and the Hernandezes, got caught in the middle of it. One of them is rich and the other one is poor. There was bad blood already between them because of that, and when the war started up again in the seventies, they ended up on different sides. People in that country started killing each other and it spread to their families too.

"Eric Hernandez fell in love with the Soto girl, but from the beginning it wasn't going to work. I don't know if he killed the girl's father and brother, the way Victor Soto says. Soto is slippery and his son is worse. Give the bad blood between the families, they would accuse Hernandez of any-thing. It also seems like Gloria Soto was mixed up with some other bad eggs, like this Julio Saenz, the smuggler of illegals whom I have to see.

"Still, it looks like Eric Hernandez killed the girl. The ammo boxes, the ballistics test, the fact that he's nowhere to be found. He had been through a lot, like Stacy Stoner said when she was trying to convince me it wasn't him. All his dreams were wrapped up in Gloria Soto. When she kissed him off, he snapped."

He sat for several more moments staring out the win-dow at the San Francisco skyline. Then he closed the file, gathered his coat and headed for Julio Saenz's house.

THE SAENZ PLACE on Twenty-ninth Street was a small green pastel house in a row of small pastel-colored houses a couple of blocks off Mission. The old woman who answered the door wore a cross around her neck and also a small idol that looked Mexican, as if she were covering all her bases, both Christian and pagan. She wore wire-rimmed glasses and told Cruz that Saenz was not at home.

"Maybe he's at Joe Ortiz's place," she said with a heavy accent.

"Where's that, ma'am?"

"The Cantina Bar on Twenty-eighth Street. Maybe he's there. His girlfriend she was killed and he doesn't feel good."

"Gloria Soto."

The woman nodded her head, yes, and said, "I don't know her. Julio he didn't bring his girlfriends to the house." This aspect of Saenz's deportment didn't sit well with the lady. You were supposed to bring *novias* home for inspection by the family.

"Did Julio see the girl Friday?" Cruz asked.

The woman shook her head. "Julio was out of town." To Cruz, it didn't appear the woman was lying.

"When did he get back?"

"He come back last night. Then they tell him. It was terrible." The woman shook her head, her face full of misery.

"Yes, it was," Cruz said. "Do you know where Julio was?"

"Julio was down in Los Angeles on business, he had something to pick up," she said. She tapped the Mexican Indian idol hanging around her neck, a cheap, poorly carved piece of onyx that went for pennies down in Mexico.

"Julio is in this business of the *artesanias*, the handicrafts. Clothes, blankets, jewelry. He brings them up here from down south." She got a canny, mischievous look on her face and rubbed her thumb and forefinger together suggestively. "He makes a lot of money, Julio."

"That's good for Julio," Cruz said. "I'm glad to hear he is doing well. I know he works hard and is always going down south."

"Two times a week, sometimes more," she said. "He works hard, Julio. He's a good boy."

"Yes, he's a very good boy," Cruz said.

He thanked her, climbed into his car and headed for the Cantina. During Cruz's days on the beat the building had housed a war veterans' hall. Now there were neon beer signs shining in the windows, salsa music sounding from inside and a couple of fetching brown-skinned women, dressed to the teeth, tottering on spike heels, making for the door. Among the parked cars was a red Firebird. Elvira Hernandez had said Saenz owned one, bought with "vulture money."

Cruz walked into the Cantina, just as a salsa group, all dress in cranberry shirts with puffed sleeves, swung into a tune by Sonora Mantancera.

The place was designed to look like a typical cantina from south of the border. It was brightly colored and rustic with bullfight posters on the walls and those square aluminum tables Mexican beer companies pass around to advertise their products. In the middle of the one large room was a good-sized dance floor strewn with sawdust—it reminded Cruz of a cock ring—and overhead were strung Japanese lanterns. The place was packed and the music was loud.

Cruz found a spot at the bar and watched the crowd on the dance floor. It was like watching a complicated piece of machinery, with all parts synchronized to the pulsing rhythm. Arms pumped, heads rocked, shoulders shimmied, hips writhed and swiveled. Cruz watched the faces; some danced happily, some seriously, and others wore faces that reminded you of sex.

One red-haired woman, in a low-cut flowered dress, tight across the hips, came dancing out of the crowd toward the bar, one hand on her stomach, her hips swiveling, her eyes shining. She danced right up to Cruz, until she was inches from him, smiling into his eyes. Then she reached past him, picked up a drink on the bar, drank from it, winked at him invitingly and then turned and danced back into the crowd, her hips swaying rhythmically. Down the bar, several men burst out in wolf calls and raucous laughter.

The bartender was a lean, fastidious-looking older Hispanic with a few strings of white hair on his chin that made him look like an old wise Chinese. Cruz ordered a beer and then yelled into his ear, asking for Julio Saenz. The old guy worked the tap, giving Cruz the once-over with a cool, practiced eye.

"Julio had a friend who died and he doesn't want to be disturbed," he said, serving up the beer. He wiped the counter, waited for payment and studiously avoided looking at Cruz.

Cruz took two dollars out of his billfold and then let it flap open to his shield. The old guy glanced at it without emotion.

"Is he here?" Cruz yelled.

The old Hispanic Confucius thought it over a minute as he polished a glass and then flicked his eyes toward the back of the room.

"Last table," he said.

"Thank you," Cruz yelled. "Keep the change."

He grabbed his beer and threaded his way back through the aluminum tables. At most of the tables there were several people sitting around enjoying themselves with a quart of whiskey or rum, a bucket of ice, limes and mixers. Seated at the very last table next to a door that said "Office—Privado" was a man as big as a Sumo wrestler, sitting behind a quart of whiskey all by himself, and not enjoying himself. At first glance, he looked like some kind of Indian idol, big, ugly and lifeless. He was dark, with wiry hair that stood straight up from his shallow brow. His face was flat like the faces of gods carved into enormous boulders. His eyes were small, narrow and blank. He wore a brightly patterned Indian blouse as big as a tent, and around his bull neck hung a thick gold chain, carved jade, onyx and other charms, like offerings left there by worshipers who were afraid he might destroy the world. He stared blankly at his subjects now as if the music and the dancing were in his honor.

Cruz flashed his shield at the man and offered him a business card.

"I'm investigating the death of Gloria Soto," he said.

Only the idol's eyes moved at first, glancing at the badge as if it were another shiny offering. Then he took the card and stared at it for a while before putting it on the table, where it began to soak up spilled liquor.

"What is there to investigate?" he said sullenly. "Go find the Indian she used to go with, the guerrilla. That's who killed her." He talked like a recording at reduced speed, slow and wobbly.

Cruz sat down across the table from him. It was like sitting across from a jukebox.

"We're looking for Eric Hernandez, Mr. Saenz, but I'm also trying to establish Miss Soto's movements that night. I'm checking with other people who might have seen her before she was killed."

Saenz poured part of his drink down his throat. "I wasn't here. I was in LA."

"That's what they tell me."

"If I was here, she wouldn't be dead," he said. "I would have killed that guy." Saenz's expression turned fierce, as if he were imagining Eric Hernandez and what he might have done to him.

"I'm sure you would have," Cruz said, looking at the man's shoulders, which were like rolling hills. "I'm told you cared for her very much."

Saenz nodded, his big boulder of a head tottering on his shoulders.

"I heard you card for her so much that you were the one who brought her up here from Los Angeles," Cruz said.

Saenz nodded again, but wariness had crept into his gaze.

"You cared for her so much, in fact," Cruz said, "that you only charged her a few hundred dollars and along the way you stopped and molested her."

Saenz turned and looked at Cruz for the first time now, as if Cruz were a species of animal that had never spoken before.

"I didn't molest nobody," he said finally.

"Uh-huh."

"If we did anything, it's because she wanted."

"Yes, I'm sure she did," Cruz said. "A handsome guy like you. She couldn't remember how to tie her shoes when she came up here, she was so screwed up, but she certainly knew a movie star when she saw one."

Saenz crunched ice between his teeth.

"I stopped at a motel to take a shower and she wanted one too," he said. He shrugged his mountainous shoulders as if to say, the rest is history.

"I guess she needed a shower pretty bad by that time, didn't she," Cruz said. "She's just come all the way from her country and crossed over from Mexico on foot. Then she was in the trunk of a car for a while and then in your truck. So you did her a favor and offered her a shower, didn't you, Mr. Mule?"

Saenz glared at him. "I don't know what you're talking about." He tilted the glass and crunched ice between his teeth as if it was Cruz's bones he was munching.

"You don't know what a mule is?" Cruz asked. "A mule goes hee-haw like an animal and charges scared people big money to bring them to the big city. Except that sometimes he takes the money and he leaves them in the middle of nowhere, sometimes in the desert to die."

"I never done nothing like that," Saenz said. "I'm an American citizen and a legitimate businessman. I bring merchandise, crafts, to sell here. That's how I make my living."

"You bring merchandise all right, merchandise like Gloria Soto. People desperate to escape the war down there.

And you squeeze them for every penny. You get rich off the war, off other people's suffering."

"I got nothing to do with the war down there," Saenz said. "It's this Hernandez and his friends, the ones involved in that war. I don't get mixed up with politics. Some people been telling you lies."

"Who would do something like that?" Cruz reached over to the jewelry hanging around Saenz's neck and fingered the shark's tooth. "This piece of merchandise is exactly right for you. Did you give one as a present to your friend Victor Soto? I saw him with one."

Saenz was sneering at Cruz.

"Victor Soto is a respected person, a legitimate businessman like me."

"What makes you and Soto such good friends?" Cruz asked. "Was he selling you his niece, or what? I can't see her doing it on her own."

The idol's eyes smoldered. Stacy Stoner had been right: Julio Saenz was not only ugly, he was an evil spirit. That petite, beautiful Gloria Soto had gotten together with this god of ugliness meant there was something strange going on, something very wrong in the universe.

As if he could read Cruz's thoughts, Saenz said: "Gloria and I liked each other."

"Yeah, that's why she was walking around scared out of her mind, because she was in love with you," Cruz said. "She was thrilled by your every touch."

"It's Hernandez she was scared of. He's the one who's crazy." He poured himself more whiskey, not bothering to invite Cruz.

The band swung into a cumbia and the energy of the place was jacked up another notch. In the midst of it, Saenz sat glum and grim-faced. The god of bad business. Even the women who passed to and from the nearby ladies' room didn't attract his attention, as fetching as they were.

"Maybe they'll sacrifice one of these girls to you," Cruz said, "maybe that would make you feel better."

Saenz glowered. "Whatchu talkin' about? I don't sacrifice nobody."

"Gloria was sacrificed," Cruz said.

Saenz guzzled his whiskey. "I don't know anything about it."

"Where were you Friday night and early Saturday?" Cruz asked.

"I told you I was in LA."

"Where in LA? Who did you see? I want to know every address you stopped at and every person you talked to."

"I was picking up merchandise. Jewelry and stuff. I can give you the names of the suppliers. I picked up Friday and came back Saturday."

Cruz picked the shark's tooth off Saenz's chest and let it fall again. "You're gonna tell me that you make a living selling this kind of garbage? You want me to believe that watch and your fancy car come from selling this junk?"

"It's a good business," Saenz said.

"Where did you stay Friday night?"

Saenz's hooded eyes feigned thought. "I don't remember the name of the place."

"That's too bad."

"But I have a receipt," Saenz said. He picked up the front of his Indian blouse and revealed a money belt strapped around the folds of his gut. He took out a piece of paper, unfolded it, and handed it to Cruz. It said "Traveler's Hideaway, Rte. 101, Santa Barbara"; it was dated Friday, made out to Julio Saenz and signed by the clerk, who had even taken the trouble to print his name clearly beneath his scrawl. His name was Joseph Allen.

"The clerk will remember me," Saenz said. "I gave him a little statue of the rain god."

"I'm sure he could never forget you," Cruz said. He

frowned at the receipt. "This is very convenient, isn't it? Receipt and all."

"I get them for tax purposes. Business expenses."

"Do you have a receipt for the people you brought back too? Ten refugees: three thousand dollars."

His brow furrowed again, like a growl.

"I don't know what you're talking about."

"Did you stop to molest one of them the way you did Gloria Soto?"

Saenz crunched ice. "I need that paper for my taxes," he said.

Cruz wrote down the name of the motel and the clerk and laid it on the table where it soaked up some water.

"When was the last time you saw Gloria Soto?" he asked.

"Thursday night. We came here and had a couple of drinks," Saenz said sullenly. "The bartender can tell you that."

"Did she tell you she was scared of you?"

"She wasn't scared of me. She was scared of Hernandez, he was the one following her around. I wanted to punch him out, but Gloria's mother didn't want it. She didn't want trouble because maybe they would deport her and Gloria."

"Did Gloria say what she was going to do last night by herself?"

"She said she was going to stay home."

"She didn't," Cruz said. "She came in here and did some drinking, didn't she?"

"That's what they tell me. I wasn't here and they can tell you that."

"I'm sure they can. You were in LA being a legitimate businessman, weren't you?"

"That's right."

"That's right, you associate only with legitimate busi-nessmen and upright citizens." Cruz drained his beer and got up. "Too bad Gloria Soto didn't associate with legitimate people instead of an animal like you," Cruz said.

Big guys always brought out the wiseass in Cruz. He saw the muscles in Saenz's neck tense, and all over the other man's body the fat quivered with anger. Cruz thought steam would come from him, or fire out of his eyes.

"Please let us know if you plan to leave town again, I want to order some jewelry," Cruz said. "And make sure and take care of that motel receipt, since you went to so much trouble to get it in the first place. It could save your fat neck."

He gave Saenz a wink and a nod and walked away. At the bar he crooked a finger at the old Confucius and showed him a photo of Gloria Soto.

"This girl was in here Friday night," Cruz said.

The other man glanced at the photo, took a swipe at the bar with his bar rag and shot a look toward the back of the bar, toward Saenz.

"No need to look anywhere, Confucius. What time was she here?"

He polished the bar a bit more. "Maybe ten, tenthirty."

"Alone?"

He nodded. "The only person she ever come in with before was Julio and he wasn't here. He was out of town."

"I just heard all about it," Cruz said. "She ever come in alone before?"

Confucius shook his head no.

"Who did she come in looking for?"

"Nobody. She sat at the end of the bar and she drank sloe gin fizz."

"Did she talk to anybody?"

He shook his head. "A couple of guys tried to hustle her. She didn't even look at them. She just drinks her drinks. She's loyal to Julio."

"Yeah, Julio inspires devotion," Cruz said. "How many did she drink?"

"Three, maybe four. I didn't give her no more."

"Why not?"

"She shouldn't have no more."

"She looked drunk?"

Confucius shrugged his bony shoulders.

"Then what?"

"Then she left."

"By herself?"

"That's right. Just like she come in."

"What time was that?"

"About midnight."

"And she didn't come back?"

He shook his head.

"You know anybody might have reason to kill her?" Cruz asked. Confucius shook his head again. "I don't know things like that. I just work around here."

"Yeah, me too," Cruz said.

He left then, as the band swung into a merengue.

Murder on the Run

Gloria White

T 6:00 A.M. the path between Crissy Field and
the San Francisco Bay was deserted. And it should
be, I thought as I ran along the edge of the Bay. It
was too early for the walkers to be out, and everybody else
who'd run the Bay to Breakers yesterday was at home in bed,
nursing runner's knees and hangovers. Lucky them. If I'd finished the race, I'd be asleep, too, instead of working on a runner's high out here, sweating in the cold.

The only sound above the muffled rush of Monday
morning bridge traffic and the nearby wash of the waves was
the solid *crunch, crunch* of my own frayed running shoes as they
hit the gravel underfoot. After a minute I reached the pavement
and ran on in silence, letting my mind drift.

For a half-Mexican daughter of jewel thieves, I was
doing pretty good with my life: I finally had my P.I. license
and, after a year, was actually making a living doing investiga-

---

**GLORIA WHITE introduces female private investigator Ronnie
Ventana in her first novel, *Murder on the Run*. The daughter
of two cat burglars, Ventana uses her heritage to her advantage, disarming alarm systems with ease. White currently
lives in San Francisco.**

tions. Knowing the city, being a native San Franciscan, helped, but knowing how to breach security systems—from locks to burglar alarms—helped even more. Since I never take anything except information, I look at it as sort of carrying on the family trade without the guilt. But there was another pay-off, too, a reason I knew I'd found my niche: sometimes in a stranger's darkened room, with my lock picks and penlight in hand and my heart beating as fast as a hummingbird's, I'd sense my father's deep-brown Mexican eyes on me and my mom's sparkling Anglo ones, and I'd feel closer to them than I'd ever felt when they were alive.

With their memory on my mind, I ran past the Coast Guard station and the Park Service outbuildings, then up the canted road that led to Fort Point, the old Civil War relic under the Golden Gate Bridge.

It was there, when I swung out and jogged along the fat yellow line down the center of the road, that I spotted them: two men standing bareheaded against the brisk May wind. They were at the tip of the fort, not more than five feet from where Jimmy Stewart pulled Kim Novak out of the Bay in *Vertigo*. They weren't fishermen or sufers: Neither carried poles or boards, and one man—the big one—had on a suit and tie. The other guy was wearing a blue windbreaker over tan pants.

From the way they were standing, the big man towering over the other one, it looked like the little guy was getting chewed out over something.

I felt uneasy and thought about turning back, but before I could make up my mind, the little guy started shouting. The first couple of words were garbled, but he said something, something else, then "vengeance."

I drew up at the brick portals, about seventy yards away from them, but neither seemed to notice me. They just kept yelling back and forth at each other like I wasn't even there. I looked around for somebody else, but it was just me, them, and the specter of Jimmy Stewart.

Before I knew it, the man in the suit had the little guy by the throat. He jerked him bodily up off the pavement and swung him back and forth, up and down, with vicious little shakes like a terrier would a rat. The little guy flailed his arms and tried to get away, but the big man in the suit paid no attention. He just kept on shaking and swinging. Then suddenly the blue arms went limp. The legs stiffened, then they went limp too.

"Stop! Hey you, stop it!"

The big man looked up at me, surprised. I was surprised myself. Here I was, a woman half his size and about a third his weight, telling him what to do. I didn't know judo or karate or what the hell I was even doing down there. The one thing I did know was that he wasn't happy to see me.

We were close enough to get a good look at each other and that's exactly what the big guy did: he stared at me like he was memorizing my face. I had just enough time to take in his square jaw, dark hair, and a streak of white at the temple before he tossed the limp body into the water like an empty candy wrapper and came after me.

He was as big as a bear, but a lot of big men could run. *Run.* I wheeled around and sprinted back down the way I'd come. *God, don't let him catch me,* I prayed, and the cold fear inside me made me fly like Pegasus.

I looked over my shoulder once, right before I ducked around the Park Service outbuildings. He was closing the distance, wheezing after me like a locomotive, but I ignored the pain in my side and doubled my speed. I didn't look back again until I dodged behind the high stand of bushes surrounding the Coast Guard station house. I flew up the three steps to the porch and slammed my fist against the door.

"Help! Help! Emergency! Open up!"

My breath came in jagged little gasps as I pounded the polished oak door. I wanted whoever was inside to hear me, but I didn't want the killer to know where I was. *"Hurry, please,"* I whispered.

The latch rattled; the door opened about an inch. I pushed, but the door wouldn't budge. I looked up. A pair of soft blue eyes, narrowed in suspicion, peered out at me.

"What is it?" a woman's voice asked from the other side.

"Please, please. You've got to help." I pushed against the door again. "Please, let me in."

She blinked and I knew she was sizing me up, trying to decide if I was going to do something weird to her if she let me in. I guess I looked sane enough because after a second the door swung open. I shoved my way inside. "Quick! Lock it. There's somebody after me."

She released the collar of her pink chenille bathrobe and locked the door while I steadied myself against the wall. I took a couple of deep breaths, then looked her over. She was just under my height, probably five-three, blond, and slender. Not exactly the mounted police, but between the two of us, I figured, we might hold our own. At least until the cops arrived.

The foyer was dark, paneled in knotty pine, and smelled of fresh brewed coffee. It had the cozy, dark feeling of a cabin below deck. I half expected the floor to surge with the lift of a wave, but it didn't. That was okay. It felt warm and safe—temporarily.

"We need to call the police," I said.

She didn't move. "Did someone jump?" The way she said it, clear and slow and patient, sounded like she was talking to a three-year-old.

"Jump?" I stared at her. My mind drew a blank. Then I understood. "No, no, he was pushed. He—"

"Sarah?" a voice called from down the hall. "Sarah, who's down there? Are you all right?"

But Sarah was already bundling a pea jacket over my clammy shoulders and hustling me out the front door.

"Hey, what the—?" I grabbed the door frame and hung on. Nobody was going to shove me back out there until the cops came.

"The station office is over there," the woman explained, pulling on my arm and pointing to the white clapboard building across the yard. "They'll send out the boats from there," she said. I let go. Over her shoulder she called out to the guy in the house, "Hurry, John. There's a man in the Bay."

WE COULDN'T TAKE the direct route, the one I'd run along because upright metal bars blocked the entrance, so we drove up a hill, around and back down again. As the Bay came into view, I heard the slow purr of the motorboats. From the way they crisscrossed the water, slowly and systematically like a couple of lawn mowers, I knew they hadn't found what they were looking for.

The jeep skimmed past the brick pillars and took us right up to where the two men had fought.

"Where'd he go in?" the captain asked.

"That's it," I said and pointed. "Right there. The little guy came from around the building right over there, and the big guy grabbed him by the neck and started choking him, then threw him in. Right here."

We all got out and stood at the end of the paved road, next to the walls of the old fortress, and stared into the frigid water. The guy who sat next to me in the backseat started taking his clothes off and ended up in a yellow wet suit. He put on headgear and a harness, then waited at the edge of the breakwater for somebody to tell him to dive in. Nobody did, though, so he just stood there, shivering in the cold. I thought about what it would be like down there, deep under the water, then pulled my borrowed pea jacket tight and looked at Captain John.

"They haven't found him yet, have they?"

"Not yet." He scanned the choppy bay with clear blue eyes.

"Could he be out there?" I motioned with my chin toward the Pacific, out past the Golden Gate.

"It's possible. We've got a flood tide, but if he goes down deep enough, the crosscurrent could carry him out. It gets as deep as four hundred feet under the bridge, but I doubt he went that far." He stared at the craggy edge of the breakwater where bay met land. "Frankly I'm surprised he's not hung up on these rocks here. If he was unconscious, it would seem likely he would."

I stared past the thick guard chain to the gray waters and tried to think positive thoughts. It didn't work.

"How long before . . .?"

John checked his wristwatch. "We'll give him another half hour. Nobody can last longer than that out there today. Especially if he went over unconscious."

"Oh."

The noise of the boats churning out there put me on edge, so I turned my back to the water and looked down the road I'd covered twice already that morning. The pavement was damp and shiny from sea spray and, off in the distance near the Park Service buildings, I could make out a couple walking their dog, a collie.

When the dog disappeared up the steep, brush-covered slope that ran parallel to the road, I felt a chill. It had nothing to do with how cold it was. It was like *he* was up there, hiding behind the trees and the bushes, watching me. I turned back to John. "Is anybody looking for the other guy?"

"Sure." On cue a siren sounded in the distance. "They should catch him if he's on his way out."

I kept my eye on the hill, and when the sirens got closer, something up there moved, a quick motion of white at the crest of the slope. I held my breath. He was up there, standing out in the open, bold as a bulldozer. I grabbed John's sleeve.

"Look! Up there. He's up there in the bushes."

"Where?" John swung around, but it was too late. He was gone. "Where?"

"Shit! He's getting away!" I started down the road, but John reached out and stopped me. "*Come on,*" I hissed, fighting his grip. "He's getting away."

"We'll never catch him on foot. They'll do it." He nodded at the police car, now sliding up behind the jeep.

John hurried over to them and pointed up the slope, but before they could pull out to chase the guy down, a second car lurched to a stop behind them. When a third one showed up a few seconds later, I knew we were sunk. John barked a few short words at them, and all three cars took off back up the road. I watched them go—military police, park police, and city police—and knew we didn't have a prayer.

"Don't look so glum," John said. "They can handle it."

"What makes you so sure?"

For the first time that morning, John grinned at me. "You don't have much confidence in bureaucrats, do you?"

"I've got every reason not to," I said. "I used to be one."

Kearny Street Ghost Story

Mark Twain

ISEMBODIED SPIRITS HAVE been on the rampage now for more than a month past in the house of one Albert Krum, in Kearny Street—so much so that the family find it impossible to keep a servant forty-eight hours. The moment a new and unsuspecting servant-maid gets fairly to bed and her light blown out, one of those dead and damned scalliwags takes her by the hair and just "hazes" her; grabs her by the waterfall and snakes her out of bed and bounces her on the floor two or three times; other disorderly corpses shy old boots at her head, and bootjacks, and brittle chamber furniture—washbowls, pitchers, hair-oil, teeth-brushes, hoop-skirts—anything that comes handy those phantoms seize and hurl at Bridget, and pay no more attention to her howling than if it were music. The spirits tramp, tramp, tramp, about the house at dead of night, and when a light is struck the footsteps cease and the promenader is not visible, and just as soon as the light is out that dead man goes waltzing

MARK TWAIN originally earned literary prominence as a newspaper correspondent and curmudgeon in California and Nevada. "Kearny Street Ghost Story" was published in a local paper in 1866, only a year after his first successful story.

around again. They are a bloody lot. The young lady of the house was lying in bed one night with the gas turned down low, when a figure approached her through the gloom, whose ghastly aspect and solemn carriage chilled her to the heart. What do you suppose she did?—she jumped up and seized the intruder?—threw a slipper at him?—"laid" him with a misquotation from Scripture? No—none of these. But with admirable presence of mind she covered up her head and yelled. That is what she did. Few young women would have thought of doing that. The ghost came and stood by the bed and groaned—a deep, agonizing heart-broken groan—and laid a bloody kitten on the pillow by the girl's head. And then it groaned again, and sighed, "Oh, God, and must it be?" and bet another bloody kitten. It groaned a third time in sorrow and tribulation, and went one kitten better. And thus the sorrowing spirit stood there, moaning in its anguish and unloading its mewing cargo, until it had stacked up a whole litter of nine little bloody kittens on the girl's pillow, and then, still moaning, moved away and vanished.

When the lights were brought, there were the kittens, with the finger-marks of bloody hands upon their white fur—and the old mother cat, that had come after them, swelled her tail in mortal fear and refused to take hold of them. What do you think of that? What would you think of a ghost that came to your bedside at dead of night and had kittens?

Photographer FRANCIS BRUGUIÉRE was primarily known for
Surrealist portraits for *Harper's Bazaar*, *Vogue*, and *Vanity
Fair* in the twenties and thirties. However, Bruguiére grew
up in San Francisco and photographed this dreamlike series
of images of his hometown. These photographs were collected
in a 1919 book, *San Francisco*.

Acknowledgments

"It's a Lousy World" by Bill Pronzini © 1968 by H. S. D. Publications, Inc. First published in *Alfred Hitchcock's Mystery Magazine* as "Sometimes There Is Justice." Revised version © 1983 by Bill Pronzini. Reprinted by permission of the author.

"Fly Paper" by Dashiell Hammett, edited by Lillian Hellman © 1966 by Lillian Hellman. Reprinted by permission of Random House, Inc.

"The Second Coming" © 1966 by Joe Gores. Reprinted by permission of the author.

Ironside by Jim Thompson was published by Popular Library in 1967.

Excerpt from *Vertigo* by Alfred Hitchcock © by Universal City Studios, Inc. Courtesy of MCA Publishing Rights, a division of MCA Inc.

Excerpt from *The Case of the Not-So-Nice Nurse* © 1993 by Mabel Maney. Reprinted by permission of the author.

"Deceptions" by Marcia Muller © 1987 by Marcia Muller. Reprinted by permisson of Larry Sternig Literary Agency.

Excerpt from *Heat Lightning* © 1987 by John Lantigua. Reprinted by permission of The Putnam Publishing Group.

Excerpt from *Murder on the Run* by Gloria White © 1991 by Gloria White. Used by permission of Dell Books, a division of Bantam Doubleday Dell Publishing Group, Inc.